SCAMBAIT

RYAN R. CAMPBELL

CEDARBROOK BOOKS

A Cedarbrook Books Publication

Published by Cedarbrook Books

Milwaukee, Wisconsin

www.cedarbrookbooks.com

Scambait

Printed in the USA

First Edition

April 2022

Print ISBN: 978-1-7363871-3-9

eBook ISBN: 978-1-7363871-2-2

This book contains references or allusions to domestic abuse.

for everyone out there doing good, even if not well

it makes a difference

CHAPTER 1
SPAM

t should be the easiest thing to delete this email, to flush it away with the already-reads, the coupon codes, the lesser spam.

But this isn't spam, no matter what the folder says.

Eric, this is your father.

My father. I haven't spoken to him in years. No one has.

It's rare to get a call from the dead—an email, rarer still.

CHAPTER 2
DOLORES

close, reopen my spam folder. The email's there. Still. Right at the top.

I select it before dragging my cursor over the trash can icon.

Nope. No. Not now. Think on it.

There's a play to be made, because here's the thing: even if they never did find my father's body, this has to be a scammer, some twisted lowlife out for revenge.

And if there's one thing I hate, it's a scammer.

If there are *two* things I hate, it's a scammer who thinks they can best me with a despicable, personalized phishing attempt like this.

While I plan my next move, I open another email and continue my work—not the job I'm paid for, mind you, but rather my true vocation.

Here is my driver's license (scan attached) and my social. Please confirm your banking details. I will wire the transfer fee immediately upon receipt, at which time I expect the prompt release of the inheritance I am owed.

The driver's license image I've forwarded is a warped, illegible scan, and the social security number I've provided is from a random number generator. The transfer fee is not a sum I intend to pay, nor do I expect the promised inheritance to ever hit an account I own.

Who do I look like, my grandma?

"Eric?"

I glance up from my screen, minimize my inbox with a keyboard shortcut. "Dolores." My tone is flat. I make no eye contact. I'm busy, can't you see? There are more pressing matters at hand, Dolores.

"Did you get that email I sent you?" she asks.

"Haven't logged in yet."

"Oh, sorry. Just get in?"

"Yeah." This, I can say at any time of day to anyone I please; thanks to carefully crafted paths to and from my desk —the Zig, the Zag, and the Long Loop—no one sees me come in, and they do not see me leave. I wear a blazer—above and beyond the office's required business casual—to ward off the pettier requests, and as the company's lone Special Advisor to Latin America, my schedule is flexible. I'm beholden to no one save for myself and the bare—and I mean bare— minimum amount of work required to not get shitcanned, so it's hard to say, day-to-day, when I might be available; it's better if you send an email.

I tell my coworkers this, especially since Grandma Amundsen's death, and on average, they listen.

Dolores, as she has made abundantly clear, does not consider herself part of *on average*.

"All right," Dolores says, "but when you have a second—"

"Yup."

Dolores steps away from the entrance to my cube, and I expand my inbox.

She returns a second later. "Hey, sorry again, but we also

never talked about that message from—" I exit my inbox. "Was that your email?"

Dolores, please. No. Stop. These aren't the emails you're looking for.

"Can you pull mine up real quick?" she insists. "It doesn't even have to be the email from this morning, but I sent you that one last Thursday—"

"About the Ampersand account? I replied to that." I didn't, no, but I did respond to the woman claiming to be former British Prime Minister Theresa May, as well as the Qatari petroleum exec to whom I've slowly revealed that the millions he plans to send me will be invested in an Ameowsment Park for cats.

To answer your question—yes, despite the wild improbability of anyone founding an Ameowsment Park, the phony oil magnate is still responding. Soon, I'll have his bank account information, which I'll phone into the bank to get the account shut down.

These people, I tell you. It's like they *want* to scambaited.

"I don't think I got that reply from you," Dolores says.

"Can you check again?"

"Is it in your sent folder?"

"Dolores, I'm sorry, but you caught me at a bad time." I pluck my blazer from the back of my chair, slide my arms through the sleeves. "I was late getting in, and I've got a meeting at—oh, would you look at the time?—I'm late for that now, too."

"We should really—"

"We'll *should really* later." I brush past her, stride for HR. "I'll check in with you after this meeting."

She says something, but I've already got my phone to my ear as if calling someone to apologize for my tardiness—not that I've dialed anyone.

I have no number to call, but I do have to do something about this dead, emailing father of mine.

CHAPTER 3
AN UNFULFILLABLE PROMISE

n a mostly empty cube in HR—downsizing, so it goes—I re-read, intend to respond to the email from my father. Or, well, my "father," this pretender who's more than likely—who *has* to be—some scammer I spurned who can't let it go.

Eric, this is your father. At least I think I'm your father. You're in the Madison area, we share a last name, and you're the same age as my son would be now. And the nose—your mother's nose. I'd recognize it anywhere.

I'm sorry if this feels like an intrusion. I've been meaning to reach out for years, but the guilt finally got to me. I found you on social media, by the way. I have no profiles of my own, not under any name you'd recognize, so I didn't message you there. You list where you work on Facebook, and after that, I went to the company's site, and, well, you get the picture. Special Advisor to Latin America? Impressive.

I know I have no right to do this to you. I'll understand if you ignore me, but I hope you don't. Please, Eric, I want to do better. I want to make up for lost time. It haunts me that I couldn't be there when your mother passed—or when my own mother passed—but I had to go. I had to. One day, you'll understand.

Can we talk? Not by email. By phone or, if you're okay with it, in person? My number's below, if you want to reach out.

I give it another read. Another. *Another,* another, and good God, man, the contents aren't going to change. Write something or don't. Deep breath. Close your eyes. Type the first thing that comes to mind.

So, here we go, clacking away at the keyboard connected to the laptop and monitors of whichever HR generalist sat in this chair before their dismissal.

First of all, how dare you.

I remove my hands from the keyboard, because what the fuck? Is my mind so a-fuck that the best I can do is essentially copypasta? And, come on, am I responding as if this guy's for real?

Try again. Clear your head. This guy isn't actually your dad, remember. Your dad is dead. Super dead. Like, only hair-and-bones-left-in-a-casket dead—not that his body ever made it to a casket—so that this is the image I've landed on means I'm in no state to handle this right now. All right. A break. I'll take a break, will press reset with a quick jaunt down the scambait hole.

Scambait hole. Gross.

I brush aside the thought of a scambait hole—again, gross—and open five new tabs in my browser. In every one, a unique account. In every one, a gold mine.

We were unable to process payment for your domain
To the moon! BIG money and much fortune waits for you
INVESTMENT OPPORTUNITY

Bad. *So bad.* And yet people fall for them, including people like, yup, Grandma Amundsen, who might as well have had a punch card with Cyber Scams Pvt. Ltd.—not a real company—where she got a refund on her tenth scam because you name it, she fell for it.

And, in doing so, she cost me a considerable inheritance.

I cannot emphasize this enough: *considerable.*

Not that the loss of the inheritance is about me so much as it is about her, because here's the thing—Grandma A had to spend her final year in a home of pitiable quality, had to remain in Wisconsin instead of retiring to Arizona, where she long intended to spend her golden years roasting in the sun instead of shivering in the cold. None of which is to mention what her getting scammed meant for Boulder—her aging, gassy Saint Bernard—who became my ward instead of farting his way through Grandma's waning hours in an old folks' home that allowed pets. Don't get me wrong: I love that dog, but the *smell* of him. Truly haunting.

Okay. Enough. I need to channel this angst, so—*knuckles crack*—let's get down to business, specifically the business of wasting as much of these assholes' time as possible. The more they spend focusing on me, after all, the less they'll have to scam anyone else, and ain't that the beauty of it all?

So—terribly sorry, I reply to the first of the emails I have open. How can I ensure payment goes through to this clearly impostor SquareSpace address? To our friend with this fantabulous cryptocurrency scheme: you'll multiply my investment tenfold in five days?! How's ten grand sound? And wow, that was fast, a reply from the schmo I requested banking details from. Let's just compare the routing number to the one on the bank's website before we drop the bank name and address into Google Maps and, sure enough, it all checks out! We've probably got a real account here, fancy that, so let's pull out the ol' cell and make a call.

While my phone connects with the bank, I catch a glimpse of that email from my dad—er, *not* my dad.

Don't let it get to you, Eric. You're not allowed to let it get to you, not now. There's one more fresh email to respond to here, after all, and—

"Southwestern Credit Union. This is Carl speaking."

"Hi, Carl," I say, my posture straightening. This is my favorite part of my job—well, *vocation*. Calling in these accounts really feels like something. Something meaningful. "I'm wondering if I can speak to someone in your fraud department."

"Oh, uh—what seems to be the situation?"

I explain to Carl, as he put it, the situation. I get emails, I tell him, attempts to goad people into passing along personal information, not to mention cash. It starts with government IDs, dates of birth, social security numbers, et cetera, before the Big Ask, as I like to call it. While I bring Carl up to speed —I've got it down to a script at this point, really—my attention drifts back to the final email of the newbies to have hit my inbox since I'd last checked.

And this one? Wow, the investment opportunity of a lifetime, and one I can't pass up: Aisha Al-Qaddafi has contacted me of all people! I support my phone between my shoulder and ear, typing a response on my keyboard while Carl puts me on hold to nab everything he needs to file a report.

Thank you so much, Mrs. Muammar Al-Qaddafi, I write, for your willingness to share you and your late husband's fortune; what can I do to make sure all twenty-seven million dollars make it to my American accounts securely?

Before I click SEND on my email to this supposed widow of the disgraced Libyan despot, I consider the attachments, open them. Standard stuff. Documents requesting bank account and routing numbers, all of it on letterhead for a bank that—yes, a Google search confirms as much—doesn't exist.

I rub my forehead. I cannot wrap my mind around how people—Grandma—get duped by these. Grandma was the first to tell you not to trust strangers on the street, but the second she got unsolicited phone calls from Microsoft and Apple tech support—from the Amazon subscription department, from the IRS and Social Security Administration—it was all *yes, of course, how can we fix this?* and *I'll gladly wire you whatever's needed to make this go away.*

Fix *what*, Grandma? Make *what* go away?

I never should have gotten her that smartphone.

"You still there, Eric?" Carl asks.

"Yup, still here."

"Okay, can you pass along that account information for me? I want to verify—"

"That it's a real account, yeah." I share the account and routing numbers the scammer forwarded to me and, sure enough, Carl confirms they're real. "I also have a name attached to the account, if you'd like that?" I ask, and of course he'd like that. It's no surprise—to me, anyway—that when I share the name of Mabel Higginbotham, Carl relays this is, yes, the name on the account.

Now, if Mabel Higginbotham doesn't sound like the name of someone who'd be out to pick the pockets of the unsuspecting, you might be right. We can look her up online, actually, and see there's a Mabel Higginbotham who lives in a twenty-five mile radius of the bank in question. She's seventy-eight years old and owns a toy poodle named Bruce —thanks, Facebook—and she doesn't look like she's walking around with Rolexes on her wrists.

Why? Because scammers are likely using her account to launder money after having scammed Mabel herself, the poor thing.

Check in on your elders, folks. Hell, check in on everyone,

but especially Mabels of the world. We can't have them winding up like my grandma. Poor. Dead. Well, we can't do anything about that last one, but you know.

The call with Carl winds down, concluding with a self-high-five and a reminder that I'm not here to think about my dad or my Grandma right now. I'm all about the mission, about the promise I made to Granny A: keep from happening to others what happened to her.

I return, then, to the contents of Mrs. Qadaffi's email, pore over its attachments one more ti—

Shit.

Those attachments. The computer in this cubicle. All of my defenses against malevolent links and other ungodliness —this laptop wasn't connected to my Raspberry Pi, the rinky-dink mini-computer I hook up to my desk's keyboard and monitors when wading through the muck.

This workstation in HR isn't safe, not like mine.

A cold sweat descends. I return my attention to the laptop before me, locate the downloads folder, wipe it clean. And then—now what? Tell IT, says a voice inside my head, but no. *No.* I'm okay. The odds are the files were harmless, were designed to encourage me to pass along sensitive personal information and nothing more. Not every scam email is some super sophisticated attempt to bring down an entire network. That's certainly not what they were out to do when they targeted Grandma Amundsen with similar shenanigans.

Besides, telling IT would only lead to questions. The wrong kinds of questions. Say, Eric, why were you on this laptop in the first place? Why were you not doing your actual job? Why would you be opening emails in your spam folder anyway? Don't you remember your IT training modules, Eric?

The list goes on.

For now, the file's deleted, and that will have to be—is —enough.

Not that my cold sweat has evaporated. Not that I'm feeling great about returning to my cubicle with Dolores skulking around the corner for what remains of the day.

So, away we go—I log out of the workstation in HR before hustling for my cube, retrieving my laptop, and taking the Zig to the parking lot. That makes for a short day, even for me, but I've got a dog to pick up at the vet.

I know. Add it to the list.

CHAPTER 4
THIRTEEN

turned thirteen the day the call came in.

"No, Glenn's not here," my mother said. "He left an hour ago. I don't understand. Slow down. Please."

I stood at the threshold between the kitchen and the living room, my ears perked.

"Oh my God. What? When? Is he—? I'm driving down."

Mom drove us, the two of us, to my father's place of employment. A sinkhole, they said, caused by a faulty water main, and everyone stay back because this is an active situation, and they'll get everyone updates as soon as they can.

Emergency lights strobed, police tape whipped and snapped, and I braced myself against the brisk October wind. The earth trembled, and the hole opened wider, swallowing another car on the surface lot.

Their best guess? My father had been in the underground parking garage when the water surged in. He didn't have a chance, they said, but it would have happened quickly. I doubted this, but said nothing; another thought consumed me.

Saturday. It was a Saturday. My father never should have

been there; we should have been at the pet store, but we weren't.

And we weren't there because of me. Because I asked too many questions.

This is how I viewed it then, anyway, when grief still whispered *you did this, you did this* every hour of every day.

On those Saturdays *before*, there was little I looked forward to more than that simple question from my dad. "Ready?"

I'd nod, already on my way to the car before we'd scoot down East Washington and dip into the Willy Street neighborhood. Then, the walk across the parking lot, the anticipation swelling. The whoosh of the automatic doors, the step inside, the smell of dog food and fish flakes, the hum of heating lamps and, during the monthly Catapalooza adoption fairs, the kittens tumbling and pawing and mewling away in their enclosures.

To me, those Saturday mornings were everything. It was time with him, with my dad, the man whose work kept him so occupied he had next to none for his wife and only son. Did I mind that he'd spend a few minutes in the back office chatting away with the store's owner, his friend? No, my dad deserved that time with his pal, and besides, he told me he'd find me later, that I was free to roam so long as I didn't pull a fast one and tell an employee I needed them to help me gather everything I'd need for an at-home aquarium, including the fish.

In my defense, I only did that once, the employee should have known better, and my father shouldn't have left me alone in the first place.

Either way, one Saturday when he returned from the back office for our customary lap around the store, curiosity got the best of me.

"Why can't I meet your friend?"

My father told me he wasn't his friend.

"Then why do you talk to him?"

"Because he's an important person," he'd say.

"Like Mom?"

My dad laughed. "Sure, like Mom."

As we passed the back office, I peered through the window. A man of herculean proportions sat in a desk chair, a girl with a bow in her hair holding tight to a stuffed animal of some kind. Even though this friend laughed, the expression he wore was calloused, always.

"Is he a bad person?" I asked.

My father said nothing, and our lap around the store was cut short. My father drove us home, straight home, without a word between us. The warmth between us dissipated, and I wouldn't return to the pet store until years later—after his death and that of my mother—to adopt Boulder to keep good old Grandma Amundsen company.

Those questions I asked of my father might have cost me those precious Saturdays. They might have even cost my father his life.

But even now, twenty years later, I'd still like answers.

CHAPTER 5
DISCORD

The traffic on East Johnson inches along, comes to a stop amid a flurry of snowfall, a slew of slush. I check my phone for the thousandth time. No reply, not yet, which, come on, people; it's been twenty minutes since I first posted to our Scambait Bros Discord server. What the hell is everyone doing that they can't help a man out when he needs it most?

Up ahead, the light changes from green to red. Traffic somehow stops even more than it had already stopped, and I slap the steering wheel. A right turn on Blair—all I want in this world is to turn right on Blair, but let's be honest: a right turn is not, in fact, all I want in this world.

I want to know if anyone has heard of a scam with an impostor father before. I want to know if it's an attempt at a ransom of some kind. I want to know if the rat bastard who emailed me earlier is actually my dad.

Oh, and I'd also like to know if I'm royally screwed after opening that attachment over in HR. Like, I'm probably not. Probably. Nothing terrible happened, at least not immediately, and I deleted all the files, so we're good.

Still, I check my phone. Again, nothing. For fuck's sake.

I stare out my driver's side window, or at least I try to. I'm in desperate need of a defrost here, and I'm furious, besides, that I never got around to having snow tires put on this bad boy. Not that I'd be the one swapping out those tires, no, I'd pay someone for that. I'd do it myself if I'd ever been taught, but, you know, I've had no dad around to teach me that kind of thing, and that's probably what dads do when they're not fake-dead. I'm assuming. Obviously.

But stop, I tell myself. Be patient. I've been without a dad for twenty years, and look at all I've accomplished!

Okay, don't go making a list or anything. That's not the point.

What I'm trying to get at is that if I've been dad-less for twenty years, I can definitely wait another twenty minutes for a reply from one of the Scambait Bros. If anyone's seen a scam or not-scam like this before—if anyone will know whether that attachment poses any real threat—it'll be one of the Bros.

Bros. God, I hate that.

Baiters. No, that's awful, too.

Scammites. There. The scammers and the scammites.

Okay, maybe not, but better. Better for now.

The brake lights ahead of me blink off. My car tires spin beneath me, failing to get traction against the snow. This is perfect timing—sarcasm—because here it is, at long last: a reply from one of my partners-in-anti-crime.

PrakashMoney: I don't know, man.

That's it? Seriously, that's it? I'm not letting—can't let—this go that easily.

BoulderIBarelyKnowHer: Very helpful.
SalchichaSimon: I'm with P-Money. We just don't know enough to know, you know?
BoulderIBarelyKnowHer: Here's the part where I'd

insert a gif of Samuel L. Jackson saying "say 'know' again."

SalchichaSimon: That's not even the original quote.

BoulderIBarelyKnowHer: That's why there's no gif of it.

PrakashMoney: Well you're obviously not too worried if you're turning to memes during these trying times.

BoulderIBarelyKnowHer: It's all memes down here. It's a coping mechanism. Ever heard of it?

SalchichaSimon: Memes can't save you now. Not even Kitboga or Pierogi can save you now.

BoulderIBarelyKnowHer: I think they're a little busy with their six bajillion YouTube subscribers to bail my ass out.

PrakashMoney: Them's the breaks. We *told* you to not scambait while at work. Fucking amateur, dude.

Some family you're born into. Some family is found.

My found family, as can be plainly seen, is about as supportive as the family into which I was born, and if you'll recall, none of them are left.

Except my dad. Maybe. But look at all the support he's been in recent years.

No time to dwell on it, because the time has come to take that right, which, after only a bit of slip and slide—handled expertly, I might add—I go *back* to dwelling on it, back to pressing these fools while I've got them online.

BoulderIBarelyKnowHer: So what do you recommend?

PrakashMoney: For your dad or the other thing?

BoulderIBarelyKnowHer: ¿Por qué no los dos?

SalchichaSimon: Por que no los dos?

BoulderIBarelyKnowHer: Jinx. Also, you forgot an accent. And a question mark.

SalchichaSimon: Says the non-native speaker.
BoulderIBarelyKnowHer: What do you think?
PrakashMoney: For your dad—play it out. Trust the process. See how forthcoming this guy is or isn't. The scientist in me says you need more data.
SalchichaSimon: And go to IT. For the other thing, that is. And STOP SCAMBAITING AT WORK, YOU—

I don't read the rest because, one, stopping my scambaiting is not an option—I made a promise to Grandma Amundsen—and two, I am literally the worst dog owner to have existed. The vet. The vet! Boulder is ready to be picked up at the vet, and here I am, an electrified nimrod, my not-so-weather-ready tires carrying me in the opposite direction. This means a U-turn at East Wash and Blair, and yes, I know, no U-turns allowed here, but riding my ass is also not allowed, something no one apparently told the douche-canoe who's about to wind up in my trunk after this fun little brake check. So, here we are—have a brake check, pal, but *what the fuck*: it was black ice, is black ice leading up to the intersection, and the light changes to red, and my every nerve is aflame as I'm pumping, pumping, pumping the brakes, but my car keeps sliding and, heaven help me, I'm about to blast through the front windows of the Korean barbecue joint when I'm sideswiped, spin, and collide instead with the stoplight in the median.

The light's metal support groans, teeters, and crashes into the middle of East Wash. Horns honk. Hazard lights flash. Commuters pull to the curb.

I test my extremities. Working, all working, but my mind is a wreck, and beneath my jacket, beneath my sweatshirt and my thermal, I sweat like no man should sweat in temperatures like these.

Am I alive? Yes, but for how much longer, I don't know; having forgotten to get Boulder, I fret how much longer everyone's favorite sickly lummox will be kenneled up at the clinic, whining intermittently, hoping every opening of the door is me come to pick him up. Christ, it's enough to have a man's eyes well over, and—

Stop. Focus.

I look for my phone. Someone's already called the cops, surely; call the vet to let them know you'll be in before they close.

Here. My phone. At my feet.

I curl my fingers around it. Tiny shards of screen embed themselves in my fingers through the thin cotton of my gloves. Smashed. Completely smashed.

Blue and red lights bounce off nearby buildings. Cars part. I wait in the cold.

CHAPTER 6
PROVE IT

t's nearly nine p.m.—nine p.m. on a hell of a day—by the time a rather unenthusiastic cab driver dumps Boulder and me in our apartment's parking lot. Ice crunches beneath my boots, and Boulder, still unsteady from the anesthesia, pauses now and then, his legs trembling. The landlords, damn them, should have already put down salt. Or sand, I guess, this close to the lakes. Whatever. In an ideal world, I'd be able to carry a Saint Bernard who weighs as much as I do, but in case this day and—*gestures broadly*—has not already made it apparent, we're a bit off the mark from *ideal world*.

Once inside, we take the elevator, the elevator with its dim yellow light and the painful screeching of cables from above and below, and wouldn't it be great if this rickety hellbox inched us upward at speeds faster than a floor a minute? It's not like I have a financial meltdown to navigate. It's not like, in the aftermath of my car's totaling, I have online car shopping to do. It's not like I'd still like to, at some point on this godforsaken day, reply to that email I've been sitting on now for—huh, it's only been six hours.

The doors part. I urge Boulder along, his weight swaying

as we navigate the hall. Here! Home. Keys jangle. Boulder mistakes them for the sound preceding a walk, which, nope. Sorry, boy. You're in no shape for a walk, and you used the facilities—so to speak—right after leaving the vet and again before we walked into the building here, so I'm going to need you to calm down. You need to rest. "Not out of the woods" is the phrase the vet used, though she did add that so long as you don't go licking the frying pan clean of bacon grease again—I'll be watching you—you're likely to be okay. Likely.

We enter the apartment, and away we go. "All right, Boulder-boy, your dad's going to post up on the couch for the foreseeable future. Get comfortable with me? Maybe I top off that water dish first?"

Once his water dish is full, I nab my laptop and make for the couch. Boulder, after a good minute of sloppily lapping from his dish, lowers himself onto my feet, which, all right, an unusual choice, but the dog's still on drugs and it's not like my toes won't appreciate the warmth.

Now, a pause. A moment to collect myself. I close my eyes, draw a deep breath. What I type in this email to this father-claimant of mine could very well shape my future, my *every-thing* going forward. No pressure, Eric. You've handled every-thing else today with grace and aplomb; surely you won't shit the bed like Boulder shat the entirety of the living room after rooting through the—okay, this is gross, and a lack of focus has already cost you umpteen times today, man. Find the email that kicked off this absolute clusterfuck of an afternoon and let's get this taken care of.

Before responding, I read the email once. Okay, twice, all in an attempt to recapture how this feels, how this really makes me feel. On the floor, Boulder smacks his lips, farts. I cover my nose with the front of my T-shirt and, at long last, type a reply.

Why in the ever living fuck should I believe you, you fucking creep? Probably some scum lord whose scam I blew up out for revenge. Special Advisor to Latin America? Nose just like my mom? Pointing out that she and my grandma are dead? You're a stalker, a cheap imitation, a lowlife with nothing better to do than harass people who've pissed you off.

And let's just say you are, in fact, my dad. What the fuck is the matter with you? Why would you think I'd want to hop on a call with you? To meet up with you? I've been fine for twenty years, but now I'm supposed to welcome you back with open arms? Get bent. All the way bent. Bent three times over, for all I care.

The rage tightening the cords of my neck, the grief welling in my chest, it's all too much. I need to walk this off, to stretch, but when I do, my shirt slips, and I gag on the stench. "Jesus, Boulder." The dog, dreaming, twitches in his sleep. I stand, slip my feet out from beneath him—sorry, buddy—and take a lap of the apartment. Kitchen, bedroom, adjoined bathroom, the other bedroom I use for, well, nothing much, but it's nice to have space when your roommate is a canine with a penchant for violating EPA emissions standards. What's important here is that circling back to the couch—and finding the surrounding airspace devoid of dog stank—grants me the clarity I need. I sit. I slip my feet back under Boulder. I delete my previous draft and try again.

Do you know how many nights I spent wishing it was a dream? How many days I hoped you'd walk back through that door? High school graduation, college, that time I finally mustered up the courage to audition for that improv team—I wished you were there for all of it, but you missed it and, holy fuck, I probably would have made the team if I hadn't spent the entire audition distracted because the man seated in the back of the auditorium looked just like you.

Fucking A. I missed you, but you missed everything, and—

I wipe one eye, then the other, and delete everything I've written. Write it, Eric. Write what you really want to know. Write exactly what it is you're after.

Two words, then. Two words before a click of the send button.

The message sends and, just confirming, it's now in my sent folder. The deed is done.

Prove it.

Now, I wait.

CHAPTER 7
BREAKFAST BAR

The sun rises. At the breakfast bar, I shift on my stool, my fried egg and coffee untouched. Even Boulder has lost interest in begging for scraps, and whatever appetite I might have had has been replaced with a sense of unease.

Vet bills are not cheap. Pre-owned vehicles are not cheap. Rent and electric and internet and dog food—none of them are cheap, but all must be paid, and paid with funds that are increasingly thin. And I just got a paycheck, for fuck's sake! I should be flush, but so it goes when your moneyed grandma gets fleeced out of an inheritance-to-be, when you're texting —or, well, using Discord—while driving, when your dog gets on his hind legs to inspect the stove, unaware he's about to consume enough fat to overwhelm his doggy innards and unleash a slurry of indogstrial waste into the carpet.

No wonder my fried egg remains untouched.

But it's fine. I'll make it work. I always have, and even if I have to find a roommate or downsize to a studio, it'll be temporary. Let's say I haggle my way into a deal when I visit the car dealership this weekend, that'd be a good start. Yeah, everything's coming up Eric!

I glance at my egg. My stomach growls. I raise my fork, set it down just as fast.

Boulder lifts his head.

"No," I say, giving him a rub with my knuckles, "that doesn't mean you can have any."

Boulder whines a low whine.

"You and me both, bud." I check the time. I should be at work, at my desk, pretending to email my way through the day. Well, technically, I do email my way through the day, just not how the gods of American-made medical devices would prefer. Perhaps that's why I find myself here, smitten—smote?—by the vengeance-bent deities of electroencephalograms and electromyograms. *Prostrate yourself before us, mortal, and reap the rewards of the plots you have sown!*

I suppose I could be good at my job, just this once.

Just this once for the first time in months, technically. I haven't always been this way.

So, fine—I slide my plate aside, retrieve my laptop, and splay it open before me.

"What's the damage, Boulder? How many unread emails am I sitting on, you think?"

The sudden stench answers for him.

"Good Lord, Boulder." A familiar scene: me, my shirt over my nose, carrying my laptop to the couch, where I sit. "If you didn't want to play, you could have guessed one email so you wouldn't go over. Though I suppose I didn't say we were playing by *Price is Right* rules. A safe assumption, though."

I settle into the couch, and, this is interesting—my email still hasn't loaded, which means maybe I'm having trouble connecting to the company VPN? Not that I should need VPN access to read email, but—oh. Wow.

God damn it.

One thousand four hundred thirty-one unread emails. Read that number again. I'll wait.

Okay, maybe it's not that bad. A nonzero number are

probably from Microsoft Analytics, and then there's the approximately seven billion bulletins HR sends out every week in the interest of *fomenting an exuberant corporate culture*—oxymoron, much? And let's not forget the group threads I get cc'd into and never need to read, the weekly sales updates from Shawn, and, hey, throw in a thousand mostly inane emails from Dolores, and suddenly it's not that bad.

Except for this email from Dolores. This one. Right here. Right at the top.

Just checking you've reviewed my email from last Thursday. Caio is on-site as of this morning, so—

Caio. On-site. Like, *at* Nortex. As in Caio of the Ampersand account is visiting from Brazil, a country whose accounts I'm at least partially responsible for.

It's fine. A visit like this isn't normal, but it's fine. It's probably a routine corporate check-in; the two of us have never met face-to-face despite frequent—if not daily when I'm actually doing my job—conversations by email and phone, so Caio must have been due for a visit to his biggest supplier. Me. Well, Nortex. Nortex, who I represent.

"This has to be what Dolores was prattling on about." Near the breakfast bar, a smash, a clatter. "Boulder, what the —?" I lunge from the couch seconds too late. He's eating—has eaten—the whole of my fried egg. "Come on, man." I sigh, retrieving the plate and fork from the floor. "I'll crack a window so you don't asphyxiate during the day."

In the end, I leave the windows closed—it's damn cold out, and I can't have the heat bill any higher than it already will be this month—but I do take a moment to check my email once more before hustling to the bus stop.

No. Nothing. Nada from my father. My *definitely not my* father.

Scammers always turn tail when you call them on their shit.

CHAPTER 8
CATCHING UP

Today, the Zig.

Once at my desk, I fly into my chair, connect my Raspberry Pi to my monitors, keyboard, and mouse. I turn it on, knees bouncing while I wait.

At last, my dual monitors flash to life. I log in before realizing, good God, man, old habits die hard. Scambaiting is not what I'm here to do, not today.

Not that it would hurt to check. Just a peek.

It's been a tough twenty-four hours, okay? Let me have this.

I open one tab—not five—and the circle icon spins on my screen. *Loading, loading, loading,* it declares oh-so mercilessly, and why is the internet so damn slow today? Even if I were trying to determine when and where I should be to connect with Caio—which I'll very much do in a minute—it'd take an hour for the full contents of my email to load at these speeds. And to think people trust this company's EEGs. Can't even get the internet right.

I reach for my phone. It's not there. Again, old habits.

The circle icon ceases spinning. My screen goes black. I

give it a thwap with my palm, and presto! We're back with a new email from my father and the proof I've been waiting for.

A new email. My father. The proof I've been waiting for.

CHAPTER 9
PROOF

"Eric?"

"Dolores." I minimize my windows.

"You're late."

"For the thousandth time, Dolores, I've told you I'm on a schedule that—"

"For the meeting," she says. "Caio's eager to speak with you. Sean and Shawn are waiting, too."

"Good. Right. Of course." I swivel my chair away from her, slide my Raspberry Pi from sight, and open my work laptop on my lap.

"What's that all about?" Dolores asks, nodding to my Pi.

"Oh, it's uh—" My cheeks are flush and only growing more so, I can tell. But think, Eric. Quick on your feet and with your tongue now, like those scambaiting streamers you admire. "Product testing. New motherboards for the Norseman EMGs. Neat, huh?"

"Well," Dolores says, "maybe now's not the time for testing? Considering you're late for the meeting? Again?"

"Hang on." I navigate to my inbox—my actual *work* inbox —and please, what in the actual, could my email and calendar load any more slowly?

"Internet's been awful all morning," Dolores says.

"Seems like it." My calendar loads, and wouldn't you know it? A ten a.m. meeting in conference room Excalibur. What a name. "I'll be right in."

"You know where Excalibur is, right?"

I wave her off. "I'm coming."

Dolores strolls away, which means, okay, a moment to ground myself. I close my eyes, place my hands over my stomach, try for three deep breaths. I attempt to channel *Zen and the Art of Account Management*, but instead it's all *Meeting Your Dad for the First Time in Twenty Years for Dummies*. Assuming, Jesus, do I want to meet him? See him, I mean. That's what he asked for in his first email—and now the second—a chance to talk, to explain himself, and do I even give him that chance? And this weekend? That's, like, days away.

I could be seeing my dad in a matter of *days*.

My thoughts snap back to his email. I open it again, revisit the attachment, *the proof*.

I'm thirteen years old in the Polaroid, the scanned image my father sent. Thirteen years old as of, as my mother would always remind me, 5:36 that morning.

In the photo, I sit at the kitchen table, a single candle flickering in the middle of my pancakes. My father has leaned forward, his tie dangling away from his chest, his briefcase on the floor at his feet.

I didn't want my mother to take this picture, nor did I want the one that came immediately after when my mother and father traded positions behind and in front of the shutter. I didn't want the candle in my breakfast, didn't want the wax to melt and spoil my pancakes, didn't want to be up at that hour at all.

And yet, my mother woke me. And yet, I posed. And yet, I choked down the pancakes, wax and all, while my dad kissed my mom goodbye for the last time, the Polaroid of the two of us in hand.

Now, twenty years later, I'm thankful for the sleep I lost that day.

This is the last photo anyone took of me and my father alive.

I check the time. I'm late, so late for this meeting, but I can't waltz in there looking how I feel, not with Caio and Shawn and Sean and God knows who else waiting. So—a moment to steady myself, because this is fine. This is normal. My dad is alive. So what? Other people have dads who are alive, too, except their dads had midlife crises instead of being dead for twenty years. Sometimes life's just like that. For my dad. And me now, I guess.

Okay, so not fine. Not normal, but *slow down*, remember? Let's be skeptical for a second, lest we—I—get duped like Grandma Amundsen, the legend herself. On the extremely outside chance this is still a bluff, I'd rather be in the know than the one getting hosed. Or something.

This Polaroid, for starters. Only one copy existed unless my dad had one made on his way into work that morning. The likelihood of that aside, could you even make copies of Polaroids in the early 2000s? Let's say you could have. Let's say my dad had an extra copy on him when he died. What would it take for that copy—or even the original, I suppose— to wind up in the hands of someone I just so happened to have scambaited previously?

A lot. A hell of a lot. We're talking a series of events like my dad scanned a Polaroid within a one-hour window, and years later, the file became compromised by someone who realized this photo featured me, the scambaiter who wasted their time despite the fact that, are you kidding me, the people I scambait know me as nothing more than the world's most generic email addresses and randomly generated aliases.

There. Skepticism check complete, and, holy hell, this is really happening.

I steady myself, laying my hands flat on either side of my keyboard.

My dad is alive. He wants to see me. This weekend, even.

Right. This is the part, Eric, where you come up with a plan. Will you see your dad? Will you write him back? What will you say when—no, *if* you do? Again, Eric, *what's the plan?*

I wait. Nothing.

I wait. Nothing still.

I wait, and a glance at the time knocks the wind out of me —what little I had left in me. This meeting. I have to go, should have already gone, should already be there tending to my more immediate future.

Before collapsing my laptop and scampering to conference room Excalibur—wherever the hell that actually is—I take one final peek at the Polaroid.

CHAPTER 10
AMPERSAND

By the time I find the conference room, I arrive an additional ten minutes late.

"Ah, there he is," Sean says, the tool. Straight out of business school, that one, as of yet uncudgeled into indifference by the corpocracy. Meanwhile, Shawn, our VP of International Sales, sits with his arms folded at the head of the conference room table like—and I don't know why I always see him this way—a grumpy Mr. Waternoose from *Monsters Inc.*, six legs and all.

Yeah, don't ask.

Elsewhere, Dolores dares a self-satisfied grin because *of course she does.* And Caio? No Caio. Where is Caio?

I set the question aside, my chin to my chest. Please, gods of corporate America, let my attendance be perfunctory! Let this be a meeting that could have been an email! Do this for me, oh gods, and I promise I will brew a new pot of coffee when I pour the last cup from the break room carafe. I will do this in your name from now until the end of time, or at least until I retire, or at least until this crisis is averted because, let's be honest, you don't exist.

"Hey, Caio." Sean leans forward, speaking into the—oh,

come on—conference call speaker? "We've got Eric here now if you want to say hi."

"Hey, Eric," Caio says. "*Tudo bem?*"

Is everything well? Funny you should ask, Caio. "*Suave na nave,*" I lie, taking a seat. "*E você?*"

"*Ótimo.*"

Okay, if everything is great, why have I been dragged into this meeting? Why is Caio on speaker instead of on-site as advertised?

"Well," Caio says, his accent flaring up on those syllable-final Ls, "*na verdade,* my flights have been a mess."

"Again," Sean chimes in, "we're really sorry about the issue with your connection."

Dolores takes this as some sort of cue. "You know, Caio, I've never really minded the Miami airport. You could do worse. Plus, since you're staying the night now, you've got a lot of night life available to you, you know."

Caio ignores her. "Eric, tell me what we're going to do."

Me? What? This was all under control, presumably, until Caio's flights were compromised. At least I think so. It's not like I've been reading my emails. My work emails. Either way, this shouldn't be hard. Just have him fly into Madison.

"First and foremost," Shawn intervenes, "Eric will be picking you up at O'Hare when your flight gets in tomorrow."

I pinch my brows together. "O'Hare?"

"Yes," Dolores says, "because there are no connecting flights available from Chicago to Madison for days, *remember?*"

You know, I'd appreciate the expertise of Dolores's digs a lot more if I weren't the subject of them.

"So," Shawn says, picking up where he left off, "you can look forward to Eric waiting for you outside your terminal tomorrow, Caio."

I raise a finger in protest because, uh, no matter Caio's

issues with connecting flights, it'll be hard to pick him up without a car.

Sean eyes me. Shawn, too, not that his curmudgeonly ass has stopped staring at me since I arrived.

I lower my finger because, add it to the list, it looks like I'm getting a new car tonight. A *new to me* car tonight, even if, sure, I could rent one to get me through until I'm ready to buy, but why put off the inevitable? "Yes," I say. "I'll be there. When and where do you need me?"

Caio relays his flight number, his arrival time, his terminal. I make careful note of each, nodding as if he can see me, which he definitely cannot. The silence on the line is long, too long, apparently, for an impatient Caio.

"But my question?" he says. "I'd like to know what we're going to do."

"About your travel plans?" I ask. "We just—"

"Is this a joke?" Caio says. "*Se sim, pode deixar*. We have an enormous problem here, Eric."

Dolores leans forward. "Yes, Caio, Eric is aware of the situation. I put this on his radar last Thursday."

A pause. A hot flash on my brow. I throw open my laptop, navigate to my email, scroll for whatever it is Dolores tried to put on my radar last week—which was apparently *not* just Caio's presence at our facility—but it's like we're working with dial-up speeds here, which reminds me of my first computer, which reminds me of tagging along to Circuit City with my dad to shop for it, which reminds me of the photo on my Raspberry Pi's hard drive.

"So, Eric," Caio says, "a solution?"

Solutions? Even if there weren't mitigating circumstances, I don't do solutions. I do—what was the word I used during my interview?—facilitations. Solutions are up to management, not that I said *that* in my interview.

I glance up from my screen at Sean, at Shawn, at Dolores. They have nothing to add, apparently.

Improvise. It's time to improvise. What would Kitboga do? Pierogi? Pretend you're on a call with a scammer, Eric, and the floor is yours. You did it with Dolores earlier and you can do it again now. Things have gone sideways, but you're in control. Channel the best. Be the best.

"Caio," I say, removing my gaze from my laptop for a moment, "first of all, I want to apologize. I'm sure this has been an inconvenience for you—"

"More than an inconvenience, *rapaz*."

Rapaz. Boy. Every inch of my skin crawls at the word, at the implications it carries. "You're right. I'm sorry. I do want to assure you, however, that you have our full attention."

Another pause. Shawn's chair groans when he shifts his weight, his cheeks tomato red. Bad. This is bad. Scenes of dismissal at the hands of HR, of an embarrassing escort from the building flash before me. Rent. Utility bills. Boulder's overnight stay at the vet and everything that came with it, all of it on my credit card, all of it unpaid. So, back to scrolling through my inbox. Find that email. Find that damn email.

"We will need more information than this," Caio says. He's polite, but testy. "Our ability to sell in our home market is in trouble. We are having a big problem with these kinds of ANVISA violations."

Heads up from Dolores or no, if ANVISA's involved, this is above my pay grade. The FDA is tough enough, but ANVISA? Don't get me started. You think you know bureaucracy, but have you met *Brazilian* bureaucracy? Give me a break.

Please. I'm begging you. Give me a break, and where is regulatory affairs when you need them? "I, well—" I try to swallow, but my mouth is dry, so dry, and Christ, remind me why I let my inbox become so unruly.

Right. A promise. Grandma Amundsen.

Shawn clears his throat. "Caio, this is Shawn."

"Shawn?" Caio says. "You sound funny."

"It's Shawn, not Sean," Shawn clarifies.

"I didn't realize you were different people," Caio says.

Shawn shifts from red to purple at this news, but he presses on, his eyes never leaving me. "We want to make it clear that Ampersand is our top priority. You and I both know that from a South American sales perspective—particularly as it pertains to Brazil—Ampersand and Nortex depend on each other to thrive."

"Yes, well," Caio says, "This is very good, but—and I do not say this easily—there are people on my team here who have been asking about Cyberstar products, and—"

Shawn lurches from his chair. "Eric, what do you have planned to address this *now?*"

Inspiration strikes. "I'm trying to load my proposal,"—I narrow my eyes at my screen, at this proposal that is one hundred percent real and definitely not something I've made up on the spot—"but our network is so slow." Huzzah! This puts them on their heels a moment: Sean fidgets with his phone, Shawn taps his fingers on the conference room table, and Dolores, well, she's got her most smug smile trained on me, but what else is new?

For a flash, it seems as though I've fought my way to a stalemate.

Then, an awful thought, a terrible realization. "Dolores, did you say everyone's computers have been slow all day?" I ask.

Shawn intervenes. "IT is working on it."

"It's been tough," Dolores adds. "But the slowdown did give me a chance to get caught up on my stapling."

Her stapling. What does that even mean? *Her stapling?*

I never get the chance to ask—not that I would have, anyway.

"This is incredible," Caio says, his ire apparent. He curses us in English, and it doesn't get any better when he transitions to Portuguese. Incompetence, a lack of professionalism, a failure to care for customers—I bear the brunt of all these accusations and more, and even if I could argue, I wouldn't; every insult the man casts is true.

"*Então,*" Caio says emphatically, "*o quê diabos a gente vai fazer para consertar essa merda?!*"

"We'll be doing nothing to address 'this shit' today," I say.

No one chastises me for this. They, too, are speechless, their eyes glued to their screens, which I suspect are locked, the same as mine.

Caio's rage continues. "You will let Eric say this? He will speak this way to a customer?"

"Sorry, Caio," I say, my voice strained, my suit jacket suddenly hot, too hot. "There's just… we might have a bigger problem on our hands."

Dear sirs,

We have infiltrated your servers. Your files are encrypted. The encryption key will be granted only once a Bitcoin payment of 250,000 United States Dollars is remitted to the address at this link.

This sum will double every forty-eight hours, at which time ten percent of your files will be destroyed. This will continue until the sum is paid.

Yours,
Mrs. Aisha Al-Qadaffi

CHAPTER 11
DON'T CLICK THAT

stand. "Don't click that link."

"Click what?" Caio says.

"I already did," says Sean, who, what the fuck, supposedly belongs to a generation that's more tech savvy than mine.

"Yeah," Dolores says, "we'll need to know the address if—"

I abandon the room and march for IT, past row after row of questioning colleagues, of confused grumbles, of astonished gasps. They stare when my stride becomes a jog, and I'm a rounded corner away from IT when the overhead speaker system crackles to life.

"Attention all Nortex staff. IT has been made aware of an ongoing ransomware attack against Nortex systems."

I halt, my heart racing, my lungs aflame. I press my hand to the wall, lean against it.

"Please take the following steps immediately. Disconnect your laptops from their docking stations. Disconnect your laptops from any hardwired connection to Nortex infrastructure, including any connection to our intranet.

Disconnect your device's access to our wifi, and then power down."

"The links," I add under my breath, still short as ever.

"Lastly," the speaker says, "do not click any links that appear on your screen. This message will be repeated."

Before it is, I'm on my way to my cube. I throw my winter coat over my shoulder, nab my Raspberry Pi, and gun for the exit.

CHAPTER 12
CONGRATULATIONS, YOU BLEW IT

search the parking lot, pacing, the undersides of my feet burning.

Me. I did that. It was that damn download in HR from yesterday, and how in the fuck could I have been such a noob?

Because of him. My dad. He's the one who really did this. Well, he didn't *do this*, but if it weren't for him, I wouldn't have been there, in HR, away from the relative safety of my traditional scambaiting setup. This is his fault, then, and I'll have to really let him have it when—wow, so it's a *when*—we see each other, which will be never if I can't find my damn car.

Ah. My car. The one I no longer have.

"Fuck." A cloud of white accompanies the exit of the word, and, wow, it *is* damn cold out, maybe it's time I put on this jacket. And gloves. And hat.

I turn as I slide on my jacket, facing the building. What's there to do? Telling IT now won't unfuck this Digital Chernobyl. It wouldn't even help them stymie the encryption of our files. Running to IT at this juncture would be like witnessing the explosion at reactor four and, the following day, letting everyone know you were there when it happened. Like—cool, man, but we're trying to put out a fire, the likes of which the planet has never before seen, so if you could hold that thought until all of Ukraine and Belarus are no longer becoming blanketed in radioactive material, that'd be great.

Yes, I enjoyed the mini-series as much as everyone else. What can I say? I'm a sucker for disaster.

A sucker *and* a magnet for it, apparently.

So, damage control. I'd ask my Scambait Bros for help, but one, we all know how excited they'd be to play *I told you so,* and two, I remain without a phone. Maybe later, then, but first—a car. I have to pick up Caio tomorrow if I plan to keep myself on the Nortex payroll, so it's off to the dealership.

Well, it's off to the bus stop, where I realize, very cool, I have no idea when the next bus will arrive.

I stand in the cold, waiting, shivering.

CHAPTER 13
OF COURSE, SIR

"So," the car salesman—Al, I think—says, "you'll sign here, here, and initial here, and the keys are yours."

I study the paperwork in the cramped office of the used car dealership. You never can tell with these people —by which I mean peddlers of used wares. Or, to paint with a broader brush, you never can tell with anyone, really, because when it comes right down to it, everyone's got an angle they're working. Besides, can you imagine my shame if I were to get conned by a two-bit huckster like Al here? No. No way. Not happening.

Not that it looks like it's going to be an issue. The contract looks good, but what's this now? This is not the price we arrived at, no. It's off by a thousand bucks in the dealership's favor.

I set down my pen. "I thought we agreed on—"

"Yes, but once you throw in the warranty—"

"Well—" I *need* that thousand dollars; I spent the entirety of my time after the test drive haggling for it, and now they're trying to slap a grand back on the sale price in the name of some warranty that will likely overlap with my insurance? This is the kind of thing I'm always on about.

There's a reason I told them I wouldn't be financing the vehicle. Up front. Cash only. Did you really think I would pay interest to some dealership's phony bank? Be serious. Just say *no* to monthly payments! The smaller the window you give people to take advantage of you, the better. "The price we shook on is an important price for me to hold to, warranty or no."

Al slides the paperwork from my hands. "This price?" he says. "Here? At the top of the page?"

"Yeah."

"I can give you half off the warranty."

Like I said, *everyone's got an angle they're working.* "Really, the final total is what counts for me."

"We can keep the price as posted at the bottom of the page and *double* the length of the warranty."

I dip my chin, hunker down. I need that thousand bucks, if not for Boulder's vet bills, for myself. I need it for food, for shelter. I need it to maintain a sense of dignity.

I need that thousand bucks because I made a promise.

All right, then. Time to negotiate like I mean it.

"I don't know if I can be more clear," I say. "The price at the top of the page is the one to which we agreed, and I would appreciate it if—"

Al turns, drops the contract into the shredder. "Of course, sir."

While the shredder whirs, Al checks the time. I do, too. The dealership is approaching its closing hour—as will be the case once I make it to the Verizon store—but I wasn't going to let that get to me. No, sir!

Al clicks his mouse, slides it, clicks again, and the printer comes to life. "Just another moment."

I nod.

The new contract prints. I review it, and would you look at that? No more pesky warranty! No other fast ones he's attempting to pull on me! Then it's a quick signing of the paperwork and another shaking of hands before I snatch the keys and stroll for the lot.

Crisis averted. Scam evaded. Promise upheld. Though one wonders if it'd be worth scanning their Google Reviews for persistent infringement of customer expectations. There's no way most people are taking the time to read every contract line by line before signing.

I glance over my shoulder at the dealership. I'll keep an eye out, but for now, *eyes forward* because there's nothing like a pre-owned, 2014 Toyota Corolla S to make a man feel—well, it's a car. Come on. It's just a car that, admittedly, has more than its fair share of miles and a less-than-ideal clanking sound whenever the heat's turned all the way up, but this car is a win, and one I desperately needed considering the forthcoming fallout from Digital Chernobyl.

Though I suppose—that email from my dad. That photo. The invite to meet him this weekend. These were wins, too. Well, perhaps not *wins*, but advancements of the ball. Whether it'll cross a goal line remains to be seen.

To find out, I'll have to keep playing. To find out, I'll need a phone.

CHAPTER 14
BAD NEWS AND BAD NEWS

clutch my new phone, waiting while it downloads Discord. At my feet where I stand eating over my kitchen sink, Boulder licks his chops, and no, Bouldie, what's left of this very sad peanut butter and jelly sandwich is for your father and your father alone because I'm assuming you don't want another trip to the vet in your future. I set down my phone a minute and kneel for a hug—because I could really use one, dammit—which, look at that, Boulder rebuffs by licking my face instead.

"You only love me for the residual peanut butter. I see how it is."

Boulder puts his paws on my shoulders, knocking me onto my butt.

"Okay, and we're done. You can stop with the kisses because *ulterior motive*. You've got one and I'm not having it. Fine. One more. Now your dad needs to get his shit together in the aftermath of you having, quite literally, lost yours, because only one of us is allowed to be a drain on this household's finances at a time, and that person's going to be me unless I can, I don't know, reverse a Digital Chernobyl. Don't look at me like that. You know what I'm talking about."

The dog, naturally, has no idea what I'm talking about.

On that note, however—PrakashMoney and Salchicha-Simon surely *will* know what I'm talking about, and fortunately for me, Discord has completed its download. Now, to log in, and explain away.

It doesn't take long for replies to come rolling in.

PrakashMoney: How can I put this nicely?
BoulderIBarelyKnowHer: Why do I think you're *not* going to put it nicely?
SalchichaSimon: Because it's going to be bad news and bad news.
PrakashMoney: Yeah, there is no "nicely." You're fucked, man. It was only a matter of time until scambaiting on the job caught up with you.
SalchichaSimon: Remind me, P-Money, who told him that was a bad idea?
PrakashMoney: That would be you, Simon.
SalchichaSimon: *bows deeply*
BoulderIBarelyKnowHer: Cool. Thanks so much for your help.
PrakashMoney: You asked us to be honest about your chances. At this point, the only way your ass gets to keep your job is if the ransom isn't paid and the scammers delete everything. Including, you know, any evidence that you were responsible.
BoulderIBarelyKnowHer: That… is a good point.
SalchichaSimon: Don't get too excited. If they *do* delete everything…
BoulderIBarelyKnowHer: …?
PrakashMoney: If they delete everything, there won't be much of a company left to work at.

I hang my head. Boulder licks my hand. I pull it back, start a snarky reply to the—what did we decide on?—scammites, yeah, but what's the point?

I sigh into the couch and study the popcorn texture of the ceiling. "Well, Boulder, that leaves two possibilities." Boulder hops onto the cushion next to me, which, whatever. I'll allow it. "I lose my job, or I cheer for scammers to maybe hopefully possibly save my ass before still losing my job." The dog settles in, his head on my lap. "At least one of them doesn't include crossing my fingers for a scammer's success?"

Jobs, then. I'm going to need one, and sooner rather than later. I'd fetch my laptop from the bedroom, but Boulder now has half his body strewn across mine, so that's not happening. I pull up Indeed on my phone, start scrolling.

Pizza delivery. Stocker, third shift, retail. Office assistant. Cashier. Bookseller.

Been there. Nope. Nah. Flashbacks, and not the good kind. Meh.

Where are the jobs, the ones that'll pay just enough to help me hand over that money to someone else immediately after having earned it? You know—human food, dog food, rent, electric and internet and phone. The list goes on. What a system we've cooked up—an entire economy of people hustling to out-hustle the hustlers. No wonder so many turn to dishonest livings.

Not that I'm looking to empathize with those bastards.

All right. I need a reset, a quick jaunt down Scambait Lane. To the laptop! Sorry, Boulder, but all laps must be vacated eventually. Take it from me and Grandma A: life's not fair, and that's not changing soon.

With my laptop open, I stand at the breakfast bar and—shit. Here. Right at the top. The email from my dad, the attached Polaroid, his invite. I do need to reply, but what's a man to say? I called his bluff and he raised the stakes, big time. I'd be embarrassed if I weren't, well, I have no idea what it's called when one's experiencing all five stages of grief simultaneously —except for maybe depression and acceptance, because I don't think this will be real until I've seen him with my own eyes.

My fingers hover over the keyboard. He has to wait, doesn't he? He can stand by another twenty minutes while I scambait or, now that my laptop's open, do more than a half-assed job search.

"Boulder!"

His ears wiggle, but he doesn't leave the couch.

"Why didn't you think of this sooner?"

At this, he lifts his head.

"What if scambaiting *were* my job?" With my laptop in hand, I return to the couch, wedge myself into the corner Boulder doesn't occupy. "Think about it: the Pierogis, Kitbogas, and Jim Brownings of the world all have Patreons and Twitch subscribers and merch. I've got, you know, a modest background in improv. I could make some videos walking people through my scambaits, and so long as I kept them entertaining and educational, I could make a run at culti-vating a followership, right?"

Boulder, almost predictably, passes wind at the proposition.

"I take it you won't be my first subscriber." I pull my sweatshirt up over my nose, but—"Christ, Boulder." I vacate the couch and head for the bedroom, lying prone across the foot of the bed with my laptop open before me.

This is possible. This can happen. I can create a YouTube account, anyway, and start working on a header image in between combing through my favorite scambaits from the last couple of months. I mean, come on—these inboxes are veri-table gold mines of vigilante justice just waiting to be monetized.

Ah, but here it is, a pesky thought to still my fingers on the trackpad: Grandma Amundsen.

A YouTube channel might raise awareness about these

scams and the people perpetrating them, but it wouldn't be about justice and justice alone; I'd be doing it for the clicks and views. Besides, most folks aren't hanging around in their spam folders in the first place. If I really wanted to create a channel worth watching, I'd have to get out of the scambaiting-by-email game and start chatting with scammers directly by phone.

Eventually. I'd need a whole new setup for that, and money is kind of the problem right now.

Still, I have to try, even if only with some of my favorite email scambaits; my pizza delivery days are and need to remain in the past. The remote past.

Grandma would understand. She'd have to understand.

I wonder if she'd understand my father's—her son's—reappearance. Hell, do *I* understand it?

I navigate back to the scanned Polaroid, let it linger on my screen. In a window behind it, my cursor expectantly blinks on, blinks off in an empty email.

I'll never know whether Grandma would understand the reason for her son's deliberate disappearance, but I can find out how I feel about it for myself—and before I commit to any sort of face-to-face.

So, in that email, I do. I ask, anyway, and I keep it short.

Why?

Until I have reason to believe otherwise, that's all the response my dad deserves.

CHAPTER 15
I-90 EAST

speed down I-90 East for Chicago, determined to time my arrival perfectly for Caio's exit from his terminal. Is this a total pipe dream considering the rat's nest of traffic that is O'Hare and Chicagoland writ large? Yes. Is that going to stop me from trying? No. If there's one thing I *am* capable of, it's arriving on time.

When I want to.

And, again, assuming the traffic situation doesn't take a turn for the worse, which is asking a lot considering the trip from Madison to Chicago is a cool two hours, one way, under the best of conditions. By this I mean *not winter*.

Not that any of this will save my surely doomed job, which, to be fair, isn't surely doomed if the scammers follow through with their file deletion, so—and here's where I'd don a foam finger if I had one—*Go, Team Scammer!*

Ugh, disgusting. Never again. Can't even joke about it.

But none of that unpleasantness, nothing of jobs to be lost, of could-be fathers. To prepare for having Caio in the passenger seat, I switch off my favorite podcast—*Better Yet with David Macomber*—to tune into some classic-to-me MPB. *Música popular brasileira* is how I got my start, after all, how I first compared Brazilian Portuguese and the Spanish they teach in university. Marisa Monte, Adriana Calcanhotto, Rita Lee—especially that cover Rita Lee does of the Beatles' "My Life" and Marisa's "*Universo ao meu redor.*" *Meu deus*, am I actually looking forward to having Caio in the car? We'll probably default to English, but you never know. I'm feeling in touch with early 2010s Eric now, the man who confidently trekked about São Paulo and Santa Catarina and Rio Grande do Sul before dipping into Uruguay for a week.

Maybe that's what I need, a vacation. Eventually. Whenever I can afford it again, which I very much could have already had my inheritance not wound up lining the pockets of Kolkata's sleaziest scamballs.

The heater—or something—clanks. I switch it off, back on. This did the trick when it revved up earlier, but—*fala sério*—the clanking continues, and why on Caio's cursed earth am I losing speed? I check my mirrors, signal, drift across one lane and onto the shoulder.

I smash, smash, smash the accelerator, but nothing. No go. The sound of metal on metal overpowers, becomes so overwhelming that Marisa's mournful notes are drowned out, and why is that the thing most pissing me off? This car! This beautiful, sleekly-designed car!

The Corolla lurches to a stop, now heinously quiet. Marisa still sings, but the engine is off. Stopped. *Sem vida.*

I nab my phone, consider my options. A tow. I have to do it. I need a tow and a rental, and I need them *o mais pronto possível.*

While I search for a tow company, my thoughts drift back to car salesman Al, that son of a bitch.

A lemon. He sold me a lemon, and what is it we do to scammers?

You know. I know. And Al's about to find out.

On the far side of a tow, that is.

CHAPTER 16
CADÊ?

An hour and countless voicemails to Caio later, a Lyft drives me to an Enterprise Rent-A-Car in Janesville. My car, meanwhile, is unceremoniously towed back to the dealership on Madison's West Side. I call him—Al, that is—and give him an earful by voicemail before I phone his repair center to give them a heads up.

"We'll keep an eye out for it," says the mechanic. "Should have a better idea of what's wrong tomorrow." I tell him that's fine, that's fine; just don't make any repairs until you've passed along a quote. "Yeah," the mechanic says, "sure thing."

"And do me a favor, will you?" I add.

"What're you thinking?"

"Make sure Al checks his voicemail."

At last, my Lyft finally arrives at the Enterprise on Milton. Caio's plane is landing any minute, and I'm still an hour and a half—best case scenario—from the airport. As I sign the rental agreement—which includes the extra insurance and damage waiver because, wow, lessons learned about saying no to warranties—my phone rings. Caio.

"*Alô,*" I answer, doing my best to be emphatically Brazilian.

"*Cadê você?*" All right, straight to the point.

"I am, uh,"—I finish with my signatures and initials, grab the keys from the attendant, head to the lot—"my car broke down. On the way to the airport. But I'm headed for you now." Where is this rental car? What vehicle am I even looking for?

"*Sério, rapaz?*"

It's a little early for *boy*, but okay. "*Infelizmente, sim.*" I really lay it on thick, my every syllable burdened with the weight of a thousand apologies. "*Mas daqui a uma hora e meia—*"

"Whoa," Caio says. "An hour? You will make me wait one hour and a half more?"

I click the lock feature on my keys, listen for a beep somewhere in the lot. "Yes, *amigo*, I'm sorry, but—"

"No. Not acceptable." He curses something fierce under his breath. "I will rent a car and drive to Nortex myself."

Finally, a beep from somewhere nearby. "Please, Caio, that's not necessary." I press the lock feature again, keep my ears attuned to the beep's direction. "I've already rented—"

"*Até a Nortex,*" Caio says. "You might want to tell them they will have a rental car to expense."

Well, *two* of them between Caio's and the one I've rented now, though who am I kidding, they're more likely to expense Caio's than they are mine, so add it to the ever-growing list: an auto repair bill, a rental payment, the new car, the replacement phone, Boulder's vet bills. Normally, I come out a little ahead every month, but *nossa senhora do céu.* If this hole gets any deeper—well, no time for that.

"I'm really sorry, Caio. I was stuck on the side of the road for—Caio? Are you there?"

I check my phone. Caio's hung up.

But here, on my screen, a fresh notification, an email from my father.

Why I left is more complicated than you think; it always was. I had to do it. I had to. If not for me, then for you and your mother. I'm happy to tell you everything, but I'd rather explain in person.

My jaw clenches.

The good news? I'm in Chicago.

Of *course* he is.

Not far for you, or shouldn't be. The offer still stands for this weekend.

I run my hands over my chin, consider my options, but first, maybe, let's find this damn rental car because it's not getting any warmer out here.

I click my keys' lock feature one more time, and, there, my rental. A 2014 Toyota Corolla S.

I can't make this shit up.

But to the car, finally, and let's crank that heat. Whatever I choose to respond with, I'll need unfrozen fingers to make it happen. I glance at my phone's screen. Chicago. Like *only an hour and a half away* Chicago.

I can't. I shouldn't.

I have to rush back to Nortex, have to arrive before Caio, have to explain what's transpired and why I was late to pick him up. I knock my knees together in the driver's seat, bouncing while I stare through the windshield.

Through spindly, mostly naked branches, the signs for the interstate onramp taunt me. I-90 West, home to disaster. I-90 East, onward to disaster—or, maybe, reconciliation. Answers, in the very least, which is more than Nortex can offer right now.

Fuck. I'm doing it, aren't I? I'm going to lose that damn job anyway.

I scroll up to the original email my father sent me, locate his phone number, open a new text message.

What about today? A couple of hours from now?

His reply is almost immediate.

Name a place and I'm there.

I shift into reverse, pull out of my parking space, and, at the onramp, take a right onto I-90 East.

CHAPTER 17
ACCEPTANCE

I didn't visit my father's grave until I turned seventeen.

Over the years, I told my mother I wasn't ready, that I couldn't handle it, that the sight of the gravestone would only make it real, final.

All of this was true, technically, but more immediate motivations kept me away.

Girls. Video games. The school plays. All of them. Every year. These distractions granted me solace, and I basked in the people and characters whose traits I embodied in order to shed myself of my own, of the guilt I felt—feel—for my father's absence.

But one listless night in October of my senior year, my mind circled back to him, endlessly, to his resting place on the far side of town. The very thought became a gravity well, one I, in my dedication to aversion, grew determined to avoid. So, I drove to take my mind off it, off him. I sped up John Nolen Drive, the skyline increasing in relative size, the capitol rotunda a ghastly beacon amid a thousand twinkling lights, their reflections shimmering on a softly swaying Lake Monona. After a turn onto Broom, I zipped west on University, cruising through the hodgepodge of stoic campus buildings. In this light, they seemed more fallout shelter than study center, more foreboding tower than residence hall. I abandoned downtown for Midvale, then, before cutting crooked paths down side streets and winding residential roads.

Then, at long last, I found myself at the place the dead rest.

There was no more avoiding it. Avoiding *him*. The gravity of his absence became too strong a pull even for me.

I told myself the agony in my chest was a result of the guilt, that if I'd only kept my mouth shut about the damn pet store, none of this would have happened. Deep down, I knew better, but I couldn't pretend it didn't pick at me, that it didn't motivate me to pull over and, at long last, drift through the graves.

I wasn't sure I'd find it. My memories of his burial always felt warped, as if the hours themselves existed out of time. It felt as if I ever broached the subject, others would insist I invented every moment because, here, look—your father has just walked in. See? Nothing to mourn.

When I did find the grave, the levee broke at the sight of the name, of my last name and my father's first on the stone. Then I knelt, the cold wind still managing to tear at the sleeves of a T-shirt that fit me all too snugly, and I wept, not knowing if I should touch the stone, not knowing if I should trace the name or say a prayer or do any of the things one's meant to do.

The longer I sat shivering, the more a creeping awareness overwhelmed—six feet of topsoil and concrete separated me from nothing more than an empty casket.

My father wasn't in there. There was nothing in there. A box. It had only ever been a box.

Of course. They never found his body.

I knew this, yes, but denial came for me, and with it, the inkling my father was out there, not watching down from above, but observing through other means. He was keeping tabs, living, breathing, biding his time, but the longer I lingered on the notion, the more the words of my therapist became true to me—that I was oscillating between denial and anger, and one day, when I was finally ready, I'd accept my father was no longer in my life, that he was gone and gone for good.

That night, I told myself my presence at the grave was an acceptance, that this was the moment it would all click, was clicking. This was a lie, naturally, one confirmed countless times over the years, and perhaps never so starkly as the day after my twenty-sixth birthday, when I realized I had known my father as a ghost for far longer than I ever knew the man.

And in that moment, a terrible pang.

If we ever reunited, I didn't know if I would recognize the man my father might have become.

CHAPTER 18
CLOUD GATE

illennium Park's stainless steel bean distorts the images of parkgoers and passersby, their warped reflections ambling and posing and puttering during a lunch hour jamboree in downtown Chicago. It's not a party, not really, but the pavement crawls with proper Chicagoans and tourists from near and far. How packed this place is blows my mind because *good grief*, it's fucking cold, and don't you people have anywhere warmer to be? Or are you all here also waiting for your dads to show up? Great minds, they say.

I settle in at a bench—my back in the direction of Lake Michigan—and thank what few lucky stars I have that parking was merely bad and not apocalyptic, not that it'd have been the worst thing to keep the old man waiting, which he's very much making me do now.

I glance at my phone. Nothing, not that I expected it. This is the place and more or less the time, a crowded plaza where it'd be next to impossible for my dad—or, as could still be possible, Eric, the scammer pretending to be him—to pull off any funny business, even if said plaza is among the more cliched places I could have suggested. What is this, a Hallmark original movie? Oh, watch now as father and son are reunited in one of the Windy City's most recognizable locales, but hey—aren't you proud of us for not shooting a film in London or New York for a change?

Blech.

I scan the crowd for a familiar face, for an aged version of a familiar face.

No one. Not yet.

I focus on my breathing.

Nearby, a mother tells her daughter they can't go ice skating in the park. Not this weekend, anyway, but maybe next. The rink will be here for a few more weeks, she adds, and I think on this. A weekend away-but-not-away: it would be nice to get away, to stomp about and drink hot chocolate and, later, trade my boots for ice skates.

Ugh, what am I talking about? That's not me. Doing something like that alone? Doing something like that at *all?* This business with my dad is really getting to me.

"This seat taken?"

I jump at the sound of the man's voice. "What? No. No, sorry."

"Didn't mean to scare you."

"It's okay. Just didn't see you there."

The man sits. I wonder.

No. The voice is all wrong, not to mention the mustache; my father would have never, would never grow a mustache.

"You waiting on someone?" the man asks.

"Yeah."

"I can leave, then, if—"

"It's okay. Not entirely sure who I'm looking for."

"Be careful now," the man says.

"What?"

"You never know with those Craigslist people."

I laugh, and the stranger does, too, though probably not for the same reason as me, if I had to guess.

My phone buzzes, and the man at my side abandons the bench, leaves me to my business.

SalchichaSimon: You went, right? You're there?

I squeeze my phone, blacken the screen. Telling Salchicha-Simon was a mistake, or, well, no—the whole point of telling him was so *someone* would know where I last intended to go if my supposed father were not, in fact, my father, but rather someone who would, I don't know, kidnap me.

I lean forward onto my knees. Christ, what a blunder, this whole operation. Today, the past week, but it goes back even deeper than that, doesn't it? Today's the culmination of it, and the coming week, if I'm honest, isn't looking any better. What do I even expect to find here? Not my father, surely, not the man I grew up with, anyway. I'm focusing on the past at a time I need to sort out my present, at a time I need to be planning for the future.

Fuck. Yes, again, fuck.

A man in a scarf emerges from the crowd. My posture straightens.

It's him, it's him, it has to be him.

There's no mistaking the dimple in the chin, the admittedly deeper than I remember crinkliness around the eyes, the hard stubble—gray now, not brown—of his jaw line.

I swallow, my fingers and toes tingling, and when he glances up from his phone, there's no denying it. He tucks his phone away. *My father* tucks his phone away. He approaches, suppressing a smile, his eyes glistening with tears.

When he reaches the bench where I sit, he stands there, his hands at his sides. Handshake? Hug? Punch the man? I've thought about this moment during the whole drive from

Janesville to Chicago, but I'm still unsure what grief and joy and adrenaline want me to do.

My father. I haven't spoken to him in years. So I do, now, my hands in my pockets, demanding from him the bare minimum I'm owed—because I never did get an answer.

"Why?"

CHAPTER 19
TERRIBLE THINGS

s the twenty-fifth letter of the alphabet." My dad chokes as he says it. Whether from sorrow or anger, I can't be sure, but I almost lose my shit at the string of nonsense —until the memory washes over me.

"Dad, why do you drive on the right side of the road?"

"Because that's what the law says."

"Why does the law say that?"

"It just does."

"Why?"

"Y is the twenty-fifty letter of the alphabet, and if you make me get to Z—"

This is one of many such exchanges lost to time, extinguished by grief, crowded out by second-semester calculus and the art of the Portuguese future subjunctive. But I catch a glimpse of these memories now, all of them, and for the first time, it hits me.

My father is human, and if I'm anything like him—which, look at the man, of course I am—he's likely a walking, talking, mistake factory, too.

Not that it justifies abandoning one's family. Not that I

could possibly be ready to forgive. Not that one joke makes up for two decades of absenteeism.

Still, I permit myself a smile, cough up a lone *ha*.

"I should've known better," my dad says. "Wasn't funny back then, either."

He continues to loom over me. My hands remain in my pockets.

"Do you want to get something?" My dad shuffles his weight, glances toward Michigan Avenue. "To eat, I mean. Or drink. My treat."

"I, uh—" *Didn't have a plan for this* is what I keep myself from saying, not that words of any kind are coming easily. I want to reach out and touch him, or, maybe instead let's try this—I pinch myself through the fabric of my jacket, and, yes, here we are. I'm still awake and my father is still standing there, gaping at me like I'm some sort of carnival sideshow.

"If you ate already," he says, "that's fine. I just thought—"

"No." I find myself standing. "We can—sure. Let's walk."

"Let's walk, then."

We do, wordlessly, matching each other stride for stride, expelling white wisps of breath. I feel for my phone, consider a message to SalchichaSimon, but I can practically hear my dad now, *"What? Your old man not interesting enough for you?"* On one hand, it'd be annoying as fuck to hear, but on the other, I've never been admonished by him for cell phone use, and isn't that something every kid should experience at some point? No?

Either way, so long as we stay among the crowd, so long as I don't follow him into an alley or up a quiet side street—what few of them there are immediately downtown—I don't have to be wary.

I don't have to be *as* wary.

He pipes up again after a few silent blocks. "I thought you'd have more questions."

"Oh, I do."

"You're welcome to ask away."

"Be careful what you wish for." I steal a glance at him. "And on that point, it's not like we're off to a good start."

"Aren't we?"

"Still waiting on that *why* over here."

My dad dry-coughs into his shoulder. "How about Panera?"

"I—okay. That's fine." Not like it matters. I only have an appetite for answers, which he seems uninterested in serving anytime soon. Still, I let him open the door for me and step inside, basking in—ah, yes—the glorious, familiar comforts of chain-restaurant America. I'd go on, but I'm not getting paid to promote Panera, and we all know what happened the last time I shilled for a brand.

Thanks, Toyota.

I keep myself half a step behind him while we wait in line. Who is this man? Who is he, *really*? Does he drink coffee? Tea? I wager he's a salad with an apple kind of guy—at least judging by the shape he seems to be in for someone his age.

Ugh. None of this means anything, not truly, not insofar as abandoning one's family is concerned. It's not like his meal of choice at Panera Bread defines who he is as a person, will justify what he did or what he's done in the last twenty years, and suddenly my breath is catching, shallow, labored, and the walls of Panera feel as if they're inching closer, closer, closer, and who designed this house of horrors? The undersides of my feet grow hot, and—

"Eric?"

"Yeah, what?" I snap, glance from my dad to the cashier. "Oh, shit. I mean. Sorry. Nothing. I'm good. Don't need anything."

Dad pays. My lips part to offer thanks, but nah, nope, not happening, and remember, Eric, you didn't order anything. Besides, I owe him nothing until I get what I came here for, and it isn't until we find a table in the restaurant's back corner that I realize, holy shit, *this is it*. He's alive. Here. *My dad isn't fucking dead.*

He drops his wallet on the table. "Sit?"

One of the chair legs sticks to the floor when I try to move it. To buy myself a moment, I shrug off my jacket and hang it over the chair back. My dad stares at me from across the way. "What?" I ask.

His smile remains wide. "I—just—"

"You can spit it out."

"Like looking in a mirror. A mirror into the past."

"We've got a lot of past to cover. And," I add, finally managing to slide out my chair, "I'm not really the one we should be looking to for answers."

My dad's expression sobers. "Fair. That's fair."

"So." I sit at last, fold my arms. I have to be strong, have to present a front that suggests I'm not questioning whether the racing of my pulse is dangerously fast, whether I should have even come.

"You probably want me to, uh—"

"The last time I saw you," I say, channeling my anger now, "you were heading into work on a Saturday morning. My birthday, in fact."

"Yeah."

"And then you drowned. Allegedly."

"That what they said it was?"

"What do you mean?"

"I never looked into my own death. Couldn't bear it."

My palms find the table. "*You* couldn't bear it?"

My dad dips his chin. "Right. Sorry. It's… I knew what I did was wrong, but it had to be done, and the sinkhole was the best opportunity I had. A perfectly plausible accident, even if never finding my body would have made it a stretch."

I lean away, study my father when he reaches for his mug —so he *does* drink coffee!—and while he sips, I rack my brain for other forgotten moments.

None come.

"Eric," my dad says, the mug tocking against the tabletop when he sets it down, "before I tell you what happened, I have to apologize."

I chew the inside of my cheek.

"I'm sorry. I really am. It was the hardest decision I ever had to make, and easily the worst thing I've ever done."

"I should hope so."

"I've done a lot of terrible things, Eric."

"You have another family you're jumping ship on to come back to Madison now?"

"No, nothing like that, but—" He glances about restaurant, winces when a blender whirs to life, and the two of us wait out its whir. My dad hides his face behind his hand. I steeple my hands in front of myself.

At last, the blender ceases its screaming. An order is dropped off at a nearby table, and as quickly as the Panera employee arrived, he departs.

"Eric," my dad tries again, "if I hadn't left, I would have been murdered."

I scoot back in my chair.

"You and your mother, too."

CHAPTER 20
CONFIDENCE MAN

Murdered. *Murdered?*

With a pained expression, his forehead glistening with sweat—so it *isn't* just me—my father lets it all out. "I was a confidence man. A con artist. A criminal."

A scammer, he means. My dad was a goddamn scammer.

It started in the nineties, my dad explains, with him and a buddy who lost their jobs during the first Bush years. They grew desperate, and Eric, he tells me, you were so little, and your mom couldn't find additional work, so hear me out because context is everything.

His buddy—and don't worry about his name; it's not important—heard through a friend of a friend about a dry cleaning scam, about some guy in New York City who made a hundred copies of the same dry cleaning receipt and mailed them to the finest restaurants in the area, how he included a letter claiming a member of the restaurant's staff had spilled on his jacket, so here's a dry cleaning bill you'd better pay or I'll run your name through the mud.

And people paid! The restaurants paid, some of them, anyway, preferring to save face than risk insulting a customer or injuring their reputation. If it worked in NYC, my dad's buddy said, why not give it a shot here? You need money, Glenn, and I do, too, and your boy Eric needs to eat, so let's give this a shot.

I wasn't sure, but, like I said, I was horribly desperate, Eric—keep that in mind—so my buddy and I went ahead and did it. And wouldn't you know it? Checks rolled in! Not many, but enough, and every visit to our drop box yielded an extra twenty dollars here, another twenty there. Meanwhile, the job market still wasn't what we needed to get by, so we visited the library—this was before the internet, you know, and yes, Dad, I'm not a rube. But anyway, my dad goes on, my partner and I read about similar scams, about the mistakes others made to get caught. We took note and expanded our operation accordingly; the dry cleaning racket proved to be one of diminishing returns, you see.

So then what? Phony sweepstakes. Letters from psychics who offered promises of great fortune if the mark was willing to pay by mail for their insight. Fraudulent charities, many of which were all about helping schmucks like your father and my buddy find employment during the recession.

"It got out of control," my dad says.

"It was out of control the second you started," I scoff, but oh how I marvel at the irony: that my father, a—former?—con man, is the parent to someone who's spent the last couple of months scambaiting his twenty-first century colleagues. And Grandma Amundsen! That my grandmother—his mom—lost her fortune to men like him? It's scammers and scams all the way down! I nearly tell him, excoriate him for being part of the ecosystem that ruined his mother's—that's ruining *my* life—but why? He doesn't deserve to know. The less he knows about me and about his own mother's final years, the better. This isn't going to be the happy reunion he came here for, anyway.

"I thought you'd be more understanding," he says.

In this moment, I am become sarcasm. "I suppose you're right. I should understand how someone low enough to abandon his family would also be a fucking scammer."

"Eric—"

"Don't *Eric* me. Don't anything me until you've explained how, exactly, this batshit operation of yours was going to cost your wife and son their lives."

"I'm getting there if you'd let me—"

"You have five minutes."

My dad grows restless. "For what it's worth, I wanted out of the whole operation the second my buddy and I found legitimate employment."

"So proud of you."

"If you're only giving me five minutes, maybe don't interrupt?"

"Ballsy to show up in my life like this and start making demands."

He's shaken, I can tell, and good. Fucking good. He should be, the bastard, though if I'm honest, I really am curious; maybe I will just shut up for, what, another four minutes and thirty-some seconds. Well, one more question first. "So you wanted out, but I'm assuming this continued while you also, eventually, had a job?"

My dad nods. "This went on for almost a decade, not that I wanted it to. It should have stayed small, and I can't emphasize this enough, Eric: I wanted out, but my partner had other ideas."

It was as if this friend, my dad says, became an entirely different person, a man obsessed with playing the game smarter, with staying one step ahead of marks who'd grown wise, as well as the authorities. The two of them changed their drop box address more frequently, diversified their tactics, executed them in smaller, steady waves rather than in single, large bursts.

"We didn't know what to do with the money," my dad

says. "We were addicts. We were just addicted to the thrill of the cat-and-mouse game."

Relatable content, that, what with the scambaiting and all—not that I'm letting him know about that. Not that I'm letting him know anything about me he doesn't absolutely have to know. He may be my father, but he clearly can't be trusted.

Not that an inability to trust him is some new revelation.

"You were saying," I interrupt, checking a watch I don't have, "something about how this led to threats of triple homicide?"

"Okay, yeah. But first, the money laundering. You remember the pet store, yeah?"

"No."

"You don't?"

"No, I mean like *no way*."

"You asked me one day, remember?" My dad stares over my shoulder, presumably replaying the moment in his mind, too. "You asked me who my friend was, the one at the pet store."

"I did."

"That was when I knew I couldn't keep you from the truth forever. I had to do something."

Something. In other words, *leave.*

My father left because of me.

"You okay?" my dad asks.

I snap out of the haze of self-pity. "Don't act like you're suddenly interested in my welfare."

"I was interested enough in your welfare to know that after the pet store incident, I had to get out."

"Fucking spare me. As if I'm going to be a prop in your—"

"You wanted to know!"

"Fucking cut to it, then." I notice, for the first time, that we've caught the attention of nearby tables, and because I don't want to be considered complicit in whatever he spews next—how long are the statutes of limitation on this kind of thing?—I lower my voice. "Just… no more meandering justifications for your shortcomings."

A gusty sigh. "In the end, I told him. My buddy, I mean. I told him I wanted out. Your mom had long been suspicious, but she was whip smart; she knew what she needed to know —and what she didn't need to know—for her sake and for yours."

"Focus. We're talking about the, uh,"—I glance about— "*ex-nay on the iving-lay* business."

My dad reaches for his mug, sips, drums his fingers on the table. "Essentially, my partner didn't trust me to keep quiet. I'd always been soft on the operation, he said, and other peoples' livelihoods were at stake here. I couldn't just drop out."

"And *then* he said he was coming after us?"

"Not in so many words."

I rub my forehead.

"It's a lot to process, I know," my dad says, "but everything I did, Eric, I did out of love. I did it to provide a home, a happy life for you and your mother. And in the end, I did it to protect you. I'm human, Eric, and people make mistakes. You have to understand."

"There you are again with that word: understand. *Understanding.*" I rise. "All I understand is that I've been just fine" —lie of the century—"without you for twenty years." I pluck my jacket from the back of my chair, slide my arm through one sleeve, then the other. "You may be human. You may make mistakes. But a confidence man? A scammer?"

"Eric, please—"

"No." I button my jacket, tuck my hands into its pockets. "I won't have that in my life." My dad finds his feet now, too, and the look of desperation on his face—I won't indulge it; I turn my back to him and stride for the door. "Delete my number from your phone."

"What?"

"It's an expression." A meme, basically, it's a fucking meme, and is that really going to be my parting shot?

It is, apparently, as the cold now nips at my face, the wind whistling over my ears.

At least I know what happened with the pet store.

Not that I should feel bad.

I can't; I made a promise to Grandma Amundsen, and I'm keeping it.

CHAPTER 21
THE MOVE

pace city streets, weaving in between pedestrians, my mind a mess of *that was your dad* and *where did you park* and *what now, what now?*

But it's not the *what now* that sucks me in, that pulls me from my search for my rental car.

It's her. Grandma.

"You're sure you'll be okay taking care of him?" she asked. "Boulder, that is."

I remember the look on her face, the pout of her lower lip, the tears behind those gargantuan, gold-rimmed glasses of hers. I remember because I knew, deep down, it wasn't the question she wanted to ask. This wasn't how she expected it to feel, either, shuffling between boxes on the wood floor of the home in which she raised her only child.

What she really wanted to ask was *why.*

Why had this happened to her? Why did it happen at all? Why did people do what they did to her, what they did, by extension, to Boulder? To me? Why were the junk collectors wading through her things, selling what of it they could—after taking their cut—to fund her overpriced, forthcoming stay at a nursing home on Madison's southside instead of in America's southwest?

"Yes," I told her. "Boulder likes me just fine. More than fine."

A flat, sad smile.

"Besides," I added, "I've got more room for a dog his size in my apartment than you ever had for him here."

"Now who's fault is that?" She laughed when she said it, tossing in a grandmotherly brow raise, her hands on her hips, comically. She kept that same sense of humor through the bitter end.

"I know," I said. "But Boulder was the only—"

"He was the only dog left, I know, and I'm grateful to have him. To have had him."

Boulder trotted up to her. She patted him on the head while he, tail wagging, sniffed at the boxes stacked waist-high in the living room.

"It'll be okay," I volunteered.

"Yes, it will." She scratched Boulder behind the ear, oblivious I meant for *her*, not the dog.

Though I like to think it's been okay for him, too.

"Well," I said, my car keys in my hand, my chest heavy with words I'd been dreading all day. "Shall we?"

Grandma knit her hands together. "I think I'd like a minute first. Alone."

"Of course. Come on, Boulder." The dog bounded after me, emerging onto the lawn where he proceeded to take one final dump—a housewarming gift for the home's new inhabitants—before rooting through the bushes in search of phantom bunnies. Or who knows? In that neighborhood, you could hardly walk out your front door without tripping over a rabbit or a real estate developer.

The house is gone now, by the way. My grandma's. The house that was once hers, bulldozed along with every other home on the block by aforementioned real estate developers, all in the name of luxury apartments they'll soon rent at preposterously high prices to Madison's aspiring young professionals. So, if you're keeping score at home, add them to the list of people who profited off a lifetime of Grandma's hard work. Add them to the list of people who erased any physical memory of the person she'd been, the place she lived.

Later, once Grandma finished inside and packed into the car with me, she kept to herself, sighing occasionally while Boulder whined in the back seat.

"You'll have to go someday," Grandma said, eventually.

"Go where?"

"Phoenix."

At this, I smiled. "Right."

"Have I ever shown you the pictures from—?"

"The Superstition Mountains? Only a million times."

"A million and one times wouldn't do them justice."

I took my eyes off the road for a flash, caught her staring wistfully into the distance.

"I always said I'd come back," she said.

I returned my gaze to the pavement. "You still could. Go back, I mean."

She slapped my knee. "Don't."

"Don't?"

"You're a sweet boy for trying, but I'm too old to be patronized." Another sigh. "Though I'm not too old to dream. You're never too old to dream."

The words hung in the space between us, the car humming along our way to the facility where she'd spend the rest of her days.

When we arrived, we were greeted, as advertised, by nursing home staff. It was all hugs and happiness and *here are your new friends*, a flotilla of seniors who stood with walkers and canes or leaned against the walls. To their credit, each of them did their best to look welcoming when what they really wanted was a nap or a damn sit in their favorite chair.

At least according to Grandma, how she told the story later.

Then, in Grandma's room, she sat by the window, gazing at the highway onramp and offramp across the way. "You don't have to stay any longer," she said.

"I can."

"Don't worry about me." She turned to face me then, that wistful look in her eyes once more. "You've got Boulder to keep an eye on now."

"I'm less worried about him and more worried about what he'll do to my apartment."

"Which is precisely why you should get a move on. Can't leave him unattended for too long. You know how he gets."

"What about you?"

Grandma snickered, placed her hands on the arms of her chair in an attempt to stand.

"Let me help you," I said, stepping forward.

She waved me off. "I can stand on my own, damn it. Let me at least stand on my own." With some struggle, she did, before taking me in for a hug with those bony arms of hers. "Promise me, Eric."

"Promise you what, Grandma?"

"Promise me you'll do good."

"Don't I always?"

"Don't get smart, now." Grandma pulled back, her tone shifting. "I appreciate everything you've done for me. I really do."

"Anything you need. Let me know, okay?"

She patted me on the shoulder. "Don't let it happen."

"I don't think I understa—"

"Don't let them do to others what they did to me."

CHAPTER 22
MARKS OF ONE'S OWN

At last, I find the rental, and it's here that it hits me.

The man who would have had my family murdered—allegedly—wouldn't have just disappeared, not given his dedication to grifting.

I turn the key in the ignition with renewed purpose.

I made a commitment to Grandma A, yes, a promise to scambait that's long seemed unfulfillable. But now? I'll come closer than ever to keeping my pledge once I'm through with that bastard.

Wherever he is.

CHAPTER 23
WAR PATH

My jaw throbs from how hard I clench it. This car, this fucking car—not mine but a constant reminder of mine, and that promise, Eric. You're always on about that promise, so do it. Call him again. It's open interstate for another couple of hours, so if there were ever a time to get it out of your system, if there were ever a time to grant yourself a distraction—

I dial the car dealership. The call is routed through the vehicle's Bluetooth, the ring thunderous.

"Haverson's Pre-Owned of West Madison."

My tone is flat. "Al, please."

"Oh, I'm sorry, Al's on the floor with a customer right now. Can I take a—?"

"Take this message to him: if he's not on the phone in the next minute, I'm filing a complaint with the state."

A pause. "Sir, is there—?"

"Anything you can do to help? Yes. Al. Phone. Now."

A longer pause. "Just a moment."

Hold music. That damn saxophone song, the one from the eighties. George Michael, maybe? George Michael. Jesus

Christ, now this'll be stuck in my head for the next four lifetimes. Thanks, Al. Thanks, Toyota.

"This is Al."

"Al!" My grip on the steering wheel tightens. "Check your voicemail much?"

"What?"

"This is Eric."

"Eric?"

"From last night. The 2014 Toyota Corolla S."

"Ah, Eric with the Corolla. Look, if you have any questions about your car—"

"Did they not tell you?"

"Did who not tell me what?"

"That mechanic. I—Jesus." I rub my forehead with the hell of my palm. "So—questions. If you're wondering whether I have questions, I do. I very much do."

"I'm sure someone in our customer care center—"

"What I want to *know*, Al, is why, for example, the damn wheels practically rolled off my car on the interstate this morning."

"The wheels rolled off?"

"It's an expression. The guys at your repair center don't know what the hell's wrong with it yet, but what I do know is it's undriveable. A lemon, Al. You sold me a lemon."

Al laughs. He laughs! "Probably a good time to have had a warranty, eh?"

"You're going to bring up the damn warranty?"

"You insisted it not be part of the package."

"So *that's* it. You knew, didn't you? You knew that car was trash, but you sold it to me anyway."

Al's greasy silver tongue goes to work for him. "None of the pre-owned vehicles on our lot are trash. They undergo a rigorous four hundred point inspection to ensure—"

"Spare me. What're you going to do to make this right?"

"I… can talk to our repair center's manager about a discounted repair?"

"Here I was thinking maybe taking the car back for a full refund would be appropriate."

Al clucks that slimeball tongue of his. "I'd say that's an unlikely resolution."

"I—what? Excuse me?"

"Look, kid." *Kid, kid.* "You bought a car. You passed on the warranty. The car broke down. Them's the brakes."

I counter. "You and I both know I've got a three-day window to return this car if—"

"Not true."

"Uh, my ass it's not true."

"The three-day window only applies if you purchased the car off-dealership. At a convention, for example."

"That can't be true."

Al snickers. "The law's funny like that sometimes."

Orange construction barrels whoosh past on either side of my rental. Behind me, a semi-truck's engine roars. Somewhere on Madison's west side, my co-workers are likely losing their damn minds over Caio's sudden appearance without me at his side. In Chicago, my dad is—fuck.

"You're just like my dad."

"What?"

"You're a crook. A crook! And if there's one thing I won't stand for in this world, it's a con man."

"Whatever your daddy issues are, I don't have time for them."

"We'll see who doesn't have time after I've filed a complaint—"

"With the state. Yeah. I heard. Good luck with that."

The call ends. My list grows by one name.

Al. My dad's partner. My dad—maybe, possibly. No, *definitely.*

No exceptions.

CHAPTER 24
THE HUNT

t's four p.m. by the time I make it back to my apartment complex. I remain behind the wheel, the engine off, the warmth creeping from the cabin.

Worth it, right? The side trip, that is, not my dad, who I now know is very much *not* worth it.

Maybe that's not true. He did lead me to the biggest prospective scambait of my life, and that has to count for something.

Please tell me it counts for something.

I retrieve my phone from the breast pocket of my jacket and remove a glove in order to message SalchichaSimon, to tell him he no longer needs to worry about me. That might be an overstatement—worry away!—but I'm no longer in danger of being kidnapped. Though who knows? With a supposed would-have-been murderer on the loose, anything's possible. Anything calamitous, anyway.

Before I make it to my Discord app: a text from—so much for deleting my number from his phone—my dad.

I'm sorry.

He's sorry. He's *sorry*? That he can't even say what he's sorry for is—well, settle down. You don't have to respond to him, Eric. Don't engage. You don't owe him shit, and you've got plenty of other cats to wrangle right now, starting with the avalanche of voicemails that have apparently accumulated while you drove.

I delete my dad's text before pressing my phone to my ear and listening.

Caio first. "*Oi, rapaz, cadê você?*"

Another voicemail. Dolores. Then Caio again before Sean and, hell, Shawn.

Just because Nortex systems are down, they say, that doesn't mean we all get a digital snow day. There are issues that need to be addressed, *Eric*, and your input is critical. Call us back and get to Nortex as soon as you can or, in Shawn's words, *your ass is grass*.

I grind my teeth, gaze up at the balcony of my second floor apartment. I'm going to lose them. My job and the apartment, anyway. But I chose this. I didn't have to see my dad. I could have driven straight from Janesville to Madison, could have tried to play the hero, could have *tried*.

But no one's said the window of opportunity has closed; I can still try, even if it's only a phone call worth of effort. I select CALL BACK next to Shawn's name—he's technically my boss in the Nortex org chart—and it rings. It rings and rings and, beep, voicemail.

"Hey, Shawn. Eric here. Really sorry I missed your calls and that I couldn't get Caio from the airport this morning. I take it he told you about my car? Broke down. Got stuck waiting on a tow and then, uh"—this doesn't account for the whole day, so get to it—"a family emergency required my immediate attention." I force down a dry swallow. "I can explain further the next time I'm in the office. Tomorrow, that is. Sorry again."

I disconnect the call, relax into the headrest. I have no idea what that family emergency is going to be—the reliable fall-back is to blame the dog, and with his urgent trips to the vet recently, that's still an option, I suppose. Speaking of, the old wind bag probably does need to be taken out, so—summoning strength—I urge myself from the car and ascend the stairs to my apartment.

Boulder bounds toward me when I enter, and yes, buddy, thank you so much. I am, in fact, grabbing your leash from the peg on the wall, but we won't be out for too long; daddy's on the war path, and vengeance will be his. No, not against you, you're perfect. Mostly perfect. Okay, pretty average as dogs go, but I love you for it, so down the stairs with us because we—you—don't piddle indoors, remember?

While Boulder tends to his business, I research who, exactly, I need to contact with the state of Wisconsin about a certain Al Haverson. Aha! It's the Wisconsin Department of Transportation and their surprisingly straightforward online complaint form. Good on you, Wisconsin, for streamlining the anti-scammer justice system. Maybe there's a job for me at the D.O.T. once the dealership has been compelled to refund me —a windfall I need pretty damn soon because, hey, cars aren't cheap even if you knock a thousand off the sticker price, and I'll gladly take my business elsewhere. I'll still need a car once this is resolved, after all.

But for now, good! Filing that complaint counts as scam-baiting for the day, though we're not done yet. Come on, Boulder, back up to the apartment, and go ahead, root around in the snow for a minute, if you must. Your dad's going to be grinding an axe for the next couple of hours, and you know how much he hates being disturbed while wielding that axe against those who would thieve others' inheritances from them.

I'm opening the door to my apartment when another text hits my phone.

If I could take it back, I would. You have to understand.

What. A. Sap.

In any other context, you'd swear my dad's texts were from a cheating partner, which, aside from being a weird analogy, makes them that much more pathetic. I mean, what does he want from me? Does he not have friends, coworkers he can talk to?

I tuck my phone away, usher Boulder into the apartment, and, minutes later—my laptop open, a mugful of hot chocolate with a generous pour of vodka at my side—I start with one simple question: what do I know about my father's partner in crime?

I open a Google Drive document and stretch my fingers.

Nothing happens. No words come, no outpouring of knowledge or leads.

Let's try again. *What do I know about my father's partner in crime?*

Scams by mail, started in early nineties. Madison, Wisconsin area. Threats became severe enough to chase my dad away about twenty years ago.

On the screen before me, the cursor blinks back at me, pregnant with expectation, and I get it, little blinky line, this is a pitiful amount of information to start with.

My phone dings.

SalchichaSimon: You still alive?

Distraction! I'll allow it. I turn my phone over in my hand and tap a reply because, the disasterpiece I am, I never did confirm how things turned out with my dad.

BoulderIBarelyKnowHer: Yes, sadly.
SalchichaSimon: That bad?
BoulderIBarelyKnowHer: Dude was a scammer.

SalchichaSimon: Like he wasn't your real dad?
BoulderIBarelyKnowHer: No, like, he *was* my real dad, but my real dad was a scammer.
SalchichaSimon: I guess the key word there is "was?"

True, true enough, though I can't be certain my dad's still not out there scamming people. I guess I never asked.

My gaze falls to the icon for my text message inbox.

What if my dad wanted—wants—revenge on the man he used to work with? We could team up, take him down together, and wouldn't that be a story for the ages: *father and son reunited by quest to bring down scammers who tore their family apart.*

I clearly don't write headlines for a living.

SalchichaSimon: You still there?
BoulderIBarelyKnowHer: Yeah, sorry. Plotting is all.
SalchichaSimon: Plotting?
BoulderIBarelyKnowHer: Against my dad's former partner, the one he used to scam with. He was planning to kill us! My family, that is. That's why my dad left. Can't remember if I told you that already or not. Anyway, trying to suss out if there's a way to find him and make his life hell for a minute. Ultimate payback, you know?

This is the first time I realize I don't have a plan. Even if I *do* catch him—or discern his identity and locate him—what, exactly, do I plan to do with that information? I pet Boulder, my thoughts on dogs, on cars chased.

SalchichaSimon: Good luck with that.
BoulderIBarelyKnowHer: Thanks? I was hoping maybe you and P-Money could help.
SalchichaSimon: And put myself in the crosshairs? No

way. And you're out of your mind if you think P-Money would be on board with this, either.

BoulderIBarelyKnowHer: Uh, why? This would be the ultimate scambait. This is the kind of thing that gets you into the Scambait Hall of Fame.

SalchichaSimon: First, again, there is no Scambait Hall of Fame.

BoulderIBarelyKnowHer: A man can dream.

SalchichaSimon: Second, he was going to *kill* you and your family.

BoulderIBarelyKnowHer: Two decades ago.

SalchichaSimon: You don't think people like that would hold a grudge? That they'd take exception to someone trying to unmask them?

BoulderIBarelyKnowHer: Fine. If you're not willing to help, I'll go it alone.

SalchichaSimon: You've proven quite capable on your own so far…

The *fuck?* Where does he get off? I toss my phone onto the carpet, wince when it slides onto the kitchen tile. I didn't hear anything shatter, so no, Boulder, you can go back to sleep.

Fucking Simon. And P-Money, too! I thought we were scambait *brothers*—not that we've ever met in real life or even know each other's real names—so, yeah, I guess this tracks. Still, all talk, the two of them! Here I am, offering the scambait of a lifetime, and they pass?

I narrow my eyes. My nearly empty Google Doc continues to mock me.

Damn it. I can't go it alone. This, I know. But who—?

"Shit, Boulder, that's how we find him!" I set my laptop aside, pace my apartment floor while sipping from this perilously alcoholic hot chocolate. That YouTube channel, the one I planned to start: it doesn't have to be for the lulz, not that anyone says that anymore. I must summon my dear sweet internet and its army of strangers with a penchant for vigilantism! Let them be turned on the enemies of the Amundsen clan!

Its lone surviving member, anyway. On paper.

But this can happen: why *not* outsource the sleuthing to an insatiable fandom of amateur detectives?

Right—because it will require me to first, you know, cultivate an insatiable fandom of amateur detectives.

Hmm. On the kitchen floor, my phone. We can do this. It can be done.

I fetch my phone from the floor—no scratches, no breakage—and set the camera mode to selfie. Then, with it propped against my mug on the coffee table, I check the lighting and, okay, it's not America's finest, but every journey starts with a single—no, who am I? Grandma Amundsen? Again?

Maybe that wouldn't be the worst thing, being more like her—aside from getting scammed out of what I deserved for my golden years.

I hit record. I drink deeply from my hot chocolate. Then I stare into the camera and ask the world a question I myself am only beginning to answer.

"What would you do if you received an email from your dad, a man who's been dead for years?"

CHAPTER 25
WOOF

The following morning, my phone vibrates on the nightstand.

If it's my dad, I swear to God.

But no: an all-Nortex text—due to Digital Chernobyl, office closed until mandatory, all-staff meeting at two p.m. That's not what it says, exactly, but I take the message's meaning along with two—make that three—Excedrin, because, as was long advertised, hangovers don't get any easier as you get older, but that they're this bad? Someone, please, just tie cinder blocks to my feet and throw me into the Yahara.

While I return the bottle of Excedrin to the cabinet in the bathroom, my thoughts flit briefly to Caio, to what the Nortex faithful are going to do with him this morning, but that sounds like a *them* problem. Today is a day to edit last night's footage. Today is a day to voiceover some of my funnier email scams. Today is a day to swing by the pet store—it goes by Kitten Caboodle these days—and start asking questions.

Two decades might have passed since my father's falling out with his partner, but the pet store is still lurking on Willy

Street. Even if ownership has turned over a hundred times—the name's changed, anyway—maybe there's someone around who can help me track down the man who used to own the joint with my dad.

Is this an ambitious list of to-dos to tackle before two? Sure. Will that stop me? No! I need more fodder for future videos. I need momentum—positive momentum—back in my life, and whatever I can manage this morning will be enough. Hopefully. No, *definitely*. If I want it, I must will it.

Boulder doesn't greet me when I exit the bedroom—maybe I'm the one who smells this morning—but I urge him outside, wait for him to use the facilities. I wait. And I wait. I wait some more.

"If you're not interested, bud, we can go back in. You look as cold as I feel, so—" He drags his paws as we trek back indoors, and I remind him all he has to do is whine while I'm working on these videos and I can have him outside in a jiff.

To the breakfast bar! To iMovie and the impeccable 4K footage I recorded last night!

Now, I edit.

Or, perhaps more apt, I realize I have no idea what I'm doing.

This program's supposed to be all click and drag, but it's really just *drag*, and that an hour has already passed and I've managed to, what, line up a couple of clips that have, for reasons beyond my reckoning, not imported in 4K? Very cool. Add Apple to the list—I really do have a lot of lists, don't I?—with Toyota, I guess.

My phone rings. Nortex? No. A number not saved to my phone.

I move to take the call, but before my thumb hits ANSWER, I pull back.

What if it's him? My dad. The scammer. He must be spoofing a 608 area code so I'll actually answer.

If that's how it's going to be, fine. Might as well let him have it.

I answer the call. "What the hell do you want?"

"Excuse me?"

"If you keep texting, if you keep calling, don't think I won't file a harassment complaint."

"Sir, this is an auto body."

Oh. Fuck. The auto body.

I apologize profusely, begin to explain myself before—Christ, Eric, they don't need your life story, and these guys work at Al's dealership, for fuck's sake—I apologize some more and ask if this is about my Corolla. It is, he says, and they can have my car ready in an hour if I promise not to file a harassment complaint—the mechanic's got a sense of humor about it, at least—and I've got a thousand bucks to spare.

A thousand bucks to spare. I ask if that's part of the gag we've got going and tell him that's not his best material, and he assures me it's no joke.

And now, the moment of truth. Do I tell him I won't be paying, that he should talk to Al about who's going to cover the cost of repair? I could, yeah, but who knows how long Al will drag his feet in doing the right thing, assuming he ever does. Meanwhile, I'm the one who'll be stuck continuing to pay for a rental car, which, yikes, is not an expense I'm interested in paying, either.

While I consider this, I tell him to hold a second so I can check my credit card balance. Fuck me, we've got fifteen-hundred to work with, and that's enough to get my car back, for starters. Besides, I can add the cost of repair to the complaint I made to the state as soon as I hear back from them, so I tell this increasingly impatient mechanic that I'll be on my way soon. By the time I catch a ride share to the dealership, the repair center should be about done with its repairs, which turns out to be exactly the case. Maybe I *am* building positive momentum.

I insert my credit card into the reader. It squawks to confirm I'm a thousand dollars deeper in debt.

Forget everything I said about positive momentum.

At least I still have enough time before the afternoon's all-hands meeting to rush home, to drop off my rental in Janesville, and to let Boulder out before taking whatever time is left to troubleshoot my ongoing video issues. The pet store will have to wait until tonight, but that's hardly a wait, all things considered.

After returning from Janesville, I reach my apartment door, my keys jangling, ready to summon Boulder for an afternoon walkabout.

But no doggy footsteps clack against the linoleum on the door's far side.

"Boulder?" I turn the key in the lock, open the door.

I gag on the wall of stench.

Rubbing my eyes, I look about. Brown. Red. A slurry of brown and red everywhere. My insides burn, feel like they might do the same that Boulder's have, loosing diarrhea and blood on the carpet, the walls, the floor.

There, on the far side of the couch, Boulder attempts to hide in the corner.

"Okay," I say, crouching, attempting to lift him. "Up we go. Vet. Vet now."

I want to weep, want to give myself a goddamn minute to process the fuck-all that is my life, but I can't. I'm drained, so drained, and though nothing should surprise me anymore, if this is it for Boulder—

No. I won't entertain the thought.

As I boost down University in the direction of the UW's Emergency Vet Clinic, I check once, twice, a thousand times over my shoulder. Breathing, still breathing. Boulder is still with me for now.

With me, too, is the blood, the feces. The smell is unbearable, and with every lurch and shift of gears, Boulder's body weight presses the mess deeper and deeper into the seats of my Corolla.

CHAPTER 26
WAITING

My staring contest with the clock is one for the ages. Who will blink first? Me, a mere mortal, or Father Time himself?

Me. It's always me.

It's been an hour of fingers tapping, of toes squirming since the vet grabbed Boulder, said they'd update me as soon as they had anything to report, and we're inching closer, closer, closer to two p.m.

I do not want to have to make this call, but I have to. I must.

Before I can depress Shawn's name in my contact list—an incoming call.

This time, yes, my dad.

It's gonna be an IGNORE from me, dog, and an emphatic one at that. That this man is somehow under the impression I've got all day to sit on my ass and indulge his emotional baggage—it's embarrassing, really, and I won't have it.

Unless—well, no, that'd be cruel. It's one thing to string along a stranger on the internet you've never met; it'd be another entirely to give my dad a glimmer of hope here and there, only to shut him down again. I'm a vigilante, not a sociopath—hopefully—and I've got to keep my eyes on the prizes here.

Boulder, number one. This two p.m. meeting at Nortex, number two.

When at last I call Shawn, he doesn't answer. Sean, either, and let's add Dolores to that list. Still, that I'll be late to—or missing in action from—the the all-hands meeting has to be phoned in. I've been reckless enough lately, thank you very much.

The main line, then. HR—what's left of it—takes those calls, I'm pretty sure, and if anyone's in the office right now it'll be them or IT.

"Thank you for calling Nortex, this is Ann Hagel."

"Ann Hagel? Ann Hagel from HR?"

"Um, yes? May I ask who's calling?"

"This is Eric." Nothing. No response. "Eric Amundsen?" I say. "Sorry, the Special Advisor—"

"To Latin America, right."

"About that meeting this afternoon—I won't be able to make it in. I'm at the vet with my dog, and—"

"That's okay."

"That's okay?"

"I'll let Shawn know." Paperwork shuffles. "Take care of your dog."

"That's it?"

Some further rustling on the line. "Well, we'd still like you to come in today. To get you caught up on the situation with IT, I mean."

"Can someone maybe shoot me an email?"

"With the system down—"

"Oh. Right." I check the time, glance at the reception desk. The receptionist waves me over. "Hey, I have to go."

"Eric?" Ann asks.

I stand, hustle over to the reception desk. "What?"

Both Ann and the receptionist speak at once. "We'd still

like you to we have come in an update about your this after-noon dog."

"Hang on," I say into the phone. Then, to the receptionist, "Come again?"

"Your dog," she says. "We have an update."

"Please tell me he's going to be okay."

"We'll need to keep him overnight."

I wring my winter hat in my hands. "But he's fine? He'll be fine?"

"The vet says he must have gotten into the garbage or otherwise eaten something he shouldn't have. Again."

"But he *is* going to be okay?"

"She's recommending a low fat diet and that he wears a cone until he's fully recovered—just to keep him from getting into anything. *Again* again."

"Okay, but for the love of God, please answer the question. Tell me he'll be all right." It feels as if every eye in the waiting room is on me—watching, waiting for a verdict.

"The vet says he will, yes."

The waiting room breathes a collective sigh.

She goes on. "But like I said, we need to keep him for observation."

"Fine. Whatever it takes. But you'll call me? You'll call if anything changes? For better or worse?"

"We have your number, yes. Someone will call when he's ready to be picked up tomorrow."

"Thank you," I say. "Thank you."

I return my phone to my ear, turn away from the desk. "You still there?"

Ann clears her throat, but says nothing.

"I'll be in soon." My attention settles on the front of my shirt, my jeans. Dried blood. God knows what else. "Maybe closer to a half hour. An hour. Is that okay?"

"We'll be waiting," she says.

I do not like that *we*.

CHAPTER 27
AN EMPTY BOX

After showering, finally, and at Nortex for the first time in days, I take the Zag past the vacant desks in HR. I'm definitely not thinking about the voicemail my dad left me, the one I left prowling about my inbox unheard. I'll delete it when I've got time, I tell myself, though walking the Zag has given me plenty of that.

It's probably nothing. It's probably as pathetic as his texts. It probably won't get me closer to his former partner, but just in case it would—I don't know. I'll leave it. For later. Maybe.

I kick any thought of the voicemail to the curb, though as I do, a creeping sense of foreboding descends: the whole of Nortex seems to have emptied out in the aftermath of this afternoon's meeting, and this place is damn eerie when photocopiers aren't running, when phones aren't ringing, when Dolores isn't doing her stapling.

At last, a sign of life, a lone light that remains on in Ann's office. I approach gingerly, rehearsing my finest apologies.

Okay. Time to shine. Time to grovel, if I must.

I knock on the door, poke my head in. "Ann? Hey, it's Er—"

As promised, Ann's not alone. She sits across from a

colleague, one I recognize from IT. He promptly stands, offers me his chair, and moves to Ann's side of the desk.

We. I didn't like that *we*, and there's no denying it now—I'm fucked. I'm one hundred percent, incontrovertibly fucked.

"Look," I say, "I can expla—"

There will be no explaining, they say. They knew, IT says, or they'd been suspicious for a while, but this ransomware attack, Eric—it really takes the cake. What led to it is a clear violation of policy and, not to mention, common sense. Yes, the attacker didn't get in via your laptop, but we know you were logged in at the station where the attack originated. Again, we get it: you've mentioned the Raspberry Pi three times now, but that's not the point; your every hour here these last two months has been a dereliction of duty. We know your grandma died, Eric, and we're very sorry to hear about whatever's going on with your dog, but no. Eric. Eric! What do your dad or his voicemail have to do with any of this? No matter the state of your personal life, this is really a long time coming, and it's best if you don't make a scene.

Yes, we're aware how challenging it is to find someone who speaks Spanish and Portuguese, but that's none of your concern. Good luck with your YouTube channel, then. No, we're not being sarcastic, Eric; we want what's best for you and for the company, and dragging this out doesn't serve either of us. Please sign here and here and here, and just confirming that no, you're not eligible for rehire. Now, if you'll turn over your key card, we'll see you out.

CHAPTER 28
SOMEONE TO BLAME

'm home now. Alone.

I have scrubbed the carpet, the walls. The stench of Boulder's insides still hangs thick in the air, and no amount of early-winter window opening chases it away.

I get off my hands and knees. The sun sets, vodka-cocoas are drunk, and my scambait inboxes swell.

I open them, close them, untouched. Who am I to scambait? Certainly not I, the miscreant who, as my unceremonious dismissal has made me realize, might as well be on the scammers' side of the conversation. Collecting months' worth of paychecks without doing my actual job? That's a scam if I ever saw one, and I've seen plenty.

So, another mug of vodka-cocoa raised high! A toast to me. To Eric Amundsen, a scammer so incompetent he didn't even know he was pulling a fast one. Like father, like son, not that this means the old man gets a second—third?—chance.

You know what I need right now? A laugh. A good, hearty laugh, so maybe it's time. That voicemail. That voicemail from that pathetic excuse for a father. Let's give it a whirl.

"Eric, look. I fucked up, but that was years ago. I want to make it up to you. Can we try again? Please? I'll even come to

Madison, if that'll make it easier. Whatever you need, Eric. Whatever you want. I'm trying. I'm trying."

The voicemail ends, and I sing out "at least he's trying" like a drunken Taylor Swift, but there's no one here to laugh, to tell me that's not even the lyric, to remind me no matter how entertaining I might find this, my dad's still a person with feelings.

Blech.

Fine. I'll entertain his voicemail. What do I need, Dad? A job. What do I want? To be left the hell alone.

I push my phone away, finish off what remains of my mug while I scroll through Netflix and Hulu. I watch nothing. I cancel both, because *money*.

And on money—that YouTube channel. I may be a damn dirty scammer, but I still need cash, so let's open iMovie, watch the raw footage. At last, I fix the video resolution, but the room is on tilt—thanks, vodka—so away with you, cursed lightbox, it's time to take out Boulder anyway, and where is he? Where is the dog?

Right. Damn it.

I recline on the couch. The ceiling ebbs, flows like cascading tide, like the nausea in my gut.

The cords in my neck strain. I feel around for my phone and, after finding it beneath me, scroll through my contacts until I find his entry. If he wants to hear from me, he'll hear from me, all right.

This is your fault, you bastard. You never should have emailed me. No, you never should have run away. You never should have become a scammer.

I stare at this text, my thumb hovering over the little arrow to send it on its merry way.

The first part's not true. This isn't my dad's fault. He was pushed into scamming by circumstance, by someone he once trusted.

So, I leave the text unsent, return to my contacts, keep scrolling.

Why did you let this happen? Why did you squander everything on such foolishness?

I pull my phone away from my face because *bright*, it's too bright. With my eyes narrowed, I re-read the drafted text and —fuck it, it's not like it's Grandma's number anymore— thumb the send button.

Is this catharsis? I think they call this catharsis.

My phone vibrates. A reply text.

New phone, who dis?

"Boulder," I say, "get a load of this," but, right, he's still not here. Of course. No one's here to laugh along with me, to see me in my shame, my sorrow.

Maybe that's for the best.

Because it's not Grandma Amundsen's fault, either. She didn't compel me to make a promise. She didn't compel me to carry it out as I have. That's not Grandma A, not what she would have wanted. That's not how she and Grandpa amassed their fortune. Hard work and a little bit of luck is all you need, she'd say, and look at me—no work and the worst luck of my life have brought me, well, here, laid low in a pool of my own pity.

A pity pool. A pity pool party.

I'll admit it: I did this to me. I did this to me with a little help from fate, but there's no accounting for fate. If there's still any hope for me, it's hope I'll need to find for myself.

Up, then. Up! Off the couch. Lights on. A full cup of water. Another. Chug, Eric, chug, because you're sobering up and getting down to business. Put on a pot of coffee because it's not like you need to set an alarm for the morning.

The coffee maker steams. The scent of coffee thickens, commingles with—and briefly blankets—the lingering stench of doggie insides. I watch on, waiting for the final drip, summoning my strength as the pot fills.

I might have, unknowingly, become a scammer. I might have made an absolute botch job of my life. I might have done both these things and more, but there's still a way out. There's a way back to the person I thought I was, to the promise I made, and doing it right this time.

Tracking down my dad's former partner is the ticket. These YouTube videos are the ticket.

CHAPTER 29

WAKE UP CALL

The blast of a train horn cutting across the isthmus stirs me. My bed shakes, and, my head throbbing, I bury myself beneath the pillows.

This fails to deafen the train's roar.

Light seeps in, too, which means no matter how my eyes burn, I've slept enough to get back to the grind. These videos aren't going to post themselves. Boulder won't be picking himself up from the vet. No one's going to go to Kitten Caboodle to finally start sniffing around—*sniffing*, ha, someone please kill me—on my behalf.

I reach for my laptop—yes, I took it to bed with me—and, somewhere beneath the twisted mass of bedsheets and comforter, I find it, open it, and press PLAY on my work from the previous night.

Video rolls. Music plays. Transitions, uh, transition, and this… isn't terrible? It might even be better than *not terrible*. Was it Hemingway who said "write drunk, edit sober?" What the hell did he know? It should have been edit drunk, you buffoon, because this video about my dad, about his appearance in my inbox and the reveals of his scammerdom at our Chicago reunion—this is impeccably arranged. Some might even say it's *compelling,* and that call to action at the end? Damn, I've still got it.

Whatever it is.

Well, shit. There's no time like the present, so to YouTube with you, along with these more run-of-the-mill scambait vids that will, hopefully, drive some traffic to the headline story sometime in the next, I don't know, *immediately* because I apparently need a thousand subscribers to start monetizing.

A thousand. No big deal.

Sarcasm.

While the videos upload, I dash to the car wash. There's a murder scene to blot out of my vehicle's vinyl, and since I still haven't heard from the vet, I've got time to do what proves to be an exercise in scrubbing the seats with vinegar, dish soap, laundry detergent, club soda, and air fresheners.

Yes, *air fresheners,* because I'd rather this car smell like cheap pine than dog shit—as would the dealership that the state of Wisconsin will certainly compel to remove this car from my care.

My forearms are saved from further strain when my phone rings. The vet has cleared Boulder for pickup, thank God.

Before I drive to the clinic—a peek at my phone, at my YouTube account.

The little circle spins at the center of the screen, a roulette wheel I need to land on black or red or however the hell roulette works. What I mean is I need views. I need comments. I need engagement. Ooh, and here it is!

Four views. One comment.

Okay, it's not all bad. A comment counts as engagement, and engagement is good, right?

hey cool video we should be friends here's my channel:
http://www.youtube.com/channel/VNEndasE…

I click the link. It's a channel, all right, but it's all anime all the time. And the dude's comment history? He leaves this comment on literally every video he can.

I squeeze my phone to keep myself from loosing it into traffic. It'll be okay. My videos have been up for less than an hour, so stop it. Stop with this. What I need is patience. These things take time, not that I've got much of that to work with before bills are due again.

So, *sigh*, I didn't want to do this—because fuck those guys—but I copy my video's link to my clipboard, drop it into the Scambait Bros Discord chat, and slip my phone into my back pocket before either of those jerks can get in a snippy reply. It's in fate's hands now, and fate's names are PrakashMoney and SalchichaSimon because we live in the upside down and nothing means anything anymore.

Whatever. Whether the Bros support me or not, Grandma Amundsen's cursed canine always will, and we're sticking together, Boulder and me—especially once we get to that damn pet store.

CHAPTER 30
I'D ADVISE AGAINST THAT

Boulder trots alongside me through the Kitten Caboodle parking lot, the edge of his plastic cone scraping against my leg.

"Think of it this way, Boulder," I say. "With all the cone-wearing you've had to do, you've probably gotten damn good at using echolocation. Maybe that's a marketable skill?" Boulder turns to face me, pressing his cone further into my thigh. "What I'm saying is you need to get a job, because your vet bills—even if they were nice enough to offer a payment plan—are going to be downright impossible to pay off starting next month."

Not that it matters. What are they going to do, repossess my dog? *Boa sorte* with that, as Caio might say. Fucking Caio. Fucking Nortex.

But anyway—down to business. The pet store, Eric, you're on your way into the pet store, and not only for the softer dog food the vet suggested but apparently didn't have available to sell directly. You've got questions for ownership. You've got YouTube content to gin up. You've got to ask about a job because you need one, of course, but also because if you're really going to do the sleuthing you've vowed to do, why not get as close to the source as you possibly can? From scambaiter to secret agent—that's me!—and who's going to get in my way?

A hiring manager, maybe, but let's set that aside for now.

Ignore, too, the swell of anticipation as you approach the building, the familiar whoosh of the automatic doors. Bask not in the smell of dog food and fish flakes, the hum of the heating lamps.

Don't think about it, Eric. Don't think about *him* and his prodding texts, his sob story voicemails. You've shopped here often enough for years without issue; don't let your dad's memory—don't let this being the first time you've been to the pet store since seeing him—get to you.

To my right, the squeaky mewling of kittens. An indoor, fenced-in playground of scratching posts, colorful catnip toys, and carpeted cat trees. And—please, no, stop—half a dozen kittens rumbling, bumbling, stumbling while larger cats laze in their cat trees, unimpressed.

Catapalooza. This weekend, starting Friday. Today.

Oh. My. God.

Boulder has the same idea I do, so, tongue lolling—him, not me—we sidle up to the Catapalooza fence line—white picket, naturally—and I hang my arm over the edge, beckoning the furry bastards my way with the classic *tchk, tchk, tchk* that we all know cats definitely always respond to.

One of them—I can't believe it—actually does respond, a furry, orange fluff ball whose clumsy padding across the tile would be an embarrassment for a drunk human but is beyond adorable for a weeks-old feline. Look at me with my words like *adorable*, with my reaching into the pen and hoisting the kitty high enough to keep Boulder from getting sufficiently close to scare the little firecracker away. And its claws! It has tiny little baby claws that—oh, you must think you're tough, huh?—swat at the pom-pom on top of my winter hat.

"Are you looking to adopt today?"

I jump at the sound of the woman's voice, spin to face her. "Who, me? I couldn't, no. This guy," I say, gesturing to Boulder with my free hand, "is enough trouble."

"It would seem so. He's had that cone on for some time."

I arch an eyebrow.

"You're here often." She brushes chestnut hair from her eyes, and it's only then that I recognize her—Bow Girl, aptly named because one, I can never remember what it says on her name tag—Adriana, I guess—and two, she wears a painfully oversized purple bow in her hair, always, the little good it does her where keeping it out of her eyes is concerned.

Assuming that's the point of wearing a bow. What would I know?

"Oh, it's you," I say.

"Beg your pardon?"

"Like—I know what you mean, now. I'm here all the time. You're here all the time. We see each other. I—sorry—long day. Week."

She furrows her brow. "About that kitten—"

"Ha! Right." That kitten. *This* kitten, the one I've been holding to my shoulder as if it were a baby in need of a burp. "No, unfortunately I'm not in the cat adoption business today."

"Ah." She reaches for the cat.

His claws catch in my jacket as she lifts him from me, his meows high-pitched.

"He seems to have taken a liking to you."

Taken a liking? And is that an English accent I detect? No, it's more of a Mid-Atlantic thing. Or a hybrid? Has she always been like this? "He has taken a liking to me, yes, but like I said—"

"Yes. You're here for your usual, then?" She unhooks the cat's claws from my jacket, returns him, gently, to the Catapalooza pen where he immediately performs a spread-eagle pounce onto the back of one of his comrades.

"No, not the usual," I say. "I, uh—you've been here for a while right?"

She ceases rubbing her hands on the front of her jeans. "I'm not sure I understand."

"Like, you've worked here for as long as I can remember."

"Yes?"

"I guess I'm—" All right, man. Slow down. Order of operations. "Never mind. I'm looking for softer food for Conehead here. Do you have—oh, where's the note on my phone?—this stuff?" I tell her the name of the brand the vet recommended, and Bow Girl—Adriana—shows me to it.

"Is that all you require?" she asks.

Cans of dog food do their damndest to escape my cradling of them. "A basket, maybe, if you can go back in time and tell me to grab one at the door."

"Time travel is impossible. And even if it were, it'd be far too dangerous."

"What?"

"You asked if I could go back in time for you."

"As a joke."

"Ahh."

We blink at each other before she repeats herself. "Is there anything further you require?"

"Uh, no. Well, I was actually wondering—"

"If you intend to ask me on a date, I'd advise against it."

Boulder's cone sways from her leg into mine.

"I—what? No," I say. She seems to take offense to this. "Sorry, I didn't mean that how it came out."

"Mmm."

"What I was going to ask is whether you're hiring."

She presses her lips together. "I would advise against that."

"You would advise against your place of employment hiring?"

"Against you applying."

I rebalance the cans of dog food, wince when one topples to the floor, rolls away. "Is it something I did? Said? I could really use a job, and—"

"Look." She fetches the can from the floor and offers it to me as if, yeah, I've *totally* proven myself capable of carrying them all on my own. "You're welcome to apply. If you insist."

"Why does it sound like there's a *but* you're leaving out?" And why did I adjust my arms to accept the return of this can, which is now wedged more uncomfortably than ever between my elbow and rib cage?

"No *but*," she says.

"No *but*?"

"Follow me."

I do, but there's a quickness to her step, and the frequency with which she glances left, right, has me feeling as though we ought to be on the lookout, strapped as if we were intent on robbing the place.

When we reach the checkout counter, she plucks a paper application from a stack on a shelf behind her. "Here you are." The store's phone rings. She answers, hangs up immediately.

"Everything okay?" I lurch forward. Dog food cans clatter on the counter.

She cowers at the sound before offering me a pen, saying nothing.

"Seriously, if this is about the asking you on a date thing, I apologize. Again. I didn't expect that to be what you were thinking, so—"

"Shall I ring you up, then?"

The phone chimes. Just as before, she removes it from the hook, only to return it as quickly as she answered.

"Uh." Boulder looks up at me, licks his chops. I stare at

the paperwork on the counter in front of me. "Go for it. Ringing me up, that is." Then, elbows on the counter, I get to work—filling out the application, yes, but taking my sweet ass time because there's no one in line behind me, and damn it all, I've got questions. "So you *have* worked here for a while, right?" I ask. "That's not just my memory playing tricks?"

"That would depend on who's inquiring." The checkout gun beeps when she scans the bag of dog food.

I keep my eyes on my application. "I'm inquiring."

"Then you know the answer to that question."

I shake my head, press on. "If it makes any difference, I knew the owners here. A long time ago. I haven't seen or heard from them in years, and I'm trying to track them down."

Again, the ringing of the phone. Again, the answer, the hang up. She relays my total.

I set down my pen, reach for my wallet. "What I'm trying to ask is whether you know the owners. Or knew the old owners. I know this place has changed names a few times, and—"

She reaches for my credit card. I pull it back. The phone rings. This time, she lets it go unanswered.

"Why are you like this?" I ask.

"I'm not like anything. I'm trying to ring you up for a rather sizable order of dog food before I see you on your way."

"You won't answer my questions?"

"Are you with the constabulary?"

"I—the what?"

"The constabulary."

The phone stops ringing.

"The fuzz," she clarifies. "The five-oh? The boys in blue? The police, as it were."

"No! No. Not at all. Look at me. The cops?"

She snatches my credit card from my hand. "Then I won't be answering any questions, and again, I'd advise—"

"Against that. I get it." I run my hand along my chin, stare at my application for employment. "This isn't going to matter, is it?" I remove the paper from the counter, wave it around like a flag.

"Legally, I'm required to consider every application."

"So you do the hiring, but you won't hire me?"

"I haven't said that." She returns my card, slides me a receipt to sign.

The phone rings. I twirl the pen between my fingers, lock my gaze with her own. "You going to answer that?"

She holds my stare, unmoved. The phone bleats on.

I blink first.

"Fine," I say, bending to sign the receipt. "But I'll be back." And I *will*, because whatever's going on here, it's damn suspicious, and if she legally has to consider my application, I'll go well out of my way to ensure it's been considered.

"I'm sure you'll be back, yes," she says. "Eventually you'll need more food for Conehead, will you not?"

"You know what I mean."

"Will you require a bag for your purchase today?"

"No, I'd like to juggle all of these cans on my way out the door."

"Well, then. Have a wonderful evening."

"I—that was sarcasm."

"Oh."

"So, uh, a bag please?"

"Of course." She uses her forearm to sweep the cans untidily into a paper bag.

I heft the bag between my arms, careful to keep my hands beneath the bottom. "I look forward to hearing from you about my application."

"Like I've said, I'd advise against—"

I turn my back, wave her off. "Come on, Boulder. I'd *advise us against* wasting any more of our time here today."

On our way to the exit, I pause, turn, sneak a peek at the checkout counter.

The phone rings once more. Her shoulders tense. She disconnects the phone from the wall before standing over a garbage can, scanning my application.

Then, with a short sigh, she disappears behind a closed door, my paperwork in hand.

CHAPTER 31
BOW GIRL

'm in the driver's seat of my car, the engine running, when I make the connection.

Bow Girl. Adriana.

I've seen her before—and not as an employee of Kitten Caboodle.

The back room. Years ago, when this place had another name. Those visits with my father, the office he ducked into while I scurried about the store's aisles.

He held Adriana at times, my dad's business partner, or at least he held a small girl with a bow, always a bow, in her hair.

It has to be her. It must.

Adriana is the daughter, and that she works at the pet store—

They're still in business. Her. Her family. Her *father*, the scamming sleaze ball who threatened my family.

"Boulder!"

He raises his head in the back seat.

"Are we going back in?"

Boulder whines a whine I can only interpret as *I'd advise against that.*

"Good point." I shift the car into reverse and back out of our parking spot. "First, you need to rest, and I need a plan. A better plan."

CHAPTER 32
VIRAL

Boulder's new food plops into his stainless steel bowl. He sniffs at it, licks at it once or twice, and abandons the bowl for the couch.

"You always were picky. And that's where *I* sit, bud. You can have—there you go—the corner. Thank you."

For the first time since the car wash, I glance at my phone. No, I *gape* at my phone.

Notifications. Dozens, if not a hundred. Discord and YouTube and Discord and YouTube, which surely means an army of *we should be friends* comments has descended on my videos like so many flying monkeys, and that P-Money and Salchicha are having a jolly old time ripping my content to shreds.

I knew I should have written them off.

But just in case—

PrakashMoney: This video—the one about your dad… it's not the worst thing I've ever watched.
SalchichaSimon: Dude, I really want to know what's up with that pet store.

PrakashMoney: Same, not that I'm fucking around with anyone in the murder business.
SalchichaSimon: @BoulderIBarelyKnowHer, you there?
PrakashMoney: He doesn't need to be. Check this shit out.

[link]
Kitten Caboodle, LLC. - Madison, WI
Kitten Caboodle is Madison, Wisconsin's premiere…

SalchichaSimon: How do you know that's the place?
PrakashMoney: I don't. I know nothing. If any murderers find this, it wasn't me.
SalchichaSimon: Bullshit.
PrakashMoney: *Maybe* I dumped the video in a few other threads. Maybe—just maybe—Noobie McNooberson forwarded me that email from his dad in a DM. The original. The one where he mentions Madison.
SalchichaSimon: For once, I'm grateful @BoulderIBarelyKnowHer is a horrible novice.
PrakashMoney: Again—I had nothing to do with turning up the name of the pet store, murderers. It wasn't me. I shared the video, sure, and whatever the lads have turned up, they've turned up.

The lads. Good God. He can pretend he didn't do anything, but PrakashMoney called in the cavalry.

I navigate to YouTube, where, holy shit, 641 views. Twenty new subscribers. Forty-eight comments.

I scroll through them, my jaw loose.

Dude, this is fucking nuts.

Thumbs-up this comment if PrakashMoney sent you here. P-Money for president!

HE DIDN'T WANT ANYONE TO KNOW IT WAS HIM, YOU EXTRAORDINARY DIPSHIT

First of all, what a shit for brains dad. Second of all, where's this pet store at?

Yeah, let me at 'em. Threatening to murder someone's family? This payback gon be gud.

Summoning Pierogi to the case in 3… 2… 1…

THE PET STORE HAS BEEN FOUND

Beneath the last of these—the website. The address. The phone number for Kitten Caboodle.

This is the reason for the inundation of calls, the subsequent hangups. This is the reason Adriana advised me against, fuck me sideways, *everything*.

And I should have listened: through that job application, I gave my address, indirectly, to a would-have-been murderer.

A would-have-been murderer who, thanks to my video, now knows my father is not dead.

CHAPTER 33
⌘ + Z

he internet is, by and large, an ocean of shitposts and porn.

And yet, I forgot.

I forgot the internet is a *sentient* ocean of shitposts and porn that can crash down on the shores of the unsuspecting at any time. So, congratulations. You did it, Reddit! Or, I guess YouTube, but either way, the point remains. Adriana and her father have been tidal-waved by unhinged internet vigilantes who just so happen to be taking action in my name.

This is what I wanted, isn't it?

Key word: *wanted*. Past tense.

"Boulder, how do you delete a video from YouTube?"

He trots past me, sniffs again at his food and, at long last, digs in.

"Thanks for your help." I abandon my phone, find my laptop, and open my channel's backend. Oh, hell—we're at 759 views on this problem child of mine, not to mention the ballooning number of comments and another two dozen subscribers. They're swarming to my other videos now, too, with comments like *insta-subscribe*.

"You hear that, doggo? We're an insta-subscribe!" I hang my head. I should be celebrating, should be steamrolling my way to a thousand subscribers—to monetization—and yet here I am, my cursor hovering over *Delete Forever*, at least on this video that's gotten completely out of control.

I pause, stroke my chin.

Deleting it is the right thing to do *if I want to protect the scammers*, but I made a promise. What could Adriana and her dad really do, anyway? If this video does blow up, I can't just get kidnapped, can I? The more popular I get, the harder it is for them to, I don't know, send some secret scammers' assassins' guild after me.

And yet, a problem. The same logic won't apply to my dad. They know about him now, the lie he kept up for years. If Adriana and her dad do go after him, he wouldn't even see it coming—and it'd be my fault.

Damn it, I need to think on this.

"Boulder, you want to go for a walk?"

Judging by the hop in his step, he's amenable. I slide on his little dog boots to keep his paws from freezing, and, after bundling up myself, we stroll through Tenney Park, snaking along the asphalt path to the metal bridge. Boulder high-steps across it, and beneath us, the snow-kissed, frozen lagoon deafens the sound of traffic on East Johnson. The ice is criss-crossed with lines from the previous evening's ice skaters, which glide my thoughts in the direction of Millennium Park, of Chicago.

They glide my thoughts in the direction, again, of my dad.

Boulder and I make it to the far side of the bridge, and he gives a tug on the leash, roots through the snow before squatting in what is apparently his ideal place for a number two.

I turn away, embracing a feeling I've been pushing down, down, down since I first saw him.

My dad, not the dog.

Because in that moment—when my dad turned, when an aged version of a familiar face illuminated with recognition—I was happy. I had hope. I thought we had another chance.

Boulder kicks about the snow, and I reach into my pocket for a bag. My pocket is empty.

I am the fucking worst.

"Hey," I say my voice low, "come on. Let's go."

I've got more pressing problems than being a shit neighbor, anyway, because I need to call my dad—need to warn him—and I'm very much not looking forward to that call.

Boulder and I do a once-around of the park, a trek that includes him stopping to lay in the snow like a total dweeb. "Your cone is full of snow now, bud. What are you gonna— oh, you're going to eat it. So long as it's fresh, I guess."

Once back in the apartment building, we take the elevator to the second floor.

My stomach drops at the sight of an envelope outside our unit.

Adriana. My job application. My address. Who the fuck else would do something so ominous?

I crouch, turn the envelope over in my hands. Boulder shakes off what snow remains embedded in his coat, his tail wagging as he waits to be let in.

"Hang on." I look to my left down the hall. Then, my right. No one. No sign of Adriana, no sign of her dad, no sign of anyone.

I unseal the envelope. Inside, a letter, and it's not from Adriana.

Instead, it's my landlord. Rent, past due. Bounced check. Five days to cure or face eviction.

Five days to cure or face eviction.

I force a dry swallow, lean against the door to steady myself.

My final paycheck from Nortex won't be enough to cover

what I owe, and even if it were, it won't arrive until the final day to cure.

I need my money back from Al, from that goddamn dealership.

It's that or I turn to my dad, the man whose life I've put in danger. Again.

CHAPTER 34
GOODBYE

t should be the easiest thing to pick up the phone, to press it to my ear, to tell my dad he needs to watch his six.

Instead—

I pace the apartment. I peer through the blinds. When he whines, I adjust Boulder's cone and, in between fresh rounds of pacing, watch as the views on my YouTube videos climb, climb, climb. I check my email for an update from the Department of Transportation. Nothing, but it's the weekend, and it's only been a couple of days since I filed the complaint, besides.

At last, my phone. I reach for it, find my dad in my contacts.

Before I can press CALL, a train grumbles on the horizon. Within a minute, it's charging through the intersection outside my window. My phone remains in my hand, limp at my side. The floor shakes. The railroad crossing clangs. A car honks, and in the parking lot outside my apartment, a sound system booms.

The train moves along. The clanging ceases. Traffic clears, and the floor steadies.

My phone remains in my hand. I glance from Boulder to my phone and finally—finally!—do the right thing.

The phone rings once. It rings again. A third time. A fourth.

Then, at what feels like the last possible moment, the call connects.

My father's voice does not fill the line.

"Hello?" I stammer. "Are you—?"

An automated message. "The number you have dialed is no longer in service. Goodbye."

CHAPTER 35
AGAIN

My father has died again.

It feels as though he's died again.

To have had him, the terrible scamming bastard, back in my life for less than a week before he blinked, again, out of existence—it's too much.

But he isn't dead, I tell myself on Saturday afternoon, on Saturday evening. I tell myself he isn't dead when I wake on Sunday morning, when I try his number again and am informed, coldly, that his number remains out of service.

I try his email, the one through which he contacted me. I ask that he call me as soon as possible, telling him only that things have changed. I check my inbox in between completing new job applications. I check in between cups of coffee, during the ad breaks in the mix of scambaiting videos YouTube has recommended me. I check in between taking Boulder out for a walk, while we're *on* the walk.

Despite the absolute clusterfuck that is my everything, I remember to bring a bag with me. Small miracles.

On Sunday night, I should be looking forward to the morning with glee. Monday is when I do my best work, my most choice scambaiting. To take the Long Loop to my desk, to plug in my Raspberry Pi, to comb through inbox after inbox with a sense of *purpose*—I'll miss it.

That night, on my mattress, I sit cross-legged, my laptop on my thighs, Boulder at the foot of the bed.

I reply to an investment banker in Benin, to a long-lost relative who would like me to incorporate a foundation in her name. It's her dying wish, you see, and if she perishes before this money is transferred to my accounts, her government will seize those funds, and orphans will go without.

After her, it's on to the crypto scammers of the world, one of whom I hook easily through one of three phony Instagram accounts. And wouldn't you know it? On one of my other accounts, an attractive woman with a salacious profile photo has decided to sext me out of the blue! What a time to be alive.

Sarcasm, people. Sarcasm.

I message her, feigning interest, knowing all the while they'll be extorting some other poor sap soon enough—assuming they aren't already. So, fine. Forget her. Back to this crypto bro, who all too predictably sticks to his script, even after I tell him I'll be using the money from my investment in crypto to fund my "chicken-flavored Kool-Aid prototype."

I should laugh, should be happy to have given myself these moments away, but when I circle back, reviewing my work, I feel nothing.

No, I feel *awful*.

This investment banker, this faux relative, this crypto bro and this amateur sextortionist—they're like me. No, I'm like *them*. Surely they wouldn't scam if they didn't have to, if they weren't desperate. My dad didn't scam until he had to, anyway, until desperation overwhelmed any sense of morality he might have had.

Not that this makes it right. Not that I would ever do the same.

My eyelids grow heavy. I toss my phone aside, close my laptop, fall asleep on top of the covers.

Monday morning, my alarm sounds, the same time as always. I check for phone calls, for emails. From him.

When I see there's nothing, I drown myself in sleep.

The sharp edge of Boulder's cone scrapes against my neck, stirring me. "What? Oh, shit. Time for you to go out. Way past time for you to go out."

On our walk, a new email. Not from my father—fuck—but from, okay, the state. I skim its contents, my heart racing.

Record of misrepresentation. Not the first time. Agreement reached with dealership. Full refund, less new mileage, in exchange for the vehicle's return.

My grip on Boulder's leash loosens. I breathe for the first time in days.

CHAPTER 36
DEALER'S CHOICE

My appointment at the dealership is at three p.m.

Al, the coward, doesn't make an appearance. Instead, I'm greeted by an inspector from the state. His handshake is firm, his demeanor sharp. He does a thrice-over of the vehicle's exterior, his face betraying nothing. At times, he writes on a clipboard, and that he does this through what are quite possibly the world's thickest gloves is damn impressive.

I do the math. Even after the mileage deduction, this refund will pay for past-due rent. It will pay for next month's, too. I can find a job in that time, a real job that doesn't put my life—or that of anyone else—in jeopardy. Other bills will languish unpaid, yes, but Boulder and I will have a roof over our heads, and this is all I can ask for in light of the alternative: cramming the whole of my life into a 2014 Toyota Corolla S. Sleeping in a reclined driver's seat while a gassy Saint Bernard reeks—yes, *reeks*—havoc through the night. A terrible cold creeping in through the windows. Fingers and toes that never truly warm.

All of this, I have imagined, and I am so not ready for it.

The inspector opens a car door, sits in the driver's seat.

He squints at the mileage, flips through papers on his clip-board, chews on the end of his pen. He exits the vehicle, opens the rear doors, shines a flashlight on the floors, on the backseat.

"Hmm."

My hands in the pockets of my jacket, I step forward. "Hmm?"

"It looks like something spilled on the back seat."

"Oh, uh—" Do not say it's blood. Blood means questions, and questions mean problems, and problems mean—

"Is this blood?" The inspector, holy shit, gets right in there and sniffs it. "And pine? Is this blood and pine?"

And dog shit, technically, not that I'm volunteering that. "I have a dog," I say. "He had some stitches open up after an operation. I had to rush him to the vet. I used a few air fresh-eners—a lot of them—while cleaning up."

"Hmm."

"Yeah, you keep saying that, but—"

"Just a moment." He strides for the dealership.

I trace his movement through the windows, watching as he struts for the welcome desk, is pointed in the direction of an office in the building's nearest corner.

Al's office.

The inspector enters, gestures to his clipboard. Al places his hands behind his head, grins, throws his feet up on his desk. The inspector frowns. Al shrugs.

This isn't happening. I won't let it happen.

I'm in the doorway of Al's office before the inspector can turn to leave. "What's the problem?" I say.

"Wear and tear," says the inspector.

"Whatever you did in that back seat, kid," Al says, "is way beyond normal wear and tear."

"So fucking what?" I say. "You agreed to take the car back for a full refund."

"You were so intent on reading the original contract," Al

says, so damn self-assured. "I'm surprised you didn't see this coming."

The inspector chimes in. "The dealership's agreement with the Department of Transportation was to accept the car back, less new mileage, assuming normal wear and tear."

I shake my head. "Then lop off a couple hundred bucks from our deal and replace the back seats."

The inspector turns to Al. "This seems reasonable."

Al considers this. He goes on considering it. He considers it for far longer than should be necessary.

"Don't hose me, Al," I say. "You know it's the right thing to do."

"The right thing?" Al laughs. "Why would you expect me to do the right thing?"

"Because—I mean, why wouldn't you?"

Al stands, his hands splayed on his desk. "I believe you called me something like a crook? A con man?"

I fold my arms. "Here's your chance to prove me wrong."

He sighs, amused. "I don't have to prove anything to you or anyone else." He looks at the inspector, shakes his head.

"What the fuck?" I say.

"Leave. Now." Al puffs up his chest, adjusts his belt. "Inspector, you'll ensure he gets his keys?"

The inspector nods, exits the office.

My feet remain planted. "Take the car back."

"I'm happy to buy it from you. How's five hundred bucks sound?"

"Oh, fuck off. I could sell it for more to the first person walking past on the sidewalk."

Al glances out the window. "Mighty cold out there. Not a lot of folks out and about."

"You know what I mean."

He reaches for the phone on his desk, presses a button. A woman answers. "Yeah," Al says, "if you could have security swing by my office—"

"You're kidding, right?" I say. "At least reimburse me for the repairs."

Al ignores me, speaking instead into this phone. "No, it's not *that* urgent." His gaze settles on mine. "At least, I don't think we're going to have further trouble, are we?"

I ball my fists, ready to knock his damn teeth out if it wouldn't mean leaving Boulder home alone while I sit in a cell.

I abandon Al's office, don't give him the satisfaction of begging him further. Out on the lot, I chase down the inspector, who's closing the doors on my vehicle. "You can't let him get away with that, can you?"

"It's not up to me," he says.

"Then what's the point of you?"

His eyes go wide. "Look, I understand your position—"

"Then get in there and shove this car back down his throat."

"Sir—"

"I don't want *sir*, I want a refund!"

"You're not going to get one!" The inspector's neck strains as he says this, and he catches himself, clearly embarrassed. "I'm sorry. It's—well. Ordinarily, I'd be as shocked as you are that he didn't take you up on your proposal, but with his dealership's license set to expire at the end of the month—"

"Wait. What?"

"He has until the end of the month to liquidate his inventory. His license has been revoked for what we'll call 'persistent infringement.'"

I reply with a series of blinks.

"What I'm trying to say is he's not especially worried about dissatisfied customers at the moment."

"That would have been good to know."

"It would have been good to know about the back seat," the inspector says, "when you first contacted the D.O.T. If we'd accounted for it in the original agreement—"

"Don't," I say. "Stop."

He sighs. "Anything else I can do to help?"

Fear and anxiety take hold. I attempt to expel both as a laugh. "Do you have any connections at the governor's office? Maybe some big cheese who could—?"

"I'm sorry, sir, but unless the dealership is willing to take the car back as is, there's nothing further to discuss." The inspector hands me my keys, ambles away.

My fingers make a fist around the keys in my open palm. From his office, Al watches me enter my car, his hands on his hips.

Al, a scammer. A goddamn scammer. A goddamn scammer protected by the law.

CHAPTER 37
MA'AM

Almost all tech support scams follow the same formula.

You receive a voicemail from Microsoft Tech Support, letting you know you were recently charged 299 dollars for antivirus software. If you'd like to cancel this service, you're asked to please call Microsoft back at this number.

These people are not Microsoft Tech Support. There is no antivirus software. No charge has been made to your credit card.

And yet, you return these calls to ask questions. You return these calls to double check you've understood correctly. You return these calls to confirm you'd like to cancel.

Okay, ma'am, to refund your money, we'll need some personal information from you.

First Name. Last. Address. Date of birth. Phone number and email address and social security number.

Is all of this necessary to cancel my antivirus subscription?

Yes, ma'am, of course. You can trust us. We're Microsoft,

and if you could now please visit the following website, we'll complete the cancellation.

The website is for TeamViewer—sometimes AnyDesk—or any software that will permit the scammer to connect to your computer, to take it over. They tell you they must do this to verify the antivirus subscription has been canceled, that they'd like to run one last security check to make sure your computer is safe before the antivirus is uninstalled.

You download the software. You give them your access information. The scammer connects to your computer.

Once they are connected, you are well and truly fucked.

They can see your screen. They can commandeer—turn on, watch you through—your webcam. They can ask you to visit your online banking portal to verify how much money is in your accounts before they pretend to issue a refund that will never arrive.

You ask them if they can see your screen. They tell you no, ma'am, your bank's security will not permit third parties to see your bank account's screen.

This is a lie.

When you log in, they make note of how much you have in your checking, your savings, your 401k.

This is when they decide how much trouble you're worth.

Through scammerly chicanery, they blacken your screen. On their side, they can still see your bank accounts. You can see nothing. Often, before blackening your screen, they send you away with your phone, tell you to take a look at your router and write down the very long serial number on the back of it.

This gives them time to work unobstructed.

They transfer funds between your accounts, edit the HTML of your online banking portal to make it seem as though you have been issued a refund. The problem? You made a mistake, ma'am, when you filled out our refund form. Do you remember that earlier, ma'am? The refund form?

Well, you must have entered an extra nine because we sent you nearly three thousand dollars instead of three hundred.

Again, no such refund has been issued. It does not matter what your screen says. It can no longer be trusted because it is under their control.

You are under their control.

Ma'am, they'll say, I'm going to lose my job if we don't get that extra money back from you, so let me check with my accounts team to see what can be done. No, ma'am, we are not permitted to just take back that money from your bank directly, but my accounts manager has told me we can work out another arrangement. Now tell me—do you have a Wal-Mart or Best Buy or Target store near you?

If you do, they will ask you to go to that store. They will ask you to purchase five 500-dollar gift cards for Google Play or the Apple Store or Best Buy or Wal-Mart.

When you are at the store, ma'am, if they ask you what these cards are for, you must tell them these are for your nieces or nephews or for personal use. No, ma'am, you cannot mention Microsoft because the store will charge taxes differently on the cards and this will cost you more money. Okay, and once you have purchased those cards, we need you to call us back on this number and share with us the codes on the back of the cards. Yes, ma'am, you will have to scratch off the back of the card first before you please share these codes with us. Do not worry that we'll only get 2,500 dollars back; you can keep the extra 200 dollars for your trouble.

If this doesn't make any sense to you, it shouldn't. None of it is real, but your flight or fight response has engaged, and you're a nice person who doesn't want "Michael Johnson" or "Todd Davidson" or any number of these—to them—American-sounding tech support droids to lose their job.

But let's say you don't have a Wal-Mart or Best Buy or Target or gas station near you. Let's say you get wise to their scheming and start asking questions. Let's say you tell them you're going to hang up because this must be a scam, and you're going to report them to the authorities.

Okay, ma'am, well then I need you to revisit your computer.

You do. It is locked. You cannot move the mouse. The keyboard does not respond to your touch.

On the screen, all of your bank accounts have been drained to zero.

Remember—none of this is real, but you will worry. Your life savings is gone, after all, and they'll tell you, ma'am, all we want back is the money we're owed. So, please, go to your bank and withdraw thousands in cash—yes, we will put this amount back in your account so you can do the transaction. You will wrap the money in foil and then take this money to a FedEx store, or UPS if that is easier. From there, you will send the cash to an address in the United States, where—not that they say this part out loud—a money mule will take a percentage of the funds for themselves and forward the rest to their operation via Western Union. No, ma'am, they'll say, we cannot give you all of your money back until you have sent us a tracking number for the package that we can confirm is valid. Only then will we return the rest of the money to your account. Only then will we release our hold on your computer.

Once you have taken these steps, they will disappear for a time—from your phone.

They're still on your computer, though—remember Team-Viewer, AnyDesk?—logging your keystrokes, the websites you visit, collecting passwords and otherwise thieving valuable personal information they can use to further take advantage of you.

This may seem farcical. Surely no one would fall for this, would fall into these traps.

But they must: there are too many call centers that do this

work, day in and day out, to possibly shut them all down, even if the local authorities wanted to. It's a numbers game.

You're a number to them, no matter how much you cry, no matter how much you wail or threaten or moan.

They are immune to your humanity. They are immune to the laws of your country. They are immune, and in this immunity is power.

Until now, I always thought I understood them. They're just scumbags, slimeballs, corrupted to the core. They're inept, lazy, or otherwise lacking the moral fortitude to do anything but scam. Bad people. They're just *bad people.*

I now know this isn't true. I now know most of them do this not by choice, but because they have no other option. They lack opportunity. They're down on their luck. They're doing what they must for their families to get by, so they can get by.

So, when I use the Google Voice account I've only just established to make my first call, I try to remind myself of this. I have no other option. It's a numbers game. I must be immune.

My call connects.

"Hello?" a woman says.

Her voice is frail, quavering. She sounds like Grandma Amundsen, the woman from whom so much was taken by people like "Michael Johnson," like "Todd Davidson." No—she sounds like the woman from whom so much was taken by people like me.

"Hello?" this woman says again.

Go on, I coach myself. You have no other option. It's a numbers game.

But I am not immune.

I hang up and, much to Boulder's chagrin, empty my insides into a toilet bowl.

CHAPTER 38
RASH DECISIONS

wipe my mouth, the taste of vomit still fresh.

What I've done is unforgivable. I didn't do it, but I meant to. I was going to.

And they did this to me—Adriana, her father. They're the fuckwads who turned me into this. They took my father from me, or, well, Adriana's old man did. Adriana, at her age—my age—couldn't have known any better, but she's still in the family. She's still complicit. She knows, protects their secrets.

Boulder nudges me with his cone, can't quite lap at my face. I extend an arm, keep him away. "You don't want any part of this, buck-o." I gag, flush the toilet. Another wave of nausea surges. I manage to get it in the toilet bowl. Most of it. I flush again, urge Boulder back from what didn't quite make it into the bowl, usher him out of the bathroom while I search for cleaning supplies.

Scrubbing away on my hands and knees in the bathroom, I attempt to reassure Boulder. "If they want this apartment back, they can have it. We'll figure it out. You and me, right? We've got each other." Famous last words, I think, considering the state of him.

Considering the state of me.

But none of that! You've got two days to cure this rent situation, Eric, and the last you checked, you had no responses to your job applications, nothing from your dad in your inbox or by voicemail, and hardly more than a hundred subscribers to your YouTube channel. You have to get. this. shit. moving.

I grab my phone. I don my jacket. I tell Boulder, no, he can't come with, not this time. I'm not going on a W-A-L-K, and though I'm going to Kitten Caboodle, I don't want to put him in harm's way. Who knows what these people are capable of? Dad's gone AWOL, remember, and Boulder deserves better. Way better.

Nightfall blankets Madison's east side. Headlights bounce and sway over railroad tracks. Traffic zips down East Washington. Revelers enter and exit bars in groups of twos and threes and fours. The capitol looms large to the west, a domed crown of illuminated white granite.

The Kitten Caboodle parking lot is empty save for one car. Adriana's, maybe. Or her dad's.

I reach into my jacket, find my phone. With the YouTube app open, I search for live, *live*, I want to go live, but okay, I guess you can only go live from the app if you have a thousand subscribers or more. Thanks.

I exit the vehicle, march for the store's front doors, hit record on my phone's camera and turn it to face me.

"Hey, it's Eric from your favorite Grandma's Revenge channel, back with a new video. You know that pet store you've been calling?" The automatic doors part. "Well, I'm here, and I've got questions." The smell of the place overwhelms, bittersweet, mostly bitter. "Want to meet the scammers themselves? You will in a minute. Hang on." I drop my phone into the breast pocket of my jacket, the camera facing outward.

At checkout, some college kid wipes down the counter, the register. "Hey," I say.

He rears back. "Oh. Didn't hear anyone come in. What can I help you with?"

I lean on the counter. "I'm looking for Adriana."

He narrows his eyes. "What's with the phone?"

"What?"

The kid nods in the direction of my phone, clearly protruding from my pocket. "That's none of your concern. Where's Adriana?"

"She's not here."

"What about the owner? He around?"

"No?"

"That a question?"

"I'm sorry. Who are you, again?"

I take a tense breath. "Who I am isn't important. I'm here to speak with—what's his name?"

"Whose name?"

"The owner."

"You mean Stu?"

"Sure, bring him out."

This kid adopts a shit-eating grin. "Look, man. I told you he's not here, and—"

"You're one of them, aren't you? You're in on it, too. You're protecting him."

"I have no idea what you're talking about, but if it makes you feel any better, I'll get Adriana on the phone." He grumbles something beneath his breath.

"What was that?"

"I said, 'she'll be pissed I'm failing to close the store without having to call her, but—'"

"So you're *not* one of them?"

He stops scrolling through his phone. "I don't even know what that means."

"Like—" I sigh. "You're not Adriana's brother or anything?"

"Hell no. I just work here, man. Trying to make a few

bucks while I'm in school."

I rub my forehead. "Just—can you—?" I motion with my hand for him to get Adriana on the line.

He completes the call. Straight to voicemail.

"Good evening," the recording says, "or good day, one supposes. You've connected with Adriana Erwahrend, though perhaps that's not entirely true, as I'm not on the line. Please leave a message, however, and I'll see to it you're phoned as soon as is reasonable."

The employee's phone beeps. He opens his mouth to begin a message.

I yank the phone away from him. "Hey, Adriana. It's Eric, the one with the conehead. The dog with the conehead. The dog with the cone around its head. You know what I mean." I stride from the checkout counter. Behind me, footsteps, the angry cursing of the kid whose phone I've stolen. "Just wanted to let you know that, hey, I'm coming for you. I'm coming for you and your dad, and ow, God damn it—"

The phone is wrestled from me. I attempt to grab it back, to complete a threat I have no idea how I'll execute. Regardless, they need to know this isn't over. They need to know they'll be made to atone. They need to know this and more, but this kid disconnects the call, holds the phone up at his side, says he's calling the cops.

"Go ahead," I say, already on my way out, "call them. Adriana will be real happy to know you couldn't close the store without getting the cops involved."

The automatic doors whir apart. Cold envelops me. I glance over my shoulder, see he's tucked his phone away.

Once in my car, I stop recording. I'll watch the video once I'm home, will determine, then, whether it'll add fuel to the internet vigilante fire or simply make me look like a fucking lunatic. I've got a strong suspicion which it'll be, but now's not the time for rash decisions.

Now's not the time for *more* rash decisions.

On the drive home, I brainstorm incendiary titles for my next video, just in case it does prove worth posting. DODGY PET STORE DRONE PROTECTS SCAM MASTERS. REVENGE IS A DISH BEST SERVED IN A DOG BOWL. THIS IS A CRY FOR HELP, SOMEONE PLEASE SAVE ME FROM THE WAKING NIGHTMARE THAT IS MY LIFE.

By the time I've pulled into my apartment's surface lot, it takes everything I have to fight back the tears. I don't have a plan—never had a reasonable plan—and now I've threatened them, *threatened them*, the family who planned to kill my family, who might have actually killed my father.

I ascend the stairs, shaking. I traverse the hall, shivering. I turn my key in the lock, numb, disappointed—but unsurprised—the place is unlocked.

But I locked the door. I know I did.

I push open the door to my apartment.

My coffee table has been upturned. My couch cushions lie scattered, torn on the floor. The television screen has been splintered into hundreds of crystalline shards. A trail of slushy boot tracks—one pair—stains the carpet, criss-crossing from bedroom to living room and back again.

Boulder is missing, gone. Taken.

CHAPTER 39

YOU'LL NEVER SEE HIM AGAIN

oulder," I call. "Boulder!"

My throbbing pulse chokes me. My vision blurs at the edges. I race from room to room, overturning blankets, peering under covers, tearing back the shower curtain, and—yeah, I don't know either—opening the dishwasher.

And he's not here. *He's not here.*

I steady myself against the kitchen counter, slipping when my hand settles on a note.

Take down the videos. Tell them you made it all up. Stay out of our business.

Fail to do this or go to the cops, and you'll never see him again.

It takes no consideration to retrieve my phone, to open the YouTube app, to delete the videos from my channel. I rush to the couch and return the cushions to their rightful position, ignoring the foam stuffing that tumbleweeds across the carpet from the speed with which I move.

Then, with the coffee table back on all fours and my phone propped up across from me, I hit record.

"Hey, folks. It's Eric with Grandma's Revenge, and…" My tongue finds the inside of my cheek, my breathing rapid, rushed. Words. Where are the words? What does it matter what I say so long as I say it? Every second wasted is another Boulder spends in their hands, so get to it, Eric, you pathetic excuse for sentient life.

I clear my throat, reset my breathing, begin again. "Hi, everyone. It's Eric with Grandma's Revenge, and I have a confession to make."

I lie. I tell viewers none of it ever happened. I tell them my dad is fine, that he was never a scammer, that he never faked his own death. I tell them I'm sorry about the pet store before I apologize *to* the pet store. I apologize to anyone I hurt, to everyone whose trust I betrayed. I also tell them, emphatically, that I never wanted anyone to get hurt. I emphasize that *no one needs to get hurt*, least of all anyone who had nothing to do with the choice I—and I alone—made in making the videos I posted. I tell the world I have no future plans for this channel, that they should forget it ever happened—that I ever existed. Please. Please don't waste any more time on me or this cause I created out of thin air. You'll only be wasting your time. You'll only be hurting people who don't deserve to be hurt.

I end the recording. I pace my apartment, looking for my laptop before finding it, of course, where I left it in bed earlier. After transferring the video I've recorded from my phone to my laptop, I hustle to upload it to YouTube, my heart slowing only once the upload begins.

Then, while YouTube servers take their sweet time processing my video, the dam finally bursts. I break down, sobbing, nearly throwing myself to the floor before I realize no, Eric, you can't. You can't give in. You can't let your guard down until you've seen this through. Boulder needs you. *You* need you, because until that smelly ass Saint Bernard is back in your care, you're all you have.

My laptop's screen refreshes. The video is finished processing, is available to subscribers.

Fifteen minutes pass. A half hour. Occasionally, my phone rattles with a new comment, some fresh admonishment or all-caps rant from a disappointed—or, perhaps more appropriate, unhinged—subscriber. Fuck 'em. They don't know the half of it. They don't know *half* of the half of it. Are they not entertained? Some balls they must have to complain about free content on the internet. It could be worse.

Understatement of a lifetime.

I urge myself from the couch, tend to my ransacked apartment, pausing intermittently to look around—to listen—for Boulder before I remember, choking back tears.

An hour after the video goes live, my phone vibrates. An incoming call. A 608 area code.

Adriana, presumably, to tell me when, where, and how I can get Boulder back.

I press my phone to my ear. "Where the hell is he?"

"What?" A man's voice. Her father, then. Stu.

"Don't play ignorant. What the fuck did you do to him? Where is he?"

"Eric, I—"

"Keep my name out of your mouth. I don't want to hear a goddamn thing from you unless it's *here's where you can get him back.*"

"I have no idea what you're talking about."

"I—" That voice. I know it. I know him. "Dad?"

"Who did you think this was?"

"This—wait. You're not dead?"

"We've been over this. You literally saw me—"

"I called you! I've been emailing."

"Sorry. New phone. Been away from email. It's a long story, but it's one you need to hear. Urgently."

I lower my phone, shake my head. "Why does this keep happening?"

"Did you say something? I couldn't—"

I draw the phone nearer again. "My life gets infinitely worse every time you show up."

"Shit, Eric. I didn't expect you to forgive me right away—if ever—but you don't have to—"

"Your buddy Stu paid me a visit."

The line goes quiet. "He what?"

"He was here. With his daughter, I'm guessing. Well, no. There was one pair of boot tracks. Maybe it was just her. I don't know. But someone was here. One of them."

"Where's *here*, Eric? Where are you?"

"My goddamn apartment."

"You need to get out of there. Now."

"They took my dog. My fucking dog, Dad."

"Eric, I'm telling you—"

"What?" I clench my jaw. "What are you telling me? You think you know better? You don't know a goddamn thing about—"

"Meet me downtown."

"If you think I'm driving to Chicago at this hour to see you of all people—"

"Madison. I'm in Madison."

"I—what?"

My dad exhales into the line. "I'm at some coffee shop. Michelangelo's. You know it?"

"Yeah, but—"

"You and I have work to do."

"Work? What work?"

"I don't know how they figured it out, Eric, but they did. They know I'm alive, and they're after me now, too."

CHAPTER 40
CHIP OFF THE OLD—

ichelangelo's is packed. Packed! As I navigate the crowd, an espresso machine steams and sputters behind the counter, and the line grows to reach the door. Every table is spoken for by laptops and textbooks and headphones, but it's a Monday night for fuck's sake; what are all of you doing flocking to a coffeehouse on a Monday night? You should be holed up in your apartments fretting the two days you have to pay back rent, should be glancing longingly at your phone for a message about your dognapped friend's return.

Okay, maybe those are just *me* things. The college crowd is here to study, to prepare for the semester's first round of exams. They're this week or next, if memory serves, and oh, how wonderful it must be to have such fleeting woes. Study away, but please, what the fuck, don't stretch your laptop chargers across the coffeehouse floor like goddamn trip wires. It's sweaty enough in here; we don't need the addition of physical challenges to—

"Eric." On my left, someone grabs my arm.

I jerk away, stumble backward into a table.

"Bro," says some Fratty McFratterson in his frayed-brim

cap, steadying his mug of coffee, which has spilled over at the edges.

"Bro yourself," I say, straightening my shoulders. He mumbles beneath his breath but returns to his study of, whatever, who the fuck cares? "Dad," I say, turning to face my old man.

"Hey." He stands, opens his arms.

I ignore the gesture, sit across from him. "You shouldn't have come here."

His chin finds his chest. "We can go somewhere else if you want."

"No," I say. "To Madison, I mean. Now sit down."

"Shouldn't we order something?"

"You paying?"

"I—uh, kind of thought—"

"Look at that line. You want to wait in that line? Just— what's in that bag of yours?" I kick the messenger bag at his feet.

"A laptop?"

"You've got more than a laptop in that bag."

"A notebook. Legal pad. I don't know. Why are you—?"

"Take it all of the bag, spread it around the table, and no one will ask any questions. Say you're studying for, I don't know, some law school thing for all anyone cares."

My dad narrows his eyes, adopts a thin smile. "Pretty resourceful of you." He sifts through his bag, does as instructed.

"Well, you need to blend in, and not just to keep us from being compelled to buy something."

He laughs. "For all the time we spent apart, you're still a chip off the old—"

"No."

"No?"

"Don't say it." I swallow, check my phone. Nothing from Adriana, from Stu.

My dad gestures to my phone. "You waiting on a call?"

"I don't know. Is your buddy Stu more of a text or a phone call guy?"

"Lower your voice."

"It's louder than a damn jet engine in here. I think we're okay."

He shifts uncomfortably. "You have no idea what we're up against."

My chair groans when I scoot it backward. "I have no idea what we're up against?"

"Don't—"

"No, that's rich. Do go on. Tell me about it. As the guy whose apartment looks like it's been run through by a triceratops on meth—and, you know, had his dog stolen—I wouldn't know anything about what we're looking at here, would I?"

"You know what I meant."

I fold my arms. Behind me, the espresso machine sputters to life again, and laughter rises from a corner of the room.

My dad seems to take my silence as a cue. "They were following me."

I throw my hands up. "And you thought getting closer to their home base was a good choice?"

"I had nowhere else to go."

"In twenty years, you didn't make a single friend? You don't have a coworker, an acquaintance from the gym, a—?"

"What are *you* doing here, then, huh?" My dad's features pinch together. "Where are all your friends? Shouldn't you be out sipping drinks with some yuppy pals of yours?"

"It's a Monday night, Dad."

He shakes his head, sighs. Then, after a glance at the door, he leans forward on the table. "What I want to know, Eric, is how they found out."

"Found out what?"

"That I'm not, you know, buried in a plot somewhere off Glenway."

I bear down, remind myself I don't owe him anything. My goal was to keep him from getting offed, but since he seems intent on putting himself in harm's way, maybe there's no saving him. If not, I can still save myself the grief of getting finger-wagged by Stu's Most Wanted by keeping the bit about the YouTube channel to myself. "I might have gone to the pet store."

"They still have that pet store?"

"It's changed names, but it's there."

"Why would you—?"

"It's where I get my dog food. *Got* my dog food."

My dad smacks his lips together. "There has to be more to it than that."

"Yeah." I swallow. "After you and I met up last week, I might have asked an employee if they knew anything about the past owners. She got dodgy, and, well, it turns out she's Stu's daughter. Adriana."

"In the history of boneheaded moves—."

"You're one to talk."

"There's a difference between making a hard choice and a bad choice, Eric."

"You seem like an expert in doing both at once, if I'm honest."

My dad gestures for me to drop it. "Going back and forth like this won't get us anywhere."

"What do you propose, then? You have mercenaries-for-hire we can use to get my dog back?"

"No, nothing like that." His shoulders rise, fall as he sighs. "Let's just take the night, you and I, to get reacquainted. When Stu calls about the dog, we'll figure out how to handle it. Together."

"Pff."

"Come on. You've got every reason to be upset with me, I

know, but I'm determined to make it right, or at least as right as I can." He checks the time on his watch, which, holy shit, is gold-plated. As I lean back in my chair, I take him in for the first time since Millennium Park—the well-ironed blazer, the carefully coiffed hairdo. He's like me when at Nortex, except not faking it. Probably.

"What do you do for a living?" I ask.

He laughs. "See? We can have a normal conversation."

"I'm sincerely asking." And not just because I'm curious, but because, if he's as moneyed as he looks, well, I could really do with a cash infusion to see me through the next week. Or longer. Longer, please.

"International banking. Super bureaucratic. Very regimented."

"Hence the getup."

"This is nothing," he says. "You should see what I wear when I go into the office."

I look away, reach for my phone. No missed calls, no texts.

"Hey," my dad says, "how about we get a drink somewhere, huh? I could use a bite to eat, too."

No, I want to say, because so long as I'm at your side, I'm at risk, too. No, I want to say, because you shouldn't be allowed to do this, to just disappear and reappear in my life whenever it's convenient or you. No, I want to say, but it's yes —it has to be yes—because I can't be alone right now, and I certainly can't go home, not by myself.

"Sure," I say. "Let's do it."

"Atta boy." My dad stands, musses my hair.

I want to tell him to fuck off, to cease and desist with the father-and-son act, but he's all I have left, and I need him—if not for the company, for the cash.

CHAPTER 41
NORMAL-ESQUE

We trudge to Coopers Tavern, only a couple of blocks from Michelangelo's. As we walk, my dad rambles. "The city's really changed since I was last here. And the east side? Don't get me started. You have no idea, Eric, how different it looks now compared to the abandoned industrial hellscape it was when you were a kid." I remind him that I do, in fact, have some idea of how much things have changed; I was here throughout the changing, remember.

This silences him until we belly up to the bar.

While we drink, I drop hints. Boulder's overnight stays at the vet. The car crash and issues with the dealership. The trouble at work—without getting too specific—and my subsequent dismissal.

"That's rough, bud."

That's rough. That's rough? All of that before my dog—his mother's former dog—is stolen, and the most compassion he can muster is *that's rough*?

Before I can drag his ass for his absolute dereliction of duty in being, I don't know, a decent person, he orders another round for the both of us, and if he's buying, fine, I won't complain, at least not about that. It'll grant me more time to pave the runway in the lead up to the big ask, anyway.

"So," he says after the bartender's dropped off our second round, "how you holding up?"

"Uh, we kind of just covered that."

"Yeah, but that's, you know—" He makes a dismissive motion with his hands.

I stare back, shake my head.

"Your grandma." He sips from his drink. "How are you holding up since she—?"

"Fine."

"Fine?"

"Shouldn't I be?"

"Well, I figured after your mom and—"

"Don't mention Mom. And I don't want another apology tour."

My dad nods, studies the chalkboard of endless beer possibilities across from us. I turn my focus to my phone, wish I'd sent myself Adriana's number from that pet store employee's contact list after leaving her that voicemail, but, very cool, I guess I'll just keep drowning my sorrows with one of the last people I'd like to be stuck here with.

Okay, that's not true. Dolores and Caio would be worse. Way worse.

"They sure do have a lot of beers here," my dad says.

Small talk. Kill me. Forget everything I said about Dolores and Caio. "Mhm."

"You're worried," my dad says. "I can tell."

"So perceptive of you."

"Do you respond to everything so sarcastically? No wonder you have no friends."

"I never said I don't have any friends."

"Trust me, you don't have to say it for people to notice."

"Okay," I say, sliding my beer away, "if this is the direction the night's headed, I think I'll take my chances—"

"Sit," my dad says.

"What am I to you, a fucking dog?"

He puts his hand on my shoulder. "No, you're someone who needs me right now. And I need you." He exhales a tense breath. "There, I said it."

I shrug his hand away. "You don't need me. Fucking off to Chicago for the entirety of my adult life proves as much."

"We're going to make this work," he says. "Just think about how much easier it's going to be to pool our resources, to find a new place to live—"

"A new place to live?"

"Well, you can't just stay in that apartment anymore, not if Stu knows about it."

I wince. "Are you suggesting we skip town?"

"Not until after we get your dog back, at least."

At this, I return to my seat.

"And honestly, Eric, I'd rather not run, not if we can help it. I'm tired of running. Stu robbed me—robbed *you*—of so much, and I think it's time he faces the consequences of his actions."

"Yeah?"

"Yeah."

"So—I mean, to be clear, we're not talking about—" I draw my thumb across his neck.

"No! God, no. Nothing like that."

"What are you thinking, then?"

"Tomorrow."

I narrow my eyes.

He slides my beer closer to me. "Tomorrow, we'll sort it all out. Your dog, a new place to live, getting a plan together for Stu. Can we just, for one night, pretend everything is normal?"

"No."

He raises his hands at his sides. "Okay, sure. Not *normal*, but, you know, normal-ish? Normal-esque?"

I don't answer, but I do sip from my beer, and it's normal —as normal as anything can be, all things considered.

CHAPTER 42
FOR DEBTS OWED

Two drinks become three, four. A fifth round is ordered—as is a sixth—and my phone never rings, never buzzes with any contact from Stu, from Adriana.

"Shit," my dad says, "we should get out of here."

The bar has emptied save for us, the bartender, and a couple on a date that's—well, they might as well be on top of each other in that booth back there. It's more than past time to head out.

"Can we close our tab?" I ask the bartender.

He nods, returns a minute later, places the bill squarely between my father and me, but my dad is already standing, is clumsily pushing his hand through a sleeve of his jacket.

My attention darts between him, the bill, and back again. "You, uh, got a Mastercard Black Card you want to throw down?"

He laughs, continues donning his jacket.

I lean away from the bar, put on my own winter gear. By the time I'm finished, my dad's shuffled to the door, his hands in his pockets while he gazes out the window at the state capitol building through softly falling snow.

I whistle.

He turns. "What?"

I wave the bill from where I stand at the bar.

"I'll get the next one."

"The next one?" I say. "You kind of owe me, you know."

"Is that how it's going to be?"

After the night I've had, after all the hints I've dropped, he's still this dense? "Don't think a couple hours of tolerable conversation make up for a decades-long absence."

"Heh." My dad waddles over, fumbles with his wallet, and slaps a card on the bar.

"That wasn't so hard, was it?"

The bartender completes the transaction, returns with the receipt. My dad signs, leaves the tip line empty, shuffles to the door.

The tip line. Empty.

Settle down, Eric—he's drunk. Maybe he forgot! But no, gross, you can't make excuses for him, even if it is better than the alternative, that accepting my dad might be a cheap bastard who can't—or simply won't—bail me out, cash-wise.

Before joining my dad outside, I add a fifty-spot to the tip line.

Just because I have to suffer my dad's return doesn't mean anyone else should have to.

CHAPTER 43
GOOD MORNING

n the night, I toss. I turn. What sleep I manage is fleeting, shallow. On the couch, my dad snores, his—deliberate?—failure to book a hotel room grating me with his every wheezing breath. I tiptoe from bed, close my bedroom door. When the wind shifts, I stir, listening closely for signs of Boulder, for signs of *them*, but my apartment's doorknob never jiggles, and the door's locked and barricaded, besides—even if only by two breakfast bar stools and a dilapidated coffee table. Sleep, Eric, sleep. You'll need what of it you can muster before a meeting tomorrow, hopefully, with Adriana and her dad, for whatever revenge you and your dad plan.

At 7:03 a.m., my phone bleats.

My eyes burning, my body sapped from exhaustion, I answer. "Hello?"

"Good morning." Adriana. For real this time.

I throw my legs over the side of my bed. "Where are we meeting?"

"One wonders why you feel entitled to an audience."

"What are you calling me for if not a meeting?"

"I'm returning your call. Your voicemail, rather. Something about how *you're coming for us?*"

In the living room, the snoring subsides. Blankets rustle. I lower my voice. "Yeah, and that was before what you did with my dog."

"I haven't the faintest notion what any of this has to do with Conehead."

"It's Boulder, and don't you—"

"Boulder, then."

"What's wrong with you?"

"I advised you against further meddling with our store's operation."

"And you think my further interference merits dognapping?"

"I believe the term is catburgling, though in any event, I'm unsure what you—"

"Are you at Kitten Caboodle right now?"

She tut-tuts. "Have you ever seen me at the store on a Tuesday?"

"I—how the hell am I supposed to—?"

"I don't work Tuesdays, nor do I have the intention of spending them entertaining your unfounded rantings."

At this, I stand. My dad yawns on the far side of my bedroom door. "Unfounded? The lack of dog in my apartment makes my accusations pretty *founded*, as does the lovely note you left behind."

"A note? Written by my hand? I assure you the presence of any such note is news to me."

"It wasn't written in any hand. It was typed, none of which matters because, what the fuck, how can you react so cruelly?"

"This isn't a reaction of cruelty. It's one of utter confusion. The whole of this is madness, if I do say so myself."

At this, I hang my head. She doesn't know. I can hear it in her voice. It's that or she's a goddamn sociopath, which, well, with what little I know of her, maybe I shouldn't discard the possibility. "So you're saying you didn't do it? Your dad didn't do it?"

"Again, if what you're implying is that I stole Conehead—Boulder, rather—your accusation couldn't be further from the truth."

"And your dad?"

"I can't speak for the actions of my father, though the animal-lover he is, I find such an act on his part quite unlikely."

A knock on my bedroom door. "Hold on," I say.

Adriana speaks up. "I won't be put on hold. It's my day off, if you'll recall, and I intend to—"

"Eric?" my dad says through the door. "You talking to someone?"

"Shut up." My tone is sharp, sharper than intended.

Adriana reacts accordingly. "Well, if that's how you'll be speaking to me, I think I'll—"

"Not you," I say. "Where—just—what are you saying? That you don't know anything about what happened to my dog?"

"Eric?" My bedroom door opens.

I throw my shoulder into it. "Naked! Changing! Boundaries! Jesus Christ!"

"Shit," my dad says. "Sorry."

I lock my door while, on her end of the call, Adriana laughs. "You're quite unusual, Eric Amundsen."

"I'm quite pissed off is what I am, and I'd like to—whatever. What are you doing with your day off? I know you said you weren't interested in entertaining my, uh—"

"Unfounded rantings, yes."

"Those, yeah, but if you didn't steal my dog—"

"Which I certainly did not."

"Sure." I pause a moment, listening for any sound from beyond my room. Water runs in the kitchen. Cupboards open, close. "Okay," I say, "can we still meet?"

"Not if you intend to further sully my Tuesday morning routine with your slander."

"No, no more slander. I just—" I remind myself to breathe. "You like Boulder, right?"

"I like him as much as any dog who comes to the store."

"Which is how much, exactly?"

"Oh, quite a bit."

I'm surprised to hear myself snickering. "Then will you help me find him? Get him back? Figure out who has him, at least? I need someone to talk this out with, and—" And what, Eric? And you have no friends? And you can't trust—or in the very least, don't like—your own father? Thankfully, I'm forced to say neither.

"I suppose my routine can still proceed if you integrate yourself into it."

"And how can I go about integrating myself?"

"You can find me where I am most Tuesday mornings."

Christ. It's like pulling teeth with her. "And where, pray tell, is that?"

"Willalby's on Williamson Street, of course."

"Yeah, *of course*." I roll my eyes for an audience of none.

"Though I should emphasize again, Eric, that if this is some ruse to harangue me further while I break my fast, I'll be quite dissatisfied."

"There'll be no need for haranguing if you can help me get Boulder back."

"Again, as I have no inkling as to the whereabouts of your canine, I make no promises, but what you do with your time is your choice and yours alone."

Willalby's it is, then. She's the only lead I have, the only person in all of this whose advice—advising me against *that*— I should have taken from the start. "Fine. See you soon," I say.

I end the call to another knock on my door.

"What is it with you?" I whip the door open.

"Uh, okay." My dad stands holding two cups of coffee.

"Here I am proud of myself for figuring out the Keurig, and you—"

"None for me." I push past him and make for the apartment's entryway. "I've got, uh—I guess I left some things behind at the office. You know, before they fired me."

My dad sets my coffee on an end table. "Want some company on the drive?"

"No." I step into my boots, lace them.

"Is it something I said?"

"It's nothing you *anything*. It's not about you. It's not all about you."

"What am I supposed to do while you're gone?"

I rub my temples, eye his messenger bag near where he crashed on the couch. "Your job, maybe? All that international banking you mentioned last night. You've got your laptop, don't you? Or here's an idea—get to work on that revenge we discussed last night or, hey, even better, look for places we might move." I slip into my jacket, wrap a scarf around my neck. "Judging by the sound of things, you had no issues sleeping last night, but I, for one, would much rather live somewhere we're not going to be swooped in on at any moment by some deranged former associate of yours."

I finish buttoning my jacket, but my father's lack of response gives me pause.

I meet his gaze. His eyes are watery, glazed over.

What I want to say is *are you seriously fucking crying right now* because, for the love of God, he's not the one whose life is in shambles—*as many* shambles—but instead, I say, "Don't take anything I'm saying right now personally."

"I told you last night that I needed your help, and you—"

"Yes, we need each other's help. But first, I have to take care of this, okay? I need time to think, a minute to be alone." My hand finds the door.

My dad's words keep me from opening it. "You weren't talking to your former employer, were you?"

"What difference does it make?" I open the door.

"I wish you trusted me."

I glance back at him. "Find us a place to live, maybe, and you can earn yourself some trust. Until then—" I slip through the door.

"Eric."

I stick my head back between the door and jamb. "What?"

"Be careful, now."

CHAPTER 44
WARM-UPS

"I don't know how many times you require me to repeat myself," Adriana says, neatly stacking her toast before biting off a piece at the corner, "I know nothing of your dog other than it's had digestive trouble."

I place my elbows on our table, the booth in which we sit the furthest from this greasy spoon of a diner's door. Through the kitchen hole, sausages sizzle, a toaster pops, and kitchenware clatters. "Order up," calls a cook, and a plateful of omelette appears in the window between kitchen and dining room.

I sip my coffee—best bang for my buck on the menu—to quell the rumbling of my stomach.

"So," Adriana says, "if your expectation was that a tete-a-tete would pry from me a confession for deeds not done, I must say—"

"No," I interrupt. "I don't know. Well, I do know. I know I'm not done because someone took my dog, and if *you* don't know anything about it, it has to be your dad."

Adriana digs into her hash browns, which are still steaming. "Whatever ill will he bears your family, my father would never resort to—if we'll permit ourselves such a term —*dognappery* to exact revenge."

"Revenge? He's the one who threatened to kill my dad. He threatened to kill me. My mom, even!"

Adriana titters, covers her mouth, dabs at its corners with a napkin. "My father? Murder? I have to say, your delusions are making for quite the entertaining morning, Eric Amundsen."

"Is that—am I a joke to you?"

"On the contrary, I pity you."

I hide my anger behind another sip of coffee.

Our server arrives as I return my mug—emblazoned with NUMBER ONE GRANDSON, because irony knows no bounds—to the table. "Can I interest anyone in a warm-up?" the server asks, already topping off Adriana's mug.

"Daniel," Adriana says, "get a load of this. Eric here is under the impression my father desired to murder his family. Can you *imagine*?"

The two of them laugh and, okay, I guess I'm taking a warm-up on that coffee.

"Is it that funny?" I ask. "Is murder funny?"

"Oh, I don't know," Daniel says. "I've never met her dad. Just, you know, playing along and—all right, well, unless there's anything else?"

I bury my head in my hands. The light shifts as Daniel departs.

"Eric, I can tell you're troubled by Boulder's disappearance—as you should be—but I must insist you've engaged the wrong party on the matter."

"Then which party do I need to, uh, engage?"

"There is the matter," she says, forking her scrambled eggs, "of your own father."

I rear back. "My dad? Why—how could he even? He slept on my couch last night, and—let me rack my memory here— yeah, no dog in my apartment. Definitely not with him."

Adriana chews, swallows. "Your father's capable of more than you realize. He thieved an untold sum from my father, after all, before absconding with it."

"You're kidding, right?" The gall of some people, to lie like they do. No, the gall of some *scammers*.

"Who do you believe, Eric? Me, someone who actively insisted you not meddle further in our affairs to spare you any grief, or your father, the man who faked his own death in order to avoid the consequences of his actions?"

"Look, my dad's not trustworthy. You don't need to tell me. But it's not like your dad's without blame here, either."

"Victim blaming, Eric? How passé."

She's been brainwashed, clearly. This is what creates the Als of the world, the Mrs. Aisha Al-Qadaffis; they convince themselves—or are convinced by others—that they're the ones who've been wronged. But *fine*. If that's what we're working with, let's see if we can tease out what she knows— what she *thinks* she knows. "Okay." I clasp my hands, lean back. "Tell me everything your dad has told you about mine."

"It's quite dreadful, really."

"Dreadful is my M.O. at the moment, in case you haven't noticed."

"Mmm." She sets down her knife and fork, stares over my shoulder. Before I can turn to see what she's ogling, she focuses again on me. "It started with the pet store, I believe."

She goes on, detailing—*lying* about—how her father and mine elected to go into business sometime in the mid-nineties. A pet store, they decided, was exactly what this neighborhood needed, and they quickly learned how right this suspicion of theirs had been. Sky-high sales made for a thrilling first year in business, and subsequent years proved equally profitable. They'd struck gold, it seemed, and life was but a dream. Our fathers spoke of new homes on Lake Mendota, of cabins up north, of snowmobiles and vacations abroad. They discussed expanding their enterprise, including franchising. This amount of success with a pet store? Unfathomable!

"There's probably a reason for that," I say.

"For what?"

"That they couldn't believe their success. That it was unfathomable."

"Whatever do you mean?"

I indulge myself a smirk. "Please, go on. I presume you're getting to the part where my dad steals a bunch of money?"

She is, saying it was sometime around the year 2000 that the company's accounts were drained. Drained! She recalls how disturbed her father was the day he came home after making this discovery—the cords of his neck looked as though they might snap—and he called my dad a million times, though he never did get an answer. My dad didn't show up at the pet store in subsequent days, either, and nearly half a week passed before her father saw the obituary in the paper.

"And then what?" I ask.

Adriana frowns. "He—well, my father, I presume, simply recognized how tasteless it would have been to pursue the matter further. To hound his partner's grieving widow for funds stolen in the days before he died… it would have been unconscionable."

I stroke my chin. "You have to realize that makes absolutely no sense."

"I beg your pardon?"

"Think about it—my dad steals a bunch of money and then just so happens to die? Your dad would have never believed mine was dead. There's no way. And did you ever consider maybe there's another reason your dad didn't talk to my mom about that money?"

Her mouth hangs open. She catches herself, closes it.

I go on. "Maybe he knew my mom didn't have the money *because it was never stolen.*"

"Don't be absurd. Why would my father invent such a tale?"

"Because, as you once said of my father, maybe yours is capable of more than you realize."

"Slander." She looks for our server, attempts to signal for her check.

"Adriana, Kitten Caboodle—or whatever it's been called over the years—has never been just a pet store. That's not how they were making all their money. No single pet store in this area could possibly be that profitable."

"I won't hear any more of it." She continues to wave at Daniel, who remains hyper focused on the doodle he's sketching on a napkin.

"I'm sure you do good business," I say, "but is the store *that* booming? Has it ever been? Most of the time I swing by, I'm the only customer there."

She lowers her hand and, her features pinched, draws in a tense breath.

I soften my stance. She's believing now, is willing to believe. Now, we reel her in. It's a scam, but in reverse. An unscam, an enlightening. "I'm not saying everything my dad's told me is true, either," I say. "The only way we're going to get to the truth—and, more importantly, make sure Boulder's okay—is if we sort this out together." I insert myself into her field of vision. "Will you let me tell you my side of the story? Or what my dad has told me, at least?"

She purses her lips, nods.

This time, I'm the one who waves down Daniel. As I do, he happens to glance up from his sketch before traipsing over a moment later. "What can I get for you?"

"Another warm-up on these coffees," I say. "I think we're going to be here awhile."

CHAPTER 45
SMALL FORTUNE

An hour later, Adriana and I emerge from Willalby's. Outside, car tires sluice through slush, and icicles melt on overhangs.

Adriana sidesteps a puddle as she futzes with her gloves. "You're nothing if not a spinner of yarns, Eric Amundsen."

"I wish I were making it all up."

"Time will tell, I suppose."

I step to the side for a dog walker, her German Shepherd's tongue lolling as they pass. "You're going to check, though?" I ask Adriana. "You'll see if your dad has oh-so-suddenly got himself a Saint Bernard?"

"Yes." She removes the bow from her hair, clips it to her jacket's lapel before slipping on her knitted cap. "I remain confident he'll have no such dog in his care, but I'll indulge you this as a token of my thanks for your having entertained me with your fabulism this morning."

"Call it what you want for now, but you'll see. You'll see." I turn to go.

"Ask him," she says, stopping after I've taken a single step. "Your dad. About the money."

"I told you I would."

"And you'll text me?"

I wave my phone. "I have your number."

We part ways, Adriana presumably in the direction of her father's place while I trek home to my apartment. Or, as the date on my phone is intent on reminding me, what will be my apartment for one more day. Unless, and I would be so lucky, my dad did steal all that cash from Adriana's family. In that case, if he hasn't squandered it all, maybe there'll be enough left to bail me out of my financial fuck-all.

Who am I kidding? That was years ago. Even if he did everything Adriana's father accuses him of and he was careful with whatever funds he philandered, that cash would be long gone. There's a reason he's working in wire transfers or whatever instead of having retired.

Still, I have to ask. I told Adriana I would, and whether to Adriana or Grandma Amundsen, a promise is a promise. And that these promises converge—that keeping up my end of the bargain might get Boulder back, that it might convince Adriana her dad's a scam master worth putting out of business together? All the better.

Once inside my apartment building, I pause in the hall outside my unit to steel myself. A queasiness consumes me. Too much coffee? Not enough to eat? An imminent, beyond challenging conversation with a man I don't trust? All of the above. Definitely. But I don't have to ask him right away. Segues, Eric. Think of segues. Become the scambaiter you were always meant to become, or at least the one you aspired to become. Walk the man into a confession, though, again, don't get ahead of yourself. Adriana is the one who's brainwashed. Your dad already laid his cards on the table when you first met with him in Chicago. He didn't steal that money. He wanted out. He wanted out for you and for your mom. The problem was Stu, the man who would stoop so low as to steal a dog—he wasn't having it then, and he's not having it now.

Before I touch the door handle, my apartment door swings open. I lurch backward.

"I thought I heard someone out there," my dad says. "You forget your keys or something?" He waves me in.

I enter the apartment, shed myself of my jacket. "Just took me a second to find them in my pocket."

"Well, hey," he says, his mood patronizingly bright, "I've got good news."

"Uh, okay? Shoot."

He leans against the breakfast bar. "I found us a place to live."

It takes more strength than it should to keep myself from collapsing with relief. "You have no idea how much that helps." He also has no idea this essentially disproves Adriana's theory: if my dad orchestrated Boulder's disappearance, he wouldn't fear Stu enough to feel like we have to move. Double relief. Double prizes!

"Yeah," he says, "and we can move in, like, immediately."

"That's unheard of. Is it a sublease or something? Where is this place?"

"It's up near the capitol."

"Sounds fancy." I brush past him and make for my room where, on my hands and knees, I throw clothes into what few suitcases I have.

From the living room, my dad continues. "I figure we might as well set ourselves up in style if we're going to take down those bastards for good."

"Definitely."

My dad pokes his head into my room. "So, uh—oh, you're packing already?"

"Shouldn't I be?"

"Sure. Of course. It's just, well, we have to sign the paperwork and write a check for the security deposit before anything is written in stone."

"Okay." I ball up a sweater, attempt to wedge it in between a pile of socks and underwear. "Can you take care of that while I pack? I mean, you don't have a ton of stuff with you right now, right? I assume you'll get your things from Chicago another day?"

His eyebrows pinch together. "I—what? Why would I be the one taking care of the security deposit?"

I toss in my phone charger, my Raspberry Pi, start zipping my suitcase. "I guess you—hmm." I abandon my zipping operation, regard my dad for a moment, the cheapy peepy he is. This isn't exactly how I wanted to ask my old man to open his wallet for his failure-factory of a son, but here we are. "How can I put this?"

"If you're going to play the *I owe you* card, you can cut the crap."

"Cut the crap? How is it crap for me to expect some help after you fucked off for twenty years, made an honest living for yourself, and then showed back up in my life, only to fuck it up again? That feels an awful lot like owing me one. More than one, in fact."

"I expected better from you."

I raise my hands at my sides, gesture to a jury box that is absolutely not in the room with us. "Ladies and gentlemen of the jury, the aggrieved, missing-in-action father believes his broke-ass son should aspire to *better*. Better! Can you imagine, folks?"

"Wait," my dad says.

"No, *you* wait. Where do you get the nerve? Where do you get off?"

"Did you say 'broke-ass son?'"

"Have you not listened to a word I've said?" I storm from my room, tear through the junk drawer in the kitchen until I find the notice from my landlord. "Here. One day. I've got one day left to catch up on rent in this place or I'm evicted. And do you know why? For all the reasons I tried dropping hints about last night! Vet bills. Getting canned after that ransomware attack. The absolute devastation of my finances at the hands of a crooked car dealership. And you wonder why I was so pissed when you first told me you were a con man. People like Stu and Al—"

"Who the fuck is Al?"

"Keep up! The goddamn car salesman."

"Right."

I heave in a breath. "It's people like Stu and Al—it's people like you—who are keeping me from getting my life back on track."

My dad inspects the notice from the landlord. "I don't see the problem."

I slap my hand down on the counter. "How is this so hard for you?"

"Just pay your bills."

"With *what money*, Dad?!"

"Oh, I don't know," he says, the sarcasm practically dripping off of him, "maybe the hundreds of thousands of dollars you inherited from my mom? Money that, by the way, would have come directly to me if I hadn't skipped town to save your li—"

"What?"

"The inheritance. From your Grandma. Pay your damn bills. Pay for the security deposit. Spare us another night in this hellhole. I mean, Jesus Christ, that you're living in a place like this—"

Before he can go on, I'm overcome. Disbelief bubbles within me, escapes as a laugh.

"What's so fucking funny?" my dad asks. "They kidnapped your damn dog, Eric. They threatened to kill me, you, your mother. How is any of this—?"

"There was no inheritance."

"Excuse me?"

I sigh, attempt to reset, but I can't keep the smile from my face. It's incredible, really, but it makes perfect sense. The timing of his first email was no coincidence. He must've known his mother died, must have been keeping tabs or watching for obituaries. He didn't want to make amends. He wasn't, after all those years, suddenly interested in a relationship with his son. He was after what he was always always after—money.

"You obviously didn't hear the news," I say.

"Don't tell me you blew all your grandma's money. Already? How the hell did you—?"

"Grandma blew all of Grandma's money."

"On what? Lotto tickets? Don't be a jackass."

"Grandma gave all her money to people like you."

In an embarrassingly dramatic gesture, my dad turns the pockets of his jeans inside out. "Look at me, swimming in cash."

"What I mean is Grandma gave all her money to scammers."

"No."

I throw my hands up, exasperated.

"No," my dad repeats, his complexion purpling. "How did she—?"

I walk him through the broadest brushstrokes, pointing out, what a time saver, he doesn't need an explanation of the scams themselves because he knows how they work, doesn't he? He's swindled hundreds out of fortunes large and small, surely—a fact that, when I point it out, has his hands curling into fists, has him pacing back and forth like some furious, caged orangutan.

"How could you let this happen?" he asks.

"Me? How is this my fault?"

"You should have been keeping a closer eye on her."

My head rocks back. I shake it, my gaze trained on the ceiling. "Wow. Wow! You are something else."

"What are you saying?"

"I'm saying, Dad, that I'm fucked. There is no money. There will, soon enough, be no roof over our heads, not here in Madison, anyway."

His attention flits about. This is, if anything, a man on the verge of panic—or rage, for whatever reason, because this isn't his problem. He's fine. His financial future's not under threat.

"Like I said last night," I go on, "you shouldn't have come here in the first place. Once we get Boulder back, we'll be safer in Chicago, so—"

"Chicago's not an option."

"Why the fuck not?"

"I don't have a place in Chicago."

I take a step back. "Excuse me?"

"I lost my goddamn place in Chicago, Eric!" His fist collides with the wall. Drywall crumbles, tumbling down the wall and collecting in the carpet.

I press my back against the refrigerator, my breathing shallow.

"Why do you think I came here?" my dad says. "I fucking *knew* it would be less safe. I'm not a goddamn moron!"

I flinch when his fist opens another crater in the wall.

"What about your job?" I ask. "Don't you still—?"

"There is no job, Eric. There was never a job."

"Oh, God damn it."

"God damn it is right." His shoulders rising and fall with his every agitated breath. "These fucking scambaiters—"

Fuck. Of course. How didn't I see it? Dead men earn no honest livings, especially not in the world of finance. International banking—a euphemism for what he was really doing, what he's still doing: scamming. And his sudden appearance in Madison? He's on the run from someone, and not just Stu. There must be creditors, the kind who would only lend to someone who's been legally dead for the majority of this millennium. That I could be so blind is—well, it's not surprising at all, really. I've more than clearly demonstrated my aptitude for poor judgment. Forget I brought it up.

"—compromising my operation," my dad says. "I swear, the amount of time I've lost. I'll wring their necks."

Good thing I deleted those videos.

He turns to me. "What are we going to do?"

"We?" I ask. "After what happened to Grandma, I have a pretty strict *no sympathizing with scammers* policy." Except for that one time where, you know, I almost became one.

"I'm your father!"

"Biologically."

This word seems to cut him more than anything that's come between us. His expression slackens and, for an instant, he appears to accept defeat.

And then—the wrinkling of the brow, the lowering of his chin, the determined march toward me.

"Dad, what are you—?"

He casts his hands out on either side of me, pinning me between himself and the refrigerator. "Listen to me, you little shit."

"Fuck you." I swat an arm away.

He wrestles it back into place, this time holding me down by the shoulders. "I lost everything when I, as you keep putting it, fucked off to Chicago, but here's the thing, Eric: I wanted you to join me. Your mother, too. With that small fortune from—"

"Small fortune?"

He shakes me, and my head clatters against the freezer. "Shut the fuck up and listen." He pushes away, the pain in my shoulder rising from the pressure. "That was always the problem—no one listening. Not you, not your mother, not Stu. Well, he got what he deserved. He should have seen it coming. That he didn't—"

"I have no idea what you're talking about."

"Because you're not listening!" Another fist flies—and this time, it's aimed at me.

I duck, my father yowling when his punch collides with the freezer door. While he shakes out his hand, I dart for my bedroom, collect one of the suitcases I've packed, roll it behind me into the living room, the kitchen.

"Where are you going?" he demands.

I grab—not bothering to put on—my winter gear. "None of Your Fucking Business Island." Also known as I Have No Idea Where I'm Going Island, not that he needs to know, not that it matters.

"Look, Eric. I'm sorry. You don't know what kind of pressure I'm under."

"Wow."

"What's that supposed to mean?" He rushes over, attempts to put himself between me and the door.

Because, fuck it, I'm more than done with this shit, I swing my suitcase at him, catching him in the gut. His eyes bulge. Spittle flies. He stumbles backward, the wind knocked from him.

While he sputters, I dash down the stairs, fumbling for my car keys while I carry my suitcase over my shoulder, while my winter gloves tumble from the bundle beneath my opposite arm.

"You can't go," my dad rasps from my apartment's entrance. "How will I—?"

I don't hear the rest. I've burst from the building and into the cold, have readied a call to 9-1-1 in case it comes to that, have darted for my car with uneasy footsteps on the ice.

I make it to my car. My dad has not followed.

Once in the driver's seat, the heat running, the car in reverse, I see the text—no, the *texts*, plural—from Adriana.

We must speak. Immediately.

Above the first of her messages: a picture taken, presumably, from her limp hand at her side.
Boulder. Alive, conehead and all.

CHAPTER 46
FIGURATIVE LANGUAGE

Adriana arrives at Tenney Park within minutes of my return text.

As she pulls into a parking spot, I exit my vehicle, bracing myself against the wind cutting cross the frozen lake. She looks shaken, her eyes wide when she finally approaches, her hand pressed to her hat as if worried the wind will carry it away. "We've much to discuss," she says.

"We do, but are you all right?"

"I'm doing quite poorly, in fact."

"*Tell* me about it."

"I certainly intend to."

"I meant that as a manner of speaking. Like, uh, *me too*."

"I don't do well with figurative language, Eric."

"Noted."

She leans against my car and stares, as I do, through swaying branches onto a snowy, frozen Lake Mendota.

"What did he say?" I ask. "About Boulder, I mean."

"He said many things. I'm sorry I couldn't get him back for you."

"I didn't think you'd be able to. What would your excuse have been?"

Adriana hangs her head. "I might have said—"

"That was rhetorical, sorry."

"Mmm." She holds herself tight. "He lied. My father *lied* to me."

I want to tell her of *course* he did, that she should have seen it all along, but then, I remember. I remember how I felt when, all those years ago, I first questioned my dad about the man he spoke with at the pet store. I remember how it felt to hear from my father's own lips that he'd been a con man. I remember his hand on my shoulder, his fist set to collide with my face. I know the pain this bullshit brings on, and to see her confronting it now for the first time—she needs time to wrap her head around it all.

After a long moment, I break my silence. "I'm sorry."

"Don't be sorry. I should have believed you."

"For what it's worth, I don't think the story your dad told you about mine was entirely untrue."

She turns, glances up at me.

I explain what my dad said, that there'd been a small fortune, that he intended to escape with me and my mom at his side.

"So," Adriana says, "your dad did pilfer funds from my family."

"Probably."

"And my father—if he'd lie to me about the origins of a dog—"

"What did he say?"

"Something about how he'd seen it, sick, at the humane society. That he wanted to adopt it in order to, and these are his words, I assure you, 'give it a good life for what days it has left.'"

I push away from my car. "What?"

"I'm simply informing you—"

"No, like—do you think that was a threat? He's not going to hurt Boulder, is he?"

"Frankly, I'm no longer sure I understand my father to sufficiently judge his character." With her hand, she brushes the hair from her eyes. "I'm not sure I ever did."

"We have to get Boulder back."

"Naturally. Though my concerns are more, shall we say, longitudinal."

I shake my head. "I don't do well with, uh, *that* language. Whatever it is."

"Say we manage to return Boulder to your care. What am I to do with what I know now about my father?"

"We're in the same boa—er, I'm confronting a similar situation."

She narrows her eyes at me.

"My dad is currently in my apartment, a space I'll be evicted from if I'm not caught up on rent by the end of the day tomorrow."

"One presumes you're unable to pay this rent?"

"'Naturally,' as you might say."

"And to confront homelessness with only your father at your side…" She nods. "Yes, I'd say you're facing quite the predicament."

I want to say this is the part where we make a plan, but there's something to this figurative language, to unspoken implications she's not picking up on—at least not without reassurance. "What I'm saying, Adriana, is we have to do something about our dads. Like, we—I—need Boulder back, but if we're going to deal with the more *longitudinal* concerns, those concerns all revolve around our dads."

"Right."

"So"—my teeth chatter—"can we do that? Somewhere that isn't here, maybe?"

"We have the means to do that, yes. Perhaps my home will be satisfactory?"

"More than satisfactory. I can follow you there?"

She nods, sighs.

"You okay?"

"No."

"Hey," I say. "We'll figure this out."

"I'm certain we will." With a huff, she starts for her car. "This really isn't how I intended to spend my day off, is all."

CHAPTER 47
ARE YOU FAMILIAR?

Adriana's place is a gem, an east-side abode—tucked just off Willy Street—that I would have figured to be well beyond her budget. But, hey, there's nothing a scamming family's laundered money can't afford, and people surprise you, including when you walk into their home to find deliberately arranged Pokémon plush dolls on shelving inlaid to a living room wall.

"Oh, shit," I say. "Charmander. I used to love this guy." After kicking off my boots and shedding myself of my jacket, I pluck him from the shelf, turning him over in my hand. "Do his eyes light up or something?"

Adriana gawks at me, her jaw loose.

"Like"—I open the velcro pouch on its underside—"did it have a battery pack in here at one point or—?"

"Please don't," she says, at last finding her words—and a damn serious tone. "I'd appreciate it if you didn't move—mmm. I'm sorry. I'm not accustomed to having others in my space. But the point remains. Please don't touch—"

"I'll add that to my notes." I return Charmander to the shelf, eyeing instead the rows upon rows of neatly arranged hardcover books on the opposite wall. "Have you actually read all of these?"

"Naturally."

"That's a lot of Dickens."

"I was always more partial to Wilde. And Brontë, for that matter."

"Is that where you get the, uh—?" I want to say *manner of speech*, but no. It's not worth it, and it doesn't really matter, in the end.

Adriana, skipping out on further pleasantries, steps deeper into her home before sitting at the kitchen table. "So," she says, still seemingly shaken by what I guess we'll call the Charmander Incident. "A plan."

I sit across from her. "We need to get our dads in the same room."

"Why would we do that? Why would they agree to such a proposition?"

"I can't answer the second question yet."

"Until you can, it seems this plan is unlikely to succeed."

I rock back in my chair. "Hear me out, okay? One step at a time."

She interlaces her fingers in front of her.

"*If* we can get them in the same room together—under a pretense we'll develop together, the two of us—we can get them to talk out their differences."

"This seems like a plan that's more about them finding peace than either one of us finding the same."

"That's why, at least at first glance, it might get them in the same room."

"But again—that won't solve our problems."

"Not unless," I say, slipping my phone from my pocket, "we record the conversation."

She raises an eyebrow.

I go on. "Like, if we can get our dads to talk out the specifics of their differences—the stolen cash, the mentions of scams, my dad faking his own death, the kidnapped dog—we'd have enough on them to go to the police."

"I don't want my father to go to prison, Eric."

Somewhere, a radiator clanks to life. "What—then how are we supposed to—?"

"I don't *want* him to," she says, "but that doesn't mean he doesn't deserve it, I suppose. If it's true that the pet store's profitability has its origins in the picking of others' pockets—figuratively speaking"—she winks, Jesus Christ—"then perhaps your plan is one worth entertaining."

The tension leaves my shoulders—or what tension can, anyway, considering the bruise I'd likely discover on my back if I bothered to look. "Good."

"Except our fathers still have no reason to enter into one another's company. My father feels yours owes him quite a sum, and one imagines your father would fear for his life in the presence of mine." She pulls a face. "None of which is to mention presenting them with the opportunity to parley might seem odd."

"How so?"

"Neither of them know we've made one another's acquaintance. Not in this capacity."

I run my hand through my hair. "I'm worried I'm the one who's not picking up on the meaning of things now."

She titters, covers her mouth with her hand. "Won't it seem odd to them, Eric, if we present ourselves as having been in cahoots?"

"Yeah, it, uh—it sure would." So what, then? Give up? Demand to know where her dad lives so I can kick down the door, fetch my dog, and hightail it out of town? No. That's not it. There's nowhere to run, no safe harbor save for the shit-stained interior of a car I'm now—and I can't believe I'm only just realizing this—super grateful the dealership didn't take off my hands; it's now the only thing separating me from total homelessness once the calendar rolls over to tomorrow.

Thanks, Al, you rat bastard.

"Perhaps I'm misreading you," Adriana says, "but are you about to cry?"

"No," I say, though I one hundred percent absolutely-definitely am. I wipe away a tear, then another, and curse myself for every decision I've made. That smartphone for Grandma Amundsen. Not checking in on her more often. Letting her words—letting the anguish and disappointment she wore—get to me. Becoming obsessed with vengeance I'd never be able to secure. Entertaining that email from my dad. Running off to HR without my Raspberry Pi, opening that damn attachment from Mrs. Aisha Al—"Wait."

"I'm confused. Are you crying? Am I to wait for you to cry?"

"No. Never mind. Is your front door unlocked?"

"I fail to see the releva—"

I stand. "What I'm asking, Adriana, is whether I'll be able to get back inside if I go to my car for a second."

"You can unlock the door on your way out, keep it unlocked, and then, when you return—"

"Yes, thank you. Just a second." I dash to my car, not bothering with a jacket.

Moments later, I return, the sound of my suitcase rolling across her wood flooring seeming to pique Adriana's dismay. "Am I to understand you plan to live here?"

"No."

"Thank goodness."

"Wow, thanks."

"You're welcome."

"That was sarcasm."

"Mmm."

I get on my hands and knees, unzip my suitcase, begin to tear through it. "There's something in here I need, though. Something *we* need." I know I grabbed it. I think I grabbed it. I really hope I grabbed it. "Yes!"

Adriana looms over me. "I'm unsure how—is that a circuit board?"

"It's a CPU, basically. A Raspberry Pi."

"That is most certainly not a pie."

"It's—I can explain."

"I'd be very grateful if you did."

I stand, my fingers tingling with the possibility. "Tell me, Adriana—what do you know about ransomware?"

CHAPTER 48
A FATHER'S RANSOM

"'m familiar with ransomware as a concept," Adriana says, "though I fail to understand—"

"The pet store, Adriana. We're going to lock it down. With ransomware."

"That's hardly helpful to the pet store's operation."

"And that's exactly the point." As I set it down, my Raspberry Pi clacks against the kitchen table. "We go to the pet store, unleash a ransomware attack, and say my dad did it."

"This will infuriate my father."

"And that's fine."

"It seems unwise to incense the man in possession of your dog."

"Is this a hobby of yours? Playing devil's advocate?"

She folds her arms. "I'm merely pointing out the impracticalities of—"

"Risks, not impracticalities. And we don't have many options, if you haven't noticed."

Adriana seems to consider this, at last removing her winter cap and retracing her footsteps to the front door.

In my pocket, my phone buzzes. I take a peek.

A new text from, come the fuck on, my dad.

"Have you received a phone call, Eric?"

"No," I say, clearing the text, unread, from my notifications. I'm not interested in what I can only imagine is a novel-length text full of *I'm sorry, I didn't mean it* and *give me another chance* because by all indications, the man has no concept of how to not check every box of abuser clichés.

Adriana, having removed her bow from the lapel of her peacoat, places it in her hair. "One wonders if we might save ourselves an awful lot of trouble by going directly to the police."

I return my phone to my pocket. "With what evidence?"

"Have you forgotten my father remains in possession of your dog?"

"Game that out, please. What happens after we go to the police and say he took my dog?"

"The police investigate and, after determining Boulder is, in fact, your dog, return him to you." Adriana adopts a self-satisfied grin, but oh, how she misses how little that helps us long term.

"And then what? Your dad still knows mine is alive. He knows I'm willing to endanger his operation. He gets more desperate—"

"Or he learns his lesson and returns to the life of a law-abiding citizen."

"He's had decades to learn his lesson from, say, getting fleeced by my dad. Or, if he were ever going to change, why wouldn't he have after conning people out of enough money to start the pet store?"

Her lips twist into an uncomfortable shape.

"My dad," I say. "Your dad. People like them—they don't change, Adriana." I wince as my father's words find me, that I'm, as he wanted to put it, a chip off the old block. What does that mean for me, damn it, considering my near-miss with becoming a scammer myself, the disaster of the last two weeks?

I hope people can change. Some of them. Me, at least.

"Perhaps you're correct." She draws a lock of her hair over shoulder, begins to stroke it. "So, we bring my father to heel with a ransomware attack?"

"Yes, and we set it up so he either has to pay a ransom to my dad—"

"Which he will not, under any circumstances, do."

"—or, and this is the other option, we tell him he can meet with my dad and, you know, actually return Boulder while he's at it."

"Mmm."

She's getting it. She's *finally* getting it. Though, and this is the trick, convincing my dad I did this out of the goodness of my own heart. Or, maybe better put, the badness of my own heart, because that it takes a ransomware attack on his behalf to prove my, I don't know, loyalty tells you all you need to know about the fucked-uppedness of my, uh, everything at the moment.

"The ransomware," Adriana says. "It's on this device of yours?" She indicates the Raspberry Pi.

"Kind of." I turn it over in my hand, inspecting it. "I —wow."

"That did not seem like a particularly enthusiastic *wow*."

"It wasn't." I return it to the table. I don't need it, the Pi. So long as I can access the email to which I forwarded the Qadaffi email, I've got something to work with. Not me, specifically, but someone—a Scambait Bro—who'll know how to edit the ransomware to display a message that looks like it came from my dad instead of Mrs. Aisha Al-Qadaffi.

Simple stuff. Probably. I hope.

"Our plan is compromised, then?" she asks. "We're unable to proceed?"

"No. Don't worry about it. Let me get to work on this." I slide my phone from my back pocket, open Discord, begin a message to my on-again, off-again comrades. While I type, the sound of a car stereo swells.

"Eric," Adriana says. "Can I ask you for a favor?" Outside, a car door slams.

I don't look up from my phone, but she steps closer, her fingers laced where she holds them at her chest. "Yeah," I say, "what—?"

"Please hide."

My attention snaps to her as I send my message. "Come again?"

"I believe my father is at the door."

CHAPTER 49
I BARELY KNOW HER

"The closet," Adriana says, nudging my suitcase with her foot.

My pulse blares in my ears. "What about me?"

"Are you under the impression you're unfit to hide alongside your suitcase?"

"What?"

"Ugh, the closet, yes, for you as well." She lifts my suitcase—still half-open—from the floor and presses it to my chest. A pair of socks tumbles from it, which I kick in the direction of the closet. "And stay quiet."

"I—yeah. Obviously." I throw open the slatted, sliding closet doors. Here—a narrow space in between a vacuum cleaner and a tower of plastic storage drawers.

Again, the doorbell rings.

"Go," Adriana says with an urgent whisper, and I do, wedging myself in the available space, biting back the pain as my shoulder thuds awkwardly against the wall. "Shit," Adriana says, doubling back to the kitchen table, nabbing my Raspberry Pi, and casting it into the closet before I can close it.

The Pi thwacks against the storage drawers and, on its way down, catches the top of my foot with its sharp edge.

At least my foot broke its fall. It's the little things.

Adriana's cell phone bleats. "Coming," she calls, and the knocking on her door is so loud, so terrible. I pull the closet doors shut, the light seeping through its slats taunting me with how sideways all of this could go. He'll be there. Right there. Feet away. Inches, maybe, and please, Adriana, have the sense to keep him outside, but maybe that'd be more suspicious. Who am I to judge? I've been right about next to nothing, so go ahead, Bow Girl, you do you.

Near the front door, the rustling of nylon. One thunk. Another. My jacket maybe? And boots? Please let them be out of sight. Please.

The front door creaks open.

"You okay?" Stu, to Adriana.

"Yes. Of course." Adriana's tone betrays her words. I imagine her fidgeting, stroking her hair, tapping her foot—though she's always doing that, doing something; maybe he won't notice. "I see you brought a friend," she adds.

A low whine. The jangling of a collar. Pawsteps on wood as a dog—Boulder, fuck—steps into the entryway.

"Can't leave him alone," Stu says, "considering his condi-tion." After a pause, he adds, "Seems to like you well enough."

"Yes." She coughs. "Well, you know how taken with me the canines amongst us often are."

"You gonna invite me in or—?"

"Oh, will you be staying?"

"I'd like to not be in the freezing cold, Adriana."

"Mmm."

She must step aside; the floorboards shift beneath the weight of his footsteps, which grow in volume as he nears the kitchen. I hug the suitcase tighter to my chest and close my eyes, but no, damn it, you have to see Boulder, have to know if he's okay, have to tell him—telepathically, I don't know—

that you're going to get him back, that he'll be with you again soon.

Stu—who is, as I'm only reminded now, apparently infused with giant's blood—steps into view, his back to the closet, perhaps only a foot away. "I need your help," he says.

Adriana busies herself in the kitchen. "Can I ask you to—well, it's just—"

"What? What is it?"

Boulder's nails click against the wood as he wedges himself between Stu and the closet doors. His cone's been removed, and the closet door sways as his snout presses against it. I could reach out, could slip my fingers through the slats, could let him lick them, just so he knows I'm here, that I'm okay and he can be, too, if only he can hang in there a few more hours. But no, I remind myself, for the love of God, Adriana, get your dad and Boulder away, away, away from this closet.

"I'm having a"—she glances at her sink—"plumbing issue. Would you mind taking a look? Here? It's the garbage disposal, I think."

"Adriana, I don't have ti—"

"Please, father."

Boulder whines, attempts to temper a bark.

Stu swats him with the back of his hand. "Quiet, you."

My fury surges. I rocket forward, my suitcase spilling from my lap and into the door.

"Father!" Adriana cries.

"He has to be trained," Stu says before turning to Boulder. "Look what you've done, rubbing against the door like that." He tightens his hold on Boulder's leash. "Get away from there." Boulder is yanked away from the closet, joining Stu and Adriana in the kitchen.

I still myself, listen to my breathing. I can't do that. Not again. No more careless moves. I can't let Boulder get hurt, either, but Stu, he's huge, and it's inconceivable to think I'd be able to wrestle Boulder away, that we'd be able to escape to the car before being beaten or worse.

"I need you to watch the store tonight," Stu says.

"Oh," Adriana says, "is it the dog that's keeping you? I'm more than happy to watch him for you, if you'd like."

Yes, *yes.* Say yes, you slimeball, and get the hell out of here before—

"No, that's not it," Stu says. Boulder lies prone, his attention trained in the direction of the closet. "Something's come up, and I'd like your assistance." He releases his hold of Boulder's leash.

This is, of course, the perfect time for my phone to vibrate again in my pocket.

"What was that?" Stu says.

A text from my dad, I mouth to myself, or one of what will surely be a litany of replies from my Scambait Bros, paling at my request to help with the ransomware.

"The pipes," Adriana says. "I've asked you to take a look beneath the sink for a reason."

Boulder, meanwhile, seeming to sense his leash has gone slack, trots over to the closet, sniffs at the underside of the door.

To keep her dad's attention on her—or at least I hope so—Adriana pivots, makes a scene. "You know how little I care for having my days off interrupted!"

"There's no need to shout, Adriana. I wouldn't ask if it weren't urgent."

"There's every reason to shout! You always do this."

Boulder boops the door with his snout, tries licking between slats. I extend my hand. His tail wags.

"First it's the dog," Stu says, "and now you?"

"Ask one of your employees to help."

"You *are* one of my employees, Adriana. More than that, you're family, so I'd appreciate it if—"

Boulder yelps with glee, rocks onto his back paws.

"God damn it!" Stu steps toward Boulder.

Adriana darts between him and the dog. "I don't know what's gotten into you. You adopted this dog, and if he's going to agitate you, perhaps he shouldn't be in your care."

Stu's fists unclench. "Why do you care so much about this dog?"

"Why shouldn't I, after seeing how you treat him?"

He lowers his chin. "You think you can keep control of a dog his size?"

"I certainly wouldn't lay my hands on him in order to find out."

His gaze drifts from Adriana, to Boulder, to me—to the closet. He can't see me, I know, but it's as if I've stumbled into a nightmare, the kind where you're just trying to do normal, everyday tasks in public before realizing you're not wearing any clothes. Okay, hiding in a closet isn't exactly a normal, everyday task, but that's not the point. Focus. Steady your breathing. Slip your phone from your back pocket so if you get another text, it's at least not vibrating between your butt and the wood floor.

"Is there something I need to know about?" Stu asks.

"I should ask you the same."

Stu's expression shifts. His attention drifts back to Adriana. If I had to guess, he's not used to this kind of pushback from his daughter.

I glance at my phone, and yup—another text from my dad. I clear it from my notifications, put my phone, at last, on silent.

Adriana presses her father further. "First, you adopt this dog—without any indication you had an interest in adding a pet to your responsibilities—and now you come to my home, in a rush, acting as if your priorities must be mine."

"I—uh, look. I'm sorry. I didn't realize—I didn't think—"

"Clearly."

Boulder's tail has returned to wagging, its every collision with Adriana's leg a reminder to wrap this up, I hope.

"I'll help," Adriana says.

I wince. Stu smiles.

"But I'm taking the dog with me," she adds.

Stu and I trade expressions, and I say a silent prayer, hoping that now, after Stu's been put on the defensive, he'll relent. My prayers to the gods of corporate America might have gone unheard—which, hey, no need to worry about refilling the office carafes as part of that trade-off, I guess—but if there are gracious gods of all things canine, please, I beg of you, return Boulder to me and I'll never forget a poop bag again.

From his jacket pocket, Stu retrieves his phone, glances at it, frowns. "So long as that dog doesn't go anywhere save for this house or the store, you can have him for a couple hours. But he can't leave your sight."

"Of course."

Fist pump! Silent clap! Now get the hell out of here, Stu, and let me reclaim my dog!

"I've got to go," he says, because the gracious gods of all things canine do, apparently, exist, "but I'll find you at the store in a couple hours."

"And you'll finish the shift?"

"Sure. Yes." His shoulders drop. "And thank you, Adriana. Sorry, for earlier." He glances at the door, mumbles something to himself.

"Mmm?"

"Sorry to the dog, too."

"Well," Adriana says, after noticing Boulder has taken to licking the closet doors again, "I'll see you off."

She does, and once the front door closes, once a car door slams, once a car stereo booms before it fades, I push open the closet doors, tumbling onto the floor. Boulder barks, bounding in place, and on my back, I laugh, welcoming his every doggy kiss.

He's back. He's mine. I'm never letting him go again.

CHAPTER 50
GETTING OUT OF DODGE

Back on my feet—sufficiently slobbered upon—I eye Adriana. "That was amazing. How can I thank you?" I open my arms wide, go in for a hug.

"No." She recoils, brings her arms into a defensive posture. "No thank you. I'd prefer to not be—it's that the touching—"

"Okay. Sure. Sorry. I only wanted to—"

"Say thank you, yes. Your words are more than sufficient."

I pat Boulder on the head, give him a good rub behind the ear. "Well, buddy, it's time to get the hell out of Dodge before—"

"We're not in Dodge County."

"It's an expression. Like, leave town."

"Leave town? Why would you do that?"

"Because I have my dog and my car and a suitcase, which is about all I have to my name—all I need—to get as far away as I possibly can from both my dad and yours."

"What am I to do?" She nips at her fingernails. "If my father discovers I've let the dog from my sight—"

"Tell him the dog ran away."

"Even if he believes me—even if that were true—I'll still

have to live knowing he's the man he is, that he's lied to me, is lying to me all the time. I can't keep working at the store, but I—where am I supposed to go? What am I to do?" It's as if her whole body squirms, her skin crawling.

I push past my fight or flight response—well, just flight, honestly—and try to ground myself here, in the room, with her fear. I can't abandon her now, can I, not after she got Boulder back, not knowing that going on the lam would mean our dads could continue to prey on the unsuspecting.

"Okay," I say. "I'm not going anywhere. Not yet."

Adriana nods, her energy quieting.

"We'll get the ransomware uploaded first, okay?" I add. "One thing at a time." And maybe only one thing: if we can use the ransomware to facilitate the meeting, if she's comfortable recording that meeting on her own before turning the audio over to the cops, well, by the time it happens, Boulder and I will be long gone.

CHAPTER 51
FACILITATIONS

Adriana's car sways on the ice as we turn onto Willy Street. Boulder, stretched across me in the back seat, wags his tail, and I fumble with my phone, desperate for a response from the Scambait Bros.

My desperation, as usual, quickly becomes disappointment.

PrakashMoney: Hey, Simon?
SalchichaSimon: Yeah, P?
PrakashMoney: Remember that time we helped @BoulderIBarelyKnowHer with that ransomware?
SalchichaSimon: Of course. That's the same ransomware he used to, uh… what did he do with it again?
PrakashMoney: Fuck if I know. Just thinking about how we went to prison when @BoulderIBarely-KnowHer inevitably compromised his own operation.
SalchichaSimon: Ha! That's right. "Accomplices to computer fraud and abuse." Or whatever. The look on your face when we got sentenced, though. Oh, man. Good times.

PrakashMoney: Good times.

"So," I say, patting the shoulder of the driver's seat, "I think we have a problem."

Up ahead, a light turns red. Adriana brakes. "One hopes it isn't grievous."

"Does 'keeps us from proceeding in any way, shape, or form with our original plan' count as grievous?"

"I should say so." The car comes to a stop at a red. Adriana's fingers tap-tap-tap against the steering wheel. "What are we to do?"

"Turn around and regroup?"

"There's the matter of my required presence at Kitten Caboodle. I can't shirk that responsibility unless we want my father—"

"What am I supposed to do?" I ask. "Just hang out at the pet store until close?"

"I can't answer that question for you." The light turns green, and she urges the car forward. "Perhaps an idea will strike as pressure mounts."

"That's—" *Not really helpful* is what I intend to say, but I bite it back because, let's be honest, it's not exactly helpful to say that, either.

Adriana squirms in the front seat, reaches for the stereo, which is connected to her phone. "I'll need a moment to ready myself before my shift begins. I'm sure you won't mind indulging me this habit?"

Gazing out the window at foot traffic, I gesture listlessly. "You do you."

The stereo booms to life with a blast of poppy synthesizers and a throbbing kick drum. Boulder leaps from my lap, snorting, eyes wide.

"Hey," I shout, "can you turn it down?"

Adriana, it seems, has gone deaf to anything but this tune, which is almost certainly—no, definitely—K-Pop. I hug

Boulder close, and he calms despite the swell of harmonized vocals. I rub the back of his neck, shaking my head while I stare out the window, trying oh-so-hard to not start tapping my feet. I've lost enough in the last two weeks; let me keep my taste in music unsullied.

Not that I have a taste in music, per se. Not that I have *taste*, per se.

Jesus, I really need to get a life.

Adriana's car climbs an easy slope in the direction of Kitten Caboodle, and I dig, dig, dig for some solution, for some way out, for some carrot or stick we can lord over either of our dads to get them to the proverbial table.

"Ooh," I call into the din, "what about a financial incentive?"

Adriana rocks to the beat, singing along, and does she speak Korean? Stop. No. That doesn't matter right now. Keep workshopping solutions—facilitations—because there might be something to this whole financial incentives thing.

"I'm just saying," I go on, my voice straining, "we could tell your dad that mine is going to refund all the money he stole if your dad will let him—and me and the dog—live in peace. Huh? Eh? What do you think?"

She drums on the steering wheel, claps her hands three times when the audio track does the same.

"Your feedback is invaluable." I stroke my chin, ball a wad of Boulder's fur in my other hand. The scenario I've put together could work, except, you know, even if everyone winds up in the same room—everyone except me and Boulder, because we'll be long gone—Adriana won't have any way to refund anyone any money. This would further piss off both of our dads, and, yeah, it only spirals out of control from there.

Maybe telling the folks at Nortex I didn't do solutions, just facilitations, was more true than I realized.

Fuck.

I tap my forehead against the frigid car window—to the beat, God help me—trying to think of something, of anything even remotely useful. Whatever we ultimately do, whatever she does, has to be actionable. There has to be something only either of us can do for this to wo—

"I've got it!"

The vehicle slows as Adriana pulls into the Kitten Caboodle parking lot.

"Hey," I shout, "I know how we can pull this off."

Adriana's car drifts into a parking space, and, even once stopped, she leaves the car running, letting the song play out as she taps and sings and thrashes to the beat.

"We need to turn around," I try. "We need my Raspberry Pi from your place."

I reach out to tap her on the shoulder but pull back—no touching, right, and there was something about routines, too. Let her have this, then. Lean back and wait this out with Boulder. Bask in a moment of peace—almost peace—before everything goes to hell again because, at some point, you know it will. But not now. Not this plan. This, at least, is going to work. Believe in the plan. Believe in yourself. Settle in and settle down.

I do, my feet tapping to what remains of the song.

CHAPTER 52
TRUST

relay the plan as we exit Adriana's car.

"If you're confident this business with your Raspberry Pi will work, I shan't stand in your way." She adjusts her scarf, reaches for Boulder's leash.

I move the leash farther from her. "What?"

"Perhaps I've misunderstood. You'll need to return to my abode if you're to fetch this item, correct? Would you like the keys first?"

"I—well, I'd like the keys, yes, if I'm going to grab the Pi from your place, but Boulder's coming with me."

"That isn't possible."

I narrow my eyes at her, and the wind kicks up, stirring snow to glimmer between us in the dimly lit parking lot.

"Oh," she says, "the keys. Of course." She fishes them from her pocket, lanyard and all, and extends them to me.

I take them and step toward the driver's side door. Boulder stays close. "Thanks."

"Ahem."

I stop. "Did you just say *ahem*?"

"There's still the matter of the dog."

"Insofar as I'm concerned, there is no matter with the

dog." The car beeps when I press the unlock button on her keys.

When she touches me on the shoulder, I pause because whatever this is, it must be serious—not that it wasn't already. It's my dog, for fuck's sake, and if she thinks I'm letting him out of my sight—

"Eric, I'm no fool."

"I haven't said you are."

"You're acting as if I am." She raises her chin. "If you and Boulder leave me here, alone, nothing stops you from returning to your own vehicle and, as you've put it, getting the hell out of Dane County."

"Dodge. The expression is Dodge. And you don't say the *County* part."

"As you wish."

I shake my head. "That's not what I intend to do. That's not what we're going to do. You have my word."

"You know how I am with words."

"I'm not your father, okay?"

"Certainly not."

I heave a sigh. "What I mean is I know your dad has lied to you—that he's been lying to you—but I'm not here to deceive you. We're in this together."

"If that's true, you'll trust Boulder to my care for the ten minutes it will take you to grab your device from my home and return here with it."

"Adriana—"

"I'm trusting *you*, Eric, with my car and with entry to my home, and you know how I am about—well, why it's important to me that my things not be disturbed, so, please, if you wouldn't mind indulging me some degree of reciprocity."

Damn it all. Boulder and I *could* skip town if we leave her sight, not that I actually planned to do so. Either way, she's right to mistrust me, the man who came storming into Kitten Caboodle twice in the last week, once to demand a job application and another time, unhinged, raising hell about getting an audience with her. She knows me as a random customer first, the son of her father's rival second, and the person who's opened her eyes to the true nature of her dad's business third.

Not to mention we don't have time for this. Her dad could be back, well, who knows when, and every second I waste mulling this over is one fewer I have to pull off an operation I'm not even sure I have the knowhow to engineer in the first place.

I squat, careful to keep my knees out of the snow when I lean forward, hug Boulder. His tail wags. "Look, bud. You know Adriana here, right? From the pet store?" His tail wags even quicker at the words 'pet store.' "Well, she's going to take you into the pet store for a few minutes while I get something from her place, okay? I'll be gone for five, maybe ten minutes, all right? You okay with that? Maybe you can pay a visit to the other dogs and cats while you're in there, huh?"

Boulder's tongue lolls from his open mouth, his eyes on the Kitten Caboodle facade.

"I'll take that as an *I'm cool with that*." I stand, extend Adriana the leash.

When she takes hold of it, I have to force myself to relinquish my grip.

"Good," she says. "Thank you."

I try not to dawdle, stepping into her car and sitting in the driver's seat without another glance at Boulder.

"Make haste, Eric Amundsen," she says.

"Mhm." I close the door, turn the key in the ignition, and reverse out of her parking spot.

Before I pull into traffic, I glance at my rear view mirror, my throat thickening as Adriana disappears into the store, Boulder at her side.

CHAPTER 53
NO DOUBT

wait to turn across traffic. Cars creep along, bumper to bumper. I curl my toes in my boots. I check my rear view mirror, again, in case Adriana and Boulder have abandoned Kitten Caboodle, in case she's changed her mind and is willing to let him come with me.

The doors to the pet store remain closed. No one stomps through the parking lot.

My turn signal clicks on, clicks off. Snow falls gently, the flurries visible only when snowflakes enter the beams from my headlights, as they pass beneath the streetlights.

"Come the fuck *on*," I say, what little it's going to do me. Some event downtown must have let out, which means I'm stuck, stuck, stuck here until there's a break in traffic headed east.

Antsiness picks at me. My mind races. Before me flash visions of Adriana entering the pet store, of her dad having abandoned whatever previously urgent errand he had to run. He takes Boulder back, and by the time I return with the Raspberry Pi, they're gone.

But Adriana wouldn't do that. She'd put up a fight. She'd have to. She cared, cares enough to at least take some sort of stand before just surrendering Boulder to her dad. I have no reason to mistrust her.

Except she's a scammer, or has long been an accessory to one. Did she really never know? Did she never have her suspicions? It's in her blood, maybe. Who knows with these people? They don't change, remember, except I did—or I'm trying to—and even then, I wasn't like them, was never truly one of them.

"Fuck it." I silence my turn signal, taking a gap in traffic headed the opposite direction of Adriana's. I'll drive around the block, will take advantage of a stoplight that'll eventually let me head toward her place instead of farther from it.

By the time I round the block and sneak into the glacially paced traffic, ten minutes have passed since bidding Boulder goodbye. Goodbye for *now*, that is, and I'm definitely not entertaining further thoughts of Adriana turning on me, of her protecting herself over our operation—over Boulder—if her dad showed up. Nope. I'm not in a spiral of what that would mean, of how one hundred percent incontrovertibly fucked I'd be if I wound up without my dog again and without access to that computer in her dad's office.

At the first opportunity, I dip onto a side street, attempt to surge toward Adriana's more quickly than I could on the main drag. But with stop signs at every intersection, with traction as shit as it is—snow tires would have been helpful—progress comes in fits and starts.

When at last I pull into her driveway, I pause. It's been twenty minutes. That's twenty fewer to execute a degree of scambaiting fuckery I've never before attempted, even if I had all the time in the world. Or, hell, even a couple of hours.

I could still head to the cops. I have a witness now, have someone who'll say Boulder is my dog, not Stu's. If we timed everything right—if we told them Stu seems willing to, Jesus Christ, actually follow through on the threat he made in the note he left on my counter—we could get Boulder back and have her dad locked up, easy peasy.

Again, assuming I can trust Adriana to do the right thing, assuming she's willing to testify openly against her dad, which, holy shit, she's going to have to do anyway. And I'll have to do the same to mine, not that I'll have an opportunity to see justice served if we go to the cops now, if we only have evidence against Adriana's dad, not mine.

This has to work, then. I have to get that Pi.

The jaunt into and out of Adriana's is short, thank fuck, though mostly because—with all apologies to her exceedingly tidy floor—I don't bother to take off my boots. Sorry-not-sorry, time is of the essence here.

The return trip is a smoother affair—by which I mean icy —but having totaled my own car just last week, the odds of avoiding an accident are in my favor. Not that odds work that way, but, hey, stay positive. Stay distracted. Stay on the road and turn right, now, into the Kitten Caboodle lot, which, you have to be kidding me.

Full. The lot is full, as if every last person in the neighborhood with a cat, dog, bird, turtle, or zebra has decided to venture out at the onset of the snowstorm before getting stuck at home, which, honestly, makes a lot of sense. Line at the grocery store too long? You'll be surprised how far a tin of cat food will get you when it comes right down to it!

I pull up alongside the building—if anyone asks, it's a parking spot—and turn off the car before grabbing my Raspberry Pi from the passenger seat and slipping into Kitten Caboodle.

I'm met by two walls—one of heat, and one of sound.

Shoppers criss-cross each other's paths with carts and baskets full of dog food, with feathery cat toys and, why not, scratching posts. I suppose if you're here, you're here. Your cat'll be just as bored as you are cooped up for the next day or two; give 'em something to scratch at.

Up ahead, the line to check-out snakes along the side of the counter. Adriana keeps her head down, the steady beep-beep-beep of her checkout gun efficient, impersonal.

I glance about for any sign of Boulder. Nothing. Nowhere.

Then, over Adriana's shoulder, I see it. In the back office, a light.

Boulder. Or no—her dad. He's here. What if he's here? All those cars, all these customers—Adriana would have needed, *needs* help to get this impatient line of peeved pet owners under control. If she called her dad, I mean, fuck.

I tuck my Raspberry Pi into the inside of my jacket, concealing it without crunching it against my chest. Then, a hop in my step, I skip to the front of the line and slip behind the counter.

"Excuse me, sir?" A restless patron, three or four spots back in line, flags me down.

I avert my gaze, attempt to peer instead around the edges of the shade that have been drawn in the back office.

"What are you doing?" Adriana says.

"Making sure the coast is clear."

Again, the worked up woman chimes in. "Sir! Can you open another register?"

"What coast?" Adriana asks.

"It's a figure of—"

Adriana glares at me. "Just do your job."

"Hmph," says the customer who, come on, is now one place closer in line than she was a second ago. "That's right."

I reach into my jacket, flash my Raspberry Pi, rely on a technique I've seen countless IT drones use to avoid conversation in the corpocracy. "Just here to fix a computer."

Then, with a deep breath—and please, lady, I don't need you grumbling over my shoulder—I open the door to the back office, unsure what, or who, awaits.

Tattered blue carpet. Disheveled wire shelving. A desk with—yes, thank God—a tower computer, a chonky monitor, and scattered, used mugs, napkins, and plastic silverware.

And smack dab in the middle of the floor, it's Boulder, his ears perked, glancing up at me while he chews on a dog treat —or what I worry is a dog treat, which, oh God, it's a dog treat toy, and whatever he's been licking at will surely have him sent straight back to the doggy ER, courtesy of Adriana.

Then, I see them—on the nearest shelf, just out of his reach if Boulders's on his hind legs, a bag of low fat doggie chewables, tightly sealed.

Adriana. I never should have doubted her.

CHAPTER 54

THE PI'S THE LIMIT

The plan is simple, really. If we can't pull off an actual ransomware attack, we'll fake one—and, you know, hope Adriana's dad can't tell the difference.

What? I didn't say it was a good plan. I said it was a simple plan.

"You have enough treats to keep yourself busy, boy?" Boulder rolls onto his side, resumes his attempts to tongue dog treats from the inside of the toy Adriana left him. "I'll take that as a yes."

I throw myself into the ratty desk chair and get to work.

First, to connect my Raspberry Pi. I hook it up to the monitor, keyboard, and tower; a blocky, immense waste of desk space—not that I'm here to critique their setup, because what the hell do I know?

I boot up and, one-two-three, the monitor comes to life.

Username. Password. I need a username and password, one of each for the store. For an employee. Stu, probably, and if Adriana doesn't have a set of her own for this computer, that's it. Game over. I am officially out of ideas, at least insofar as this exact configuration is concerned.

I dash from the chair and to the office door, opening it a smidge. "You have a password for this thing?"

Adriana raises her middle finger at me.

"What's the matter with—?" Oh. That's a single finger, an index finger as in *one second*. I hang my head, avoid eye contact with anxious customers while Adriana scribbles on a Post-It, turns and extends it to me.

"How much longer do you need?" she asks.

"I've hardly started."

"Took you long enough to—"

"You're not helping." I pluck the Post-It from her, dip into the office, and shut the door behind me.

Then, back in the rolling chair, I examine what we're working with.

Username: KittenCaboodle
Password: pineappleonpizza123

Pineapple. On pizza. Scammers, they're really just the worst.

I type in both the username and password, log in, and get to work, by which I mean do a Google search.

Okay, okay. It looks like this is possible. It's going to take some painstaking attention to detail—and we all know how good I am at that—but this can be pulled off. At some point, we'll need to download Putty and RealVNC viewer, so let's get that started while I hook up, fuck, an SD card adapter? Who the hell just has an SD card adapter laying around?

Not ideal. Not. Ideal.

If I had time—or if there were an electronics store nearby— an SD card adapter would be no problem, but since neither is the case, we'll have to go simpler. Yes, even simpler, which means the likelihood of being found out is that much greater, but what do you want from me? What does anyone want from me?

Boulder nudges my hand with his snout. "What? Are you all out of treats?" He barks, his tail wagging, and I give him a pat on the head. "I have to concentrate here, okay? Can you keep yourself occupied with—?" I look around, find a chew toy wedged between the floor an empty milk crate, of all things. "Here." I toss the toy to the far side of the office, and Boulder bounds after it, or bounds as much as a dog his age is able to bound. Once he catches up, he tears into it, a piercing *squeak-squeak* sounding from the toy with every clench of his jaw.

That was a mistake.

But, like I said to Boulder, I need to concentrate. Time remains very much not on my side, though there is some good news: the simplest version of this operation, despite the exceptional odds of it collapsing under the barest amount of scrutiny, should take far less time to setup.

So, while keeping my Pi connected to the keyboard and monitor, I unplug it from the pet store's tower, which means anyone interacting with the monitor won't be operating the real computer at all. Instead, they'll see whatever I tell this Raspberry Pi to display.

I reboot, access the Windows 10 virtual machine on my Raspberry Pi, and get on with the customizations. First, a new desktop background, one I design in, you guessed it, Paint. We'll use the paint bucket tool to create an intimidating red background, over which we'll draw and center an angry-looking yellow rectangle because, as Bob Ross would say, everyone needs a friend. And now, the text, menacing and quite unfriendly in the midst of it all.

YOU HAVE MESSED WITH THE WRONG FAMILY.

MEET US, TOMORROW, AT 7:00 A.M. BURY THE PAST. DROP YOUR THREATS.

DO THIS, OR THE AUTHORITIES WILL BE GIVEN A COPY OF YOUR HARD DRIVE.

I lean back, inspect my work. *Squeak-squeak.* It's not the worst —*squeak-squeak*—thing I've ever—*squeak-squeak.* "Boulder!"

He stops, his eyes on mine. Then, with no regard for the gravity of the situation, dares one more *squeak-squeak.*

"Okay, bud." I romp over to him, attempt to dislodge the toy from his jaw. He growls, playfully, crouching as if we're here to play Tug of War and not, you know, Escape the Weight of a Thousand Escalating Calamities. "Give it up. Yeah. Please. Come on." He does not, as I've asked, *come on.* "Ooh, take a look at this." I release my grip on the squeaky-squeak, make for the formerly treat-filled toy in the middle of the floor. "Remember this?" I turn my back to him, pretend like I'm adding more treats to it. "Wow, oh boy." Boulder trots over, his tail wagging. I hold the toy above my head, rile him up, and fake a couple of tosses to the opposite end of the room.

A man's voice cuts through the moment of frolic. "I don't understand the problem, Adriana."

Stu, right outside the door.

"Can you please help me?" I catch Adriana say. "I would prioritize our customers over—"

I can't pause to hear the rest. I toss the toy, Boulder thundering after it while I return to the desk chair. This Paint monstrosity could do with a few touch-ups, but it will have to do as-is. I save the file, set it as the desktop background, hide all of the desktop icons.

"I just want to check in on the dog," Stu says, his voice low. "I'll be back in a minute."

"The dog is fine, father. Do you not trust me?"

"Adriana—"

Shit, shit. Triple-shit, but calm down. Steady yourself.

Okay, what next? Right. Hide the taskbar. Keep the Pi from automatically going to sleep, from displaying a screen saver. "Boulder," I say, my voice low. "Come here." If I can wrap this up, if I can leash the dog and slip out the back door before Stu comes barging in, there might be hope for us yet. "Boulder," I repeat, my voice low, not that it matters to a dog who's now obsessed with getting at dog treats that are definitely not in the toy I threw.

I stand, snapping my fingers in Boulder's direction while I appraise my, well, whatever it is I've created here.

"Wouldn't you agree, ma'am," shouts Adriana, making it painfully obvious her words are meant to be heard from outer space, "that my father opening another register right this moment would be in your best interest and that of the store? Don't you agree that maybe this is what he should be doing instead of disappearing into the office?"

So much for that appraisal. Leaving my Raspberry Pi wired to the monitor, I disconnect it from the keyboard and mouse before hooking both up to the pet store's tower again. Now, if anyone—Stu—interacts with either, the keyboard and mouse will seem unresponsive. Perfect. Good. Exactly what a ransomware attack would look like, except now that I'm really eyeing it, there's no way this passes muster with—

"I'll be right with you, everyone." Again, Stu. I glance over my shoulder. The door opens, is opening. "One second while—"

I throw myself under the desk, pull in the chair, attempt to shoo Boulder into hiding somewhere, anywhere, though a dog his size will be hard pressed to hide in a space like this.

"—I remove my jacket," Stu finishes, becoming, to me, little more than slush-soaked boots stomping across carpet. "There you are," he says to Boulder, whose ears go back before he attempts to trot over to where he saw me last. "Just making sure you're okay before I—what the fuck?"

Stu pivots my direction. He leans over the desk, snow melting off his boots inches from my toes. "Adriana!"

"I'm quite occupied," she calls. "And you've let the dog out of the office."

"What did you do to the computer? Who did this?"

"I haven't used the computer since I've been in. Why?" Her voice draws nearer. "What's—oh my."

I hug my knees to my chest while the rolling chair, still pushed in, is pressed deeper beneath the desk as Stu leans more intensely against it. He clicks the mouse frantically. The keyboard clickety-clacks in fruitless bursts. Adriana stands back, no doubt gobsmacked by my disappearing act, before she calls to Boulder, attempts to calm him down wherever he's run off to in the store proper.

Her father's cursing, meanwhile, only escalates. "That fucking asshole," Stu says. "I should've known better."

"Father," Adriana says, "I could still use your help. With the store. With the dog."

"This is kind of an emergency." He taps his foot. "How do I restart this thing?"

"Hit the Windows key and—"

"The keyboard doesn't respond!"

"Just push the power button on the tower."

No! No, no, no. I grit my teeth, close my eyes. Restarting the tower won't do anything, which, in this case, is kind of a problem. No matter how many times Stu turns the tower on and off, he'll still see the message on the screen. When the monitor doesn't respond, he'll know the ransomware attack isn't ransomware and is hardly an attack.

What I'm trying to say is it'll be a dead giveaway this whole operation is a fraud. Emphasis on *dead*.

"Oh, here," Stu says. A clicking sound. The whir of the tower's internal fan slows, ceases. "What the fuck?" he grumbles, and the ensuing slap, I can only presume, is one of the monitor, still mocking him with my crude cave painting version of a ransomware attack.

He restarts the tower once, twice, a third time, his anger escalating with every press of the power button.

And with every press of the power button, I hug myself more tightly. Stop. Get out of here. Surrender. Just leave and come back tomorrow.

Instead, he calls to his daughter. "Adriana! Get in here."

"One moment ple—"

"Get in here!"

Adriana, if the squeak of shoes on tile is any indication, must appear in the doorway. "You're on your own for the rest of the night." He abandons the desk, joins her at the door.

"What? I—"

"And where's that dog?"

"What dog?"

"What do you mean *what dog*? The dog. My dog. Our new dog."

"He's frolicking about an aisle, last I saw."

Stu digs around in the pocket of his jeans, fumbles with his phone once he's slid it out. "Fetch him for me."

No. Not again. This—I—fuck.

Adriana does her darnedest. "If you cared one iota for our customers—"

Stu's call connects. "What do you mean *what's going on*? I should ask you what's going on, you—" Stu self-censors himself, striding from the office and into the store.

Once Stu and Adriana have disappeared from the doorway, I kick away the chair and roll out from beneath the desk, my heart in my throat. I'll beat Stu to Boulder, will race to the parking lot with the dog at my side, will load him into Adriana's car or dash back to mine at her place if that's what it takes.

I rush from the back office, nearly colliding with Adriana at the check-out counter. A customer gasps, and another places her hand on her chest, which, hey, can't blame her. A strange man has just come tearing past her, wide-eyed and sweating, his head on a swivel while he mutters the name Boulder, Boulder, Boulder to himself because I have, at long last, lost my damn mind.

There. Sanity restored! In the window's reflection near the entrance, Boulder tugs against—oh no—his leash, his leash in the hands of, fuck everyone and everything, Stu. I burst down the nearest aisle after him. My shoulder brushes against a display of dog treats, and the display—along with the foil packets on it—topples to the floor.

In the reflection, Stu pauses, glances back, his brow furrowed.

I press myself flat against the aisle's shelving and count to three. One, please don't let him linger on whatever he heard. Two, usher him on his merry way, oblivious to my approach. Three, when I resume my pursuit, *keep him* oblivious to my approach until I can, I don't know, rip the leash away before sprinting down the icy sidewalk, Boulder bounding along with me.

Again, a marvelous plan. Truly magnificent.

But three! That was three, and you need to keep moving, man, so away you go. Chase after that dog, and—oh. Deflation. Utter deflation.

Outside, Stu slams shut one of the rear doors on his Ford Explorer. As he slips into the driver's seat, the cab light illuminates Boulder in the back, his eyes trained on the store. On me.

By the time I reach the parking lot—the wind whipping at my face, the cold nipping at the nape of my neck—they're gone.

CHAPTER 55
MAKE THE CALL

embrace the cold, the sting of it a distraction from a pain far worse, because he's gone. Again. Boulder's gone again, and I let him go without a fight. I let him go, cowering. I let him go, putting off another confrontation—one with a scammer, no less.

But I made a promise. I made a plan, and even if it wasn't a particularly good one, it was working until, you know, the bit with the dog being whisked away once more.

Eventually, the winter wind overwhelms, and I turn back to Kitten Caboodle, urge myself inside. Adriana lets her attention drift from a customer laughing at his own joke, and I shake my head. She draws a steady breath, glances at the clock while I slip back into the office.

My heart sinks. Scattered dog toys await, as well as an overturned chair, an even more disheveled desk.

I right the rolling chair, slump into it, and spin myself away from the monitor, my elbows on my knees. It's an embarrassment, really, the impostor ransomware, but it did the trick. For now.

And if phase two of this operation is going to succeed, I

need to call my dad, let him know what, exactly, I've made him responsible for.

So—might as well get this unpleasantness over with because I can't get much more down on myself or on, well, *everything* than I am already. I grab my phone. More missed texts. A missed call. All from my dad.

At least he'll be happy to hear from me, I guess.

Before I can dial him, my screen illuminates. An incoming call from, yup, the old man himself. Okay, I coach myself. Put on a show. Insofar as he knows, you're working *with* your dad, Eric, even if, in the end, vengeance will be yours. Remember, be excited so your dad will be, too—this Stu guy won't know what hit him once you're done with him. Imagine you're one of the big guys, that you've got a few thousand viewers watching you mess with a scammer live on Twitch, on YouTube. It's all emotes, all for fun, and you have nothing at stake save for the entertainment of those who've tuned in.

Whew. All right.

I catch his call before it goes to voicemail. "Good news."

"Good news?" Bad start. Terrible start. He's incredulous, still in a rage, and that he's this worked up hours after having attempted to cave my face in with his fist— "How has today brought good news of any kind, Eric? Please. Tell me."

"I feel like there's something you should tell *me*. I mean, I was calling you back to let you know—"

"Where have you been all day? What, exactly, do you think you're doing?"

"I—what?" I stand, press my free hand to my forehead. "I've been scheming, working on that revenge we were *originally* going to plan and execute together. You know, before you—"

"Stop." My dad breathes into the receiver. "It's true, then?"

"What are you actually—?"

"The ransomware attack."

I rear back. "How do you know about—?"

"You actually went to the pet store and uploaded ransomware to their computers?"

Yes, I want to say, of course I did. That's the news I'm supposed to be breaking, the news that should have my dad on the hook, gleeful at the prospect of a meeting tomorrow where he'll have the upper hand, where he can tell off his partner-turned-rival once and for all. Instead, he's indignant. Furious.

And there's only one way he's heard about this ransomware attack. "Dad?"

"Answer the question, Eric."

"No," I say. "You first. Why are you talking to Stu? How long have you been talking to—?"

A shattering sound on the other end of the call. I hold my breath, expecting a skirmish, some hand-to-hand combat between him and Adriana's dad, who I can only presume found out, somehow, my dad wasn't just alive but actively living within the walls of my apartment.

No such brawl ensues, but another grunt, another smash tells me he's apparently decided to turn my apartment into his very own rage room, and at this point, what-the-fuck-ever. Tomorrow's eviction day, and if the place is in shambles, what are they going to do? Charge me more money I don't have? Charge away, what little good it's going to do you.

"You finished?" I say, my patience thin. "Think you might tell me why you've been going behind my back to—?"

"Me? Going behind your back? I've been trying to get ahold of you all day."

"I've been kind of busy."

"Clearly."

"And you might consider, next time, that the people you try to punch in the face aren't normally inclined to take your calls."

"Eric," he says, sounding aghast at the accusation.

"What?"

"I would *never*. I can't believe you'd say—"

"Wow." My head rocks back, and I pace the office. "That's —huh. You know what? I don't even have time for that. We're not going there. We're not doing a damn thing until you explain what the fuck is going on between you and Stu."

My dad sighs, chuckles. He's like some pulpy comic villain, this asshole, and that I'm related to him sets my skin to crawling, at least until he finally gets on with it. Everything was already taken care of, he tells me, or it was until Stu returned to Kitten Caboodle to find his computer had been fucked with, that he'd been threatened by the very man who just extended him an olive branch.

"An olive branch?" I run my hand through my hair. "How did the two of you even run into each other?"

"We ran into each other," my dad says, savoring every syllable, "because he came to return your dog."

At this, I collapse into a squat, then to my ass. "He came to return Boulder?"

"He said you'd done everything he asked, and he wanted to drop him off in person to ensure there'd be no issues between the two of you going forward."

"But when you answered the door—"

"I didn't answer the door."

"Then how—?"

"I saw him in the parking lot, approaching the building. We had a nice chat, him on the ground, me on your balcony."

With my free hand, I ball a wad of my hair in my fist.

"I'll admit," my dad goes on, "that it was, I don't know, a little awkward at first—"

"No shit."

"—but I told him we didn't have to be enemies, that if I had to guess, we'd both been learning the hard way that the game has changed."

"You offered to get back into business together?"

"I told him I'd consider it if he apologized for threatening you. For threatening your mom."

"Bullshit."

"Excuse me?"

I release my hold on my hair, ease myself up with help from the chair. "He never threatened us, did he?"

"He absolutely did. Why do you think I had to go on the run? Everything I did was to protect you and your mom, Eric."

"Including stealing untold tens of thousands of dollars from him and *his* family? Does that sound familiar?"

"Who told you that?"

"It doesn't matter who told me that. What matters is I know. I know you've been lying, or at least that you haven't been telling me the full truth."

"Again, everything I did was to protect—"

"No. Don't bother. I don't need to hear it."

An uneasy pause ensues, neither of us—me, anyway— wanting to be the first to give in. But he's lied before, could be lying again, and when my mind drifts back to Boulder, I wonder.

"If Stu came to my place to return Boulder," I say, "why does he still have him? How didn't you wind up with the dog?"

My dad coughs a laugh. "Said he needed time to think on it."

"On what?"

"On the two of us teaming up again. He said he didn't know if he could trust me, that he wanted to discuss this with me further, but first he needed to get someone to cover for him at the pet store."

"God damn it."

"What?"

That's it—Stu came to Adriana's, forcing me into hiding

while he demanded she cover for him at the store. The errand he had to run wasn't some one-off stop to Target; it was a deeper discussion with my dad.

I ignore my dad's question. "Stu was keeping Boulder as leverage."

"For a day or two, he said, while he considered my proposal. While we worked out the details."

"And then, after joining you—in my damn apartment—and presumably reaching some sort of agreement, he returned to the pet store to discover you'd been fucking with him all along."

"I did no such fucking," my dad says.

"I'm saying *from his perspective* it looked like you—"

"I'd encourage you to shut the fuck up. You've done quite enough for one day."

"I—that won't be hard. There are no words. None."

"To think, Eric. All you had to do was *nothing*, and you could have your dog back, could be on the verge of getting some cash in your pocket."

"Don't."

"Don't what?"

"I *really* don't need you to rub it in."

My dad sips something, swallows. "Then what do you need? Because I know what I need, and unless you've got a plan to undo the last couple of hours, you can kiss your dog goodbye."

"Don't say that."

"You've got a lot of *don't* in you for someone who can hardly handle *do*."

"I don't know what that means."

My dad launches into some tirade, some vitriol-soaked rant intended to wear me down, to manipulate me into thinking he's my only way out of this. He's a scammer, after all—emotional manipulation is all he knows, and I'm not falling for it, not from him, not anymore.

Instead, I consider my options, the first of which is, no matter how it might pain me, to leave. Just go. Drive. Get as far as I can on a tank of gas and work for cash somewhere. I envision myself sleeping in my car, alone, beneath a pile of clothes for warmth. Once I've settled, maybe I sell my car, live in some ramshackle apartment that's walking distance from wherever I work. Start over, basically, and hope to God the creditors—and, you know, my dad and Stu—never catch up.

But none of that's an option, not really. I couldn't live like that, like my dad did for years, knowing I'd left my family behind, or, in this case, knowing I'd left Boulder behind.

I have to stay, then. I stand and fight. Not physically, obviously, but I would—will—if it comes to that. Not that I want it to. Not that I'll urge it to, but if we stick to the original plan with, yes, a few minor changes, I can still get Boulder back.

And, maybe more importantly long-term, both my dad and Adriana's can end up in prison.

I interrupt my dad. "Hey. Listen. Hey. Shut the fuck up!"

To my surprise, he does.

"You and Stu can still get back into business together," I lie.

"And how do you propose we make that happen?"

"Tomorrow," I say. "Seven a.m. You meet him here—"

"He made it more than apparent he will *not* be meeting me tomorrow morning thanks to your—"

"Tell him it was me. Tell him I alone am responsible for the ransomware and that I'm more than happy to apologize to him, in person, tomorrow." I take my dad's silence as a sign to go on. "Just tell him to bring the dog. If he brings the dog, he'll get his apology and I'll remove the ransomware. Easy. Simple. All a misunderstanding, right? Yeah?"

A long silence. An impossibly long, terribly torturous silence.

"Did you hear me? Can you try to—?"

"I'll see what I can do."

CHAPTER 56
CLEANING UP

"You know," Adriana says once the store has closed at nine, "this would go far more quickly if you helped in any capacity." She continues sweeping, her broom kicking up small clouds of dust around her heels. "I'll still have to mop once the sweeping is complete, and then there's the matter of settling receipts—"

"Here." I hop off the pallet of dog food where I've sat, brooding, and offer my hand.

"Here what?"

"The broom. Give it to me."

She stops sweeping, eyes me curiously.

"I'm saying I'll sweep and mop if you need to deal with the register."

Adriana nods, surrenders the broom, and I get to work.

"What are we to do, then?" she asks, the till dinging when she opens it. "About our fathers, that is. About tomorrow."

"Nothing's changed for you, really."

She ceases leafing through a stack of twenties. "That's untrue. I care for Boulder, you know. He doesn't deserve to be separated from you for any longer than is necessary. He doesn't deserve to be separated from you at all."

I stop sweeping, lean on the broom a moment. "You're all right, you know that?"

"I'm quite unwell, in truth." She sifts through a stack of fives, pauses. "That's not what you meant, is it?"

"It's not, but that's okay."

"Mmm."

"Mmm indeed." I return to sweeping, losing myself in the rhythm. A quarter of an hour passes, maybe, before I let myself check my phone.

"Expecting a call?" Adriana asks, wheeling the mop bucket out from the back office.

"Well, my dad was allegedly going to talk to yours."

"I can try my father, too." Water sloshes over the side of the bucket as she brings it to a stop.

"That's nice, Adriana, and I appreciate it, but don't you think it'd be weird if you called your dad to convince him to show up to a meeting you're not supposed to know about?"

She dips the mop into the bucket, wrings it out. "My father underestimates me. Many people do."

I grab the broom again, realizing I'll need to keep ahead of her if we're to get out of here sooner rather than later. "I don't see how that helps us."

"I'd call him to check in or, well, under the guise of checking in. The last I saw of him, he was storming out of the store, and wouldn't his daughter be worried about him and this terrible message on the computer?"

I nod, resume sweeping.

"If you'd like," she adds, "I can visit him tonight. This would allow me to talk to him and to verify Boulder is okay."

"That'd be… thank you."

"Mmm."

Adriana follows along, mopping where I've swept until the work is done.

Later, I stand near the exit, Adriana calling to me from the opposite end of the store. "Ready?"

"Ready."

The overhead lights go dark, aisle by aisle. Light slants into the entryway from the parking lot, and moments later, the flashlight from Adriana's phone bobs in the darkness, approaching me near the exit.

"It's snowed quite a bit," she says.

"I think they call this a metric fuck-ton."

"No. No, they do not."

"I was making a joke."

She pushes past me, opens the door with a smile. "As was I."

The return drive to her place is perilous. At least twice I'm convinced I'll be in my second accident in as many weeks, but Adriana turns down her K-Pop—far less enjoyable without a dog on my lap—steels herself, and keeps us from hopping the curb or sliding into intersections at red lights.

When at last we pull into her driveway—breathing for what feels like the first time in hours—I thank her again. "And you'll keep me posted?"

"Whatever do you mean?" She turns off the car.

"Like, when you send me another photo of Boulder? After you visit your dad?"

"Oh, I shan't be going to see him, not now."

"What?"

She reaches for the door handle. "With the roads in this state, I'm afraid the best I can do is a phone call." She opens the door, steps out.

I throw my own door open, trudge alongside her amid the flurry of flakes. "What about Boulder?"

"I'll inquire as to his condition."

"He could lie!"

"Be that as it may—"

I stop. "Adriana."

Her arms go rigid at her sides. She turns, faces me, her

gaze on the tracks we've tread through the snow. "I'm doing the best I can."

"The best you can would be to—"

"Please," she says. "Keep in mind the day I've had."

"The day *you've* had?"

"It's all relative, Eric. Everyone has a unique capacity for stress, and I should say I burned through whatever capacity I had quite early this morning. My offer to visit my father tonight, to make the phone call, even, is already being borrowed against the energy I'll have available to me tomorrow. I'm not saying this to disappoint you or to suggest that any one person's day has been worse than another's, but rather to communicate my boundaries and to insist they be respected."

I cluck my tongue against the roof of my mouth. "I—uh—"

"We will have our meeting tomorrow morning. I will make that phone call. You have my word. I want to be through with this as much as you do."

"Right." I breathe deep. "Thanks."

As I step forward, Adriana begins again. "For now, though, you should rest."

"Yeah."

Her attention drifts to my car, parked down the street.

"I—you're kidding, right? I can't sleep on your couch, or—?"

"Boundaries. Please, Eric. It's not that I don't trust you, but I'm afraid if I continue to bend any further, I'll soon break, and I do not want to break. I really do not want to break."

I rub my chin, resigned. "Can I get my things at least? Whatever's still inside your place?"

She returns a minute later, my suitcase at her side. "I'll be in touch. Tonight. Keep your phone close."

I heft my bag from her, carrying it instead of rolling it to keep snow from soaking in. "That won't be hard. You know, sleeping in the car and all."

CHAPTER 57
THANK YOU, AL

've prayed, a few times, to the gods of corporate America, that I might be spared some humiliation, that I might be saved from myself. And yet, humiliation has infected me like so much malware, and salvation has kept me at bay, has changed all my passwords and mocked me all the while.

I want to say this is a gods problem—that my faith has been misplaced—but deep down, I know better. I have for some time. I've said it once and I'll say it again: I've got no one to blame but myself, even if it still feels like we're in the upside-down because, with only this car keeping me from freezing to death overnight, sleazeball car salesman Al and his no-holds-barred approach to enterprise has somehow made him the hero here.

Broken. It's all broken. That scammers like Al and Stu and my dad are sleeping safely, that they're warm in beds of their own tonight—is there no justice in this world? The whole of their life is *lie, cheat, steal, succeed* before doing a *lather, rinse, repeat* tomorrow, except their tomorrow is now *my* tomorrow, is a day for the Erics and Adrianas of the world.

Assuming she actually texts me to confirm her dad is in. Assuming my dad says he'll be there, too.

I adjust the pile of clothes I've buried myself under in the back seat, feeling for my phone. When I find it, the light it casts is blinding. Eyes narrowed, I dim the screen, navigate to my text inbox and, would you look at that, a text from Adriana from twenty minutes ago.

My father will be in attendance. I told him I would watch Boulder while he speaks with you and your father.

Every muscle in my body relaxes before the cold reminds them, hey, maybe preserve that warmth. With Stu now set to appear, my dad's got no reason to no-show—unless, I guess, he fears for his life, which would mean, yikes, I probably should, too.

Not that it's much of a life.

Okay, wow, nope. Not going there. That's a bad place, Eric, and it's one you're not allowed to visit again. Not tonight and especially not tomorrow because you've got to keep 'er moving here. Eyes on the prize. Uh, another cliche just for good measure, not that I can think of one right now because I'm struggling to fend off visions of an untimely demise at Stu's hands in the morning.

Deep breaths. Reset. Text Adriana back and, God damn it, call Dad again.

So, I text Adriana my thanks, head to my recent calls, and highlight my dad's name.

His answer is immediate. "What?"

"Stu will be there. Tomorrow morning. The pet store."

"And?"

"Come. I've done my part. Let's fix this, move on."

In the background, a sweeping movie soundtrack plays. The heat clicks on, and I imagine my dad curled up in bed—

in my bed—having himself a great time with a pirated movie marathon on his laptop. Disgusting.

The music stops. My dad's voice strains as, I don't know, he sits upright? "How do you know Stu's coming?"

"Uh—" Right. He can't know I've been coordinating with Adriana. "You've got to trust me on this."

"You expect me to just trust you after you—"

"Trust cuts both ways, Dad." I adjust one of the sweat-shirts on my chest, keep it from sliding off. "And I'm not looking for an argument. What other choice do you have?"

"I could *not* meet with him and skip town instead."

"Very courageous of you."

"Courage has nothing to do with it."

Okay, if this asshole isn't going to come to the pet store tomorrow, I need an out. So, let's take a look, can the voice memo app on my phone be used to record calls? We're going to find out.

"You still there?" my dad says.

"Yeah, did I drop off for a second?" I open the voice memo app, start recording. "I'm kind of sleeping in my car, so my reception might not be—"

"No one said you had to sleep in your car."

"They didn't, but that's not the point." I check the recording app, see that it's picking me up. My dad, though? That's a big nope, which means, all right, it's time we try speakerphone.

My dad sighs. "Look, I'm sorry about earlier."

There! The phone is catching his voice, too, at least it looks like it if I'm reading the app correctly.

"Eric?" he says.

"Reception again," I say. "What were you saying?"

"That I'm sorry?"

I sit up a bit. "For what?"

"Earlier today."

"Hmph." More. I need more.

"What? An apology isn't enough for you?"

Not when it's insufficiently incriminating. "You ever been to a Jimmy John's, Dad?"

"What does that have to do with—?"

"Have you?"

"Sure. Yes. Many times."

"On the walls, you might have seen some signs."

"Eric, what the fuck are you—?"

"There's this one sign right near where you wait for your sub—at least at the JJ's I go to—that I always find myself reading while I wait."

Crickets on the other end of the line. Not literal crickets, but you know what I mean.

"The sign says something like 'proper apologies have three parts.'"

"Oh, fuck off," my dad says.

"First, you say what you did was wrong. Then, you say you feel bad you hurt the person you hurt. Third—"

"Since when did you become a goddamn therapist?"

I laugh. "I'm not a therapist, Dad. I'm just a guy who thinks that if Jimmy John's can get apologies right, so can you."

My dad curses under his breath before returning to the conversation. "Get on with it, then."

"The third thing is asking how you can make this better."

A mattress groans. A door creaks open. There's a thud as if he's set his phone down, and water runs—the bathroom faucet?—and it's all *splish-splash* for a moment on the other end of the call.

"You still there?" I say.

The faucet turns off. "Yeah."

"About that apology?"

"Yeah, yeah." A light switch *tocks* off. The mattress complains. My dad mumbles for a good ten seconds.

"What was that?"

"I *said*," he snaps back at me, "I shouldn't have done that—"

"Done what?"

"Are you fucking serious?"

"Jimmy John sure is." I glance at my phone, make sure it's still recording. It is.

"I don't know who raised you to be such a brat."

"I might've become less of a brat if you'd been around to—"

"Do you want an apology or not?"

"I think I've made that pretty clear." And get the fuck on with it; my phone's battery won't last forever.

"All right. I shouldn't have come at you."

No, damn it. That's not enough. "By which you mean?"

"I don't know what came over me. I'm sorry."

"That doesn't answer my question."

"You know, Eric, I was going to tell you you're welcome to —that you should come back to your place and sleep in, you know, your own bed—"

"And why do you think I don't feel safe doing that?"

"Because you're a demanding little shit."

"Some apology this has proven to be."

"What do you want from me?"

I can't wait any longer. "I want you to say it. I want you to say you took a swing at me, that you pinned me to the fridge and—"

"Don't. Stop."

"Oh, I'm sorry. Is hearing this too much for you? Is confronting the consequences of your actions too tough for you, the man who's spent his whole life running? And don't you dare pull the 'I faked my own death for you and for your mom' card. I've seen that one quite enough lately, thank you very much."

"But you know it's true."

"I don't know what to believe, Dad, but what I do know is

tomorrow morning, at seven a.m., Stu will be at Kitten Caboo-dle, waiting to talk all of this out with you. If you really want to move forward with your life, practicing your apologies now before you have to give them to Stu might not be such a bad idea."

"Who said I'm meeting with Stu tomorrow?"

At this point, I'm ready to throw open my car door and lie facedown in the snow until the earth reclaims me. Holy fuck. "You know what? Forget it."

"What do you mean?"

"Fuck your apology," I say. "I don't want it."

"Good. Fine."

"What I want instead—"

"Oh, here we go—"

"—is for you to show up at that pet store tomorrow. That's what you can do to make it better, if you're curious. You know, the third part of that apology."

He says nothing, the brat he is.

"It's that, Dad, or you spend the rest of your life in hiding. Alone. Again."

"Alone? I thought you and I would—"

"You thought wrong." But here, an opening. "Maybe I'll reconsider if you do me this favor, if you can get Stu off my ass and get my fucking dog back once and for all."

"Even if Stu and I go back into business together?"

Another opening. I press him for more. "It depends on that nature of that business."

"You know what I mean."

"Do I, though? Do I, really?"

"Cut the shit. I'll be there."

Damn it all. I didn't get everything I wanted from the recording of this call, but if he and Stu will be in the same place at the same time tomorrow, I don't need it, not when I can get so much more in the morning. "Seven a.m.," I remind him.

"Seven a.m."

"Good." I end the call before he tries to weasel his way out of it, before he tries to plead with me to return to the apartment so he can, I don't know, attempt to convince me we're better off if we hit the road together. And here we go, we stop recording on the voice memo app after a quick—but painful—replay of the audio to make sure it's clear enough to turn over to the police when the time is right.

Not bad. I mean, it's not the quality I'd want to listen to in a scambaiting video, but that's not what this is for.

It's done, then. This part of it, anyway.

My fingers frozen, I text Adriana back to thank her for everything, to confirm my dad and I will be there tomorrow.

And now, a moment to myself. A moment to stare through the rear window of my car at, well, not the stars, but the streetlight overhead. It'll have to do. It's all I deserve, really.

My mind drifts to apologies, to Jimmy John's, and it's hard not to laugh. Jimmy John's, you know? Jimmy John's and proper apologies and, apparently, inspiration to gather evidence on one's enemies.

Maybe the gods of corporate America aren't so bad, after all.

Nope. I hate that. Let's chalk it up to Stockholm Syndrome.

I roll over, starved for sleep, but remind myself I can't close my eyes, not yet.

After returning to my back, I reach again for my phone.

I've got one more call to make.

CHAPTER 58
CHARITY CASE

The following morning, Daniel sets down a coffee in front of me. "Looks like we made a repeat customer out of you."

I coil my fingers around the mug, desperate for warmth.

"Sure I can't get you anything else?"

"No," I say, hunched on my stool.

Daniel remains with his elbows on the bar, glances over my shoulder at the otherwise empty restaurant. "You okay?"

"I, uh—tough day."

"It's six in the morning."

"Sure is."

A bell rings over my shoulder. A wintry gust follows soon after, and low voices trickle past, settle into a booth somewhere behind me.

Sitting so near to the door was, as the hair rising on my neck can attest, another mistake in a long line of unforced errors. I slide several stools farther from the door and bring my coffee with me. Daniel, at my prompting, takes my phone, plugs it into the charger behind the counter, thank fuck. While I sip from my mug, I keep my gaze forward, minding the clock on the wall while I study the unicorn art that frames it.

Here, a glittery pink pony with, yes, a sea-shell like horn. Next to it—one of those mass produced landscape scenes from the nineties, except this one's horse has had a horn painted protruding from its head. I expect to feel something—because of the looming meeting at the pet store, not the unicorns—but exhaustion is all I can muster. Even as the jitters creep into the tips of my fingers, the caffeine fails, flounders before doing much beyond warming me from the inside out.

Not that I'm upset about that.

The point is that where there should be fear or anticipation, instead I'm just ready for this to be over, and not even unicorns are going to change that.

I sip the last of my coffee, leave a couple of bills on the counter, wave to Daniel.

"Oh, where are you going?" Daniel asks.

I step for the door. "I've got a date with destiny."

"What about your eggs?"

From the kitchen, someone calls "order up."

"I—what?" I turn to face Daniel, ready to tell him off, that I'm not ready to be conned again, that I'm in no mood to be forced to pay for something I can hardly afford. "What's the catch?"

"No catch." With a smile, Daniel returns with a plate. "They're on the house. I hope over-easy's okay."

I fucking *hate* over-easy, but I pause, moved, unmoving.

"You okay?" Daniel asks. Then, his voice lower, "Can I get you a tissue?"

I wipe my eyes. "No. Thank you."

"Just try not to get any on the eggs." He sets down the plate where I sat at the bar. "Between you and me, they're salty enough."

I return to my seat, sniffling a laugh and thanking him again before wolfing down the whole plate in a few bites, horrible yolk goo and all.

And it's genuinely one of the best breakfasts I've had.

Minutes later, as I toss my used napkin on my empty plate, I, a broken record of gratitude, thank Daniel once more. He returns my phone to me and tells me to swing by whenever I need a warm-up: coffee or to just escape the cold.

That he can tell I'm in such miserable shape—I must look like absolute shit.

But no time for that. Zip up your jacket, Eric, and push through into the cold. The pet store is but blocks away, and you have a date with destiny, as you put it, or at least with a couple of scammers who won't know what hit them in a half hour's time, and you'll have your dog back, to boot.

Assuming I've timed all of this right. Assuming the cavalry, as one might call them, actually shows up. Assuming Stu buys my apology, that matters don't escalate beyond my control before I can get him and my dad on record as the criminals they are.

On the sidewalk, I raise my shoulders, dip my head, march forward.

The cold tears at me from the outside, but within—coffee, eggs, a stranger's kindness.

Maybe if we had more Daniels, we'd have fewer Stus.

CHAPTER 59
THE EXCHANGE

At 6:58 a.m., I arrive, shivering, at the Kitten Caboodle parking lot.

With my back pressed to the building's windowed storefront, I wait, counting the cars slinking past on Willy Street, listening to Madison sleepily stirring to life. I check my phone. 7:02. No texts. No missed calls. No one else in the parking lot.

Time, I should've given myself more time, but they have to show. They must. They need me—or at least think they do—to facilitate whatever peace they think they're going to forge, so God damn it, let's get on with it.

On cue, a Ford Explorer turns into the lot. I retrieve my phone, start recording on my voice memo app. When I glance up, I steel myself, peering through the windshield to find Stu in the driver's seat and—fuck—Adriana at his side.

Maybe it's fine. Maybe Adriana meant she'd be watching Boulder elsewhere in the store—and not at her place—while I handle the rest of the operation. That has to be it. She'll exit the car, we'll pretend we don't know each other, and I'll try to temper my desire to bound off with Boulder before anyone can do a damn thing about it.

Stu turns his Explorer into a parking spot, showing off its broad side.

There is no dog in the truck.

Car doors swing open, slam shut, with Adriana exiting from the side of the truck nearest me. Held tight to her chest is, you have to be kidding me, her Charmander plushie, which she hugs like *she's* the one missing her dog.

"What the fuck?" I mouth at her.

Adriana keeps her gaze averted, which, okay, not unusual, but this isn't right. Something's wrong, but I swallow my protest; she and I aren't supposed to know each other.

Stu emerges from around the far side of his car, a self-satisfied grin on his face. "Good morning, Eric."

I channel my ire, blast him with it, head-on. "Where's the dog?"

"We'll discuss the dog."

I consider my phone, recording in my jacket pocket. "So you're not returning my dog?"

He strides past me, keys in hand, and unlocks the store. "I said we'll discuss the dog."

The dog, he says, and not *your* dog, but it's an acknowledgment, and that has to count for something.

Stu steps aside as the automatic doors whir open, and Adriana, her head down, the plushie still in her embrace, enters the building. Stu looks at me, gestures sternly for my entry.

I want to tell him I'll wait for my dad, that I don't intend to spend time alone in a room with a would-be murderer and his daughter. But maybe there's a window here I can use to press him further. I have to at least try to open it.

My heart thundering, I slip past Stu and into the store.

Inside, my dad is already waiting. "Eric."

I gawk at him where he stands in the open, central aisle between the entrance and the back office. "Wha—?"

"Why don't you come with us?" Stu marches deeper into the store as he says it, hardly acknowledging my dad.

Adriana continues to ignore my questioning glances and follows her father.

"No." My voice echoes amid the relative emptiness.

The three of them stop. My dad and Stu turn to face me.

"Are you under the impression you're in charge here?" my dad asks.

Stu eyes him. "Are *you*?"

My dad doesn't answer Stu. He plods toward me instead, his every step methodical.

I retreat a half-step and lean against a nearby shelving unit, leaving fish flakes on my left and the windows overlooking the parking lot on my right. While partially concealed, I use the cover to slip my phone from my pocket, to place it on a shelf amid scattered aquarium decorations.

"What do you think you're doing?" my dad demands.

I puff up my chest, distracting him from the ceramic coral reefs, the plastic treasure chests, my phone. "Not indulging you whatever this is. Not unless I know what, exactly, you think you have planned."

"Planned? That's funny," he says, as Stu appears behind him. "We were going to ask you what you and your new friend have planned."

Adriana must have been pressed by her dad, must have confessed. She must have betrayed me. The room spins, but I lean against the aisle's steel shelving, steadying myself.

"I believe your father asked you a question," Stu says.

"Not technically, he didn't." The reply escapes before I can bite it back, and now I'm on my heels, am stepping backward, am foolishly drawing them farther from my phone where it records feet away. I cease my backpedal, resolved, again, to get them talking. "Why would you be worried about our plans? Have something to hide? Something you're ashamed about?"

"Cut the shit," my dad says. Then, to Stu, "Hold him."

Stu lunges forward, wrenches my arms behind my back while my dad pats me down. "Where is it?" he asks. "Where's your damn phone?"

"In my fucking car," I lie, struggling against Stu's grasp. "Battery died. Hard to keep it charged when you're sleeping in a car."

"Bullshit," Stu says, tightening his hold.

I flail my legs, dropping to the floor in an attempt to drag him down with me.

Stu remains upright. Straining, but upright.

My dad steps back, shakes his head.

Stu releases me.

"I thought you said you knew what they were planning," my dad says to Stu.

"I said I *thought* this might be what they had in mind."

Shit. Adriana didn't tell him, then. Stu might have guessed, which, how many times do I need to be taught this lesson? Adriana has my back. She keeps her wits about her. She's on my side. *Our* side.

Huh. We have a side.

"Adriana!" Stu calls. "Get over here. Where the hell—?"

Adriana emerges into the aisle. In one hand, limp at her side, is the Charmander plushie, the velcro pocket open on its underside. In her other hand, trained on her father—pepper spray.

So much for keeping her wits about her.

"Against the fish food, all of you." She sweeps her aim from her father to mine and then, what the fuck, to me, stepping forward with an unsteady hand. "Are you under the impression what I said was in jest? Against the fish flakes, now!"

My dad and I do as she's instructed, but Stu raises his hands, dares a step forward. "Adriana, honey, this is a bad time for—"

"A bad time, father? A bad time?!" She strides forward with purpose. "Have you ever considered I might be familiar with bad times? Have you considered perhaps I don't need your lectures?"

"What I'm saying is—"

Adriana aims over her father's shoulder and activates the canister.

Stu ducks, turns away, puts himself between me and my dad against the pet store shelving. His shoulders heave, his face contorted with rage and desperation.

"A bad time," Adriana says, pacing in front of us, "is living the whole one's life dedicated to furthering the mission of a family operation that is devoted to anything but its purported purpose." She winces. Her hands, once again, shake.

Last night, she told me she didn't want to break, and now that she has—or, oh God, has she not broken yet?—strikes me still. I mean, at least it's pepper spray and not a gun, not that I'm excited about getting maced to kick off eviction day, and are mace and pepper spray even the same thing?

"Honey," Stu pleads, "I planned to tell you someday. I did."

Adriana stops, pivots hard, her chin down as she stares at her father. "So, it's true? The pet store is supported in part by theft?"

"It's not theft," Stu says.

"People *choose to* give him the money," my dad volunteers before Stu's elbow, a moment later, finds his ribs.

"In any event," Adriana says, lowering her pepper spray and raising her chin, "you're a criminal. And you confess to this? You confess to defrauding others?"

Stu stammers. "Can we talk about this another time?"

Adriana takes aim again.

"I—yeah," he says. "Just stop. Don't."

"Yeah *what*, father?"

"Yeah, it's not a clean operation, this place. It never has been, not completely."

Adriana sucks in her cheeks, seemingly shaken by the finality of her father's words. "And what of the threats on his life?" She jerks her head toward me and my dad. "The threats on their lives and that of Eric's mother?"

"It was a heat of the moment thing, Adriana. I never would have actually done—"

"Who knows what you would have actually done? You're a stranger to me, my own father!" Her shoulders rise and fall, and now I sincerely worry—even if we have a full confession on tape—where this might be headed.

I intervene. "That means," I say, daring a step forward, slowly turning to face Stu and my dad, "that you, Dad, *did* steal from Stu, didn't you?"

"I won't be made a fool," he says. "I don't know how, but I know this is some dumbass YouTube scambait shit."

"You know about the YouTube channel?" I ask, bringing myself up alongside Adriana. She must trust me—as if there were ever any doubt—now that she's heard a confession straight from the horse's mouth.

Or, if we're avoiding figurative language, her dad, the horse. I guess.

"I've been filled in on the YouTube channel," my dad says, "by an old friend of mine."

I glare at Stu. "You really didn't like that, did you? People sniffing around your operation? You didn't like accountability?"

"Shut the fuck up and tell us what you want."

Adriana steps forward before I can. "His dog, first and foremost."

Stu shrugs. "What do we get out of it?"

"You don't get pepper sprayed in the face, for starters," Adriana says.

I'd tell her to take it easy with a pat on the shoulder, but no touching. "And, to stave off mace to the face," I say, "we'd also like the full story, not what we've been able to piece together on our own."

"One also wonders," Adriana adds, "how you discerned Eric and I had become collaborators."

My dad laughs. "Eric was pretty damn adamant about this meeting, for one, when it would have been a lot easier to turn tail and run."

"Not all of us are so keen to fake our own deaths," I say.

"Not all of us have what it takes to survive."

"Some survival this is," I snap back, "cowering against a row of fish flakes without nowhere to call home once this is all over." Is there some irony in that last bit? Sure, but I'm not the one cowering at the moment, so at least I've got that.

It's the little things.

Stu ignores me and my dad, pleads with his daughter. "He called me," he says. "Eric's dad. He said Eric was anxious about this meeting, and after you phoned me about it earlier, we figured out the two of you must be planning something."

"This is why you insisted I attend this morning's festivities," Adriana says.

"It is."

"It's why you took my phone?" she adds.

"I couldn't trust you."

"How rich," Adriana says. "You, not trusting me."

"So," I say redirecting the conversation, "I believe we were discussing my dog."

"We were *discussing*," my dad says, "what Stu and I get out of this."

I cross my arms. "I'll disable the ransomware on the pet store's computers."

"That's it?" Stu asks.

No, not technically, not if the recording on my phone

proves worth anything—and not that they'll like what comes from that—but I can't go threatening them with that now. I can't—shouldn't—threaten them with anything until I've got Boulder back. "What time is it?" I ask.

"Who the fuck cares?" Stu says.

Adriana checks a wristwatch. "Seven thirty-seven."

"Fuck." I glance over my shoulder. The parking lot is empty save for Stu's truck. They're late, God damn them, and the pet store opens at eight, I think, so we need to wrap this shit up before Don and Donna Dog Owner come strolling up to the storefront in search of chew toys.

"You have somewhere to be?" my dad asks.

I shrug in the direction of Adriana, her pepper spray. "I think Bonnie here will ask the questions, thank you very much."

"Have you forgotten my name is Adriana?"

"It's—ugh. It's a reference to Bonnie and Clyde."

Adriana blinks at me.

"They were bank robbers? During the Depression?"

"I was never one for American history."

"Enough!" My dad bounds forward, catches Adriana on the elbow with his hand. Adriana shrieks, and the pepper spray hits the ground with a clank. Stu leaps for it. My balance thrown off by my dad's lunge, I flail my foot in the canister's direction, toeing it farther down the aisle.

Stu, unfazed, paces after the rolling container—until he hears the scream.

I pivot when I hear it, too: Adriana's voice shrill, despairing.

My father has her arms held tight behind her back, his eyes alight with rage while Adriana thrashes about, weeping.

"Let her go," Stu demands.

I'm surprised to find myself shoulder-to-shoulder with him—or, okay, shoulder to, like, elbow. "Dad, fucking stop it."

"Whose side are you on?" my dad says to Stu.

"I am always on the side of my daughter."

"Dad," I plead. "You can't. Don't. It's—there's this no touching thing. You can't."

"Can't," my dad says, mockingly. "*Can't* and *don't* and *stop* are all you people know." Adriana attempts to drop to the floor as I did earlier, tries to swing her legs at my dad's knees, but he wrests her back into his control. "You're weak. All of you. I don't know what I was thinking. You never had what it takes, and you never will."

I rib Stu. "So much for your renewed partnership, huh?"

Stu, rightly, ignores me, instead closing the distance between himself, my dad, and an increasingly frantic Adriana. "Release her."

Through the window, I catch the glare of the sun off a vehicle—two vehicles—pulling into the parking lot. My heart races when, fuck yes, I confirm it's *them*.

I leave the others to their scrum, rolling the pepper spray out of sight beneath an aisle with my foot.

"Hey," Stu shouts. "Hey! What the fuck?" He sees them now, too, two patrol cars from the Madison Police Department sliding into parking spaces outside.

My dad, noticing them at last, releases Adriana. She stumbles forward, but Stu catches her.

Before she realizes, apparently, who's outside—people who might, you know, actively be watching the last of this unfold—she pushes off of her father and, with an open hand, slashes my dad across the face with her nails.

The open red wounds on his face will, if we're lucky, leave scars.

Adriana, fear still her in step, puts her father between herself and mine, though she draws herself closer to me with every backward step. "I see you phoned some friends," she calls to me over her shoulder.

I breathe easily—as easily as one can, considering the circumstances—for the first time in days. "Sure did."

"Then it would seem that where our fathers are concerned"—she glances at me—"there'll be no getting the hell out of Dodge."

CHAPTER 60
I'M ERIC

Car doors slam. Uniformed officers strut for the storefront. My dad shoots me a hateful glance.

Then, he makes a run for it.

"Stop him," I instruct no one in particular, dashing past Adriana to intercept the officers as they approach the store's automatic doors.

While my rat-shit coward of a dad rushes for the rear of the store—presumably in search of an exit—Stu, visibly gobsmacked, seems to recognize the jig is up. Where the hell is *he* going to run off to? The business belongs to him, so unless he has some patsy accountant who he can blame for his money laundering, he's fucked with a capital F.

The automatic doors whir apart. An officer—Gibson, according to his uniform—is the first on the scene. "We're looking for an Eric Amundsen."

"Him," I gasp, gesturing to the back of the store. "Stop him."

Gibson's partner, Vargas, seems to see what I see—my dad dipping just out of sight as he finally jukes from store's central aisle and out of sight. "On it," she says, before demanding he stop right there.

My dad, as will come as a surprise to absolutely no one, does not *stop right there.*

Vargas chases after him, and Gibson returns to his questions.

"All right," he says, "can I get your name, sir?"

"I—what? Aren't you going to go after—?"

Two other officers enter the building. Gibson brings them up to speed, and one of them steps away to speak with Stu and Adriana. The other begins a sweep of the store because, well, what the fuck do I know, but shouldn't they have more resources dedicated to the man actively attempting to escape custody?

"Now," Gibson says, "if you don't mind, can I get a name?"

"I'm him. The guy who called you last night."

Gibson narrows his eyes and glances at his notepad, which, thus far, remains empty. Elsewhere, Stu stays quiet, embracing his right to remain silent, and Adriana, through indignant sobs, explains what, exactly, is happening here.

"You did the whole ransomware bit?" Gibson asks. "You're the guy who called in the tip?

"Should I not have? This is a slam dunk case. Like I said, Stu and my dad have been scamming people for decades, and we've now got them on tape essentially confessing to—"

"Can I see some I.D.?"

"Sure, yeah"—I fumble with my wallet, hand him my driver's license—"but is someone going to get my dog? From Stu's, I mean. At least that's where I'm assuming he's kept the dog. He's been sick, so if someone can get him? Please? Or maybe you already have other officers on it."

"Don't you worry," he says, "we've probably got his home surrounded by now."

Relief blankets me until—oh, sarcasm. "Sorry, is there something I'm not understanding? Here, let me grab my phone. Once you hear the recording, you—or, I guess the D.A. or whoever—will have everything they need to—"

"Yeah, I think we've got everything we need right here, bud." He finishes examining my license, but doesn't return it. Instead, he reaches for his handcuffs. "Place your hands behind your back."

"No," I say. "I'm *Eric*. My dad, Glenn—"

"Let Vargas worry about Glenn. For now," Gibson says, grabbing me by the wrist, "turn around."

As I do, time slows. Sweat beads on my brow. Adriana's animated gestures cease, her jaw hanging loose when we make eye contact, and Stu folds his arms, suppresses a smile.

"I don't understand," I manage.

"Eric Amundsen," Gibson says, "you're under arrest for unauthorized access of a computer."

CHAPTER 61
YOU'RE THE CRIMINAL NOW. DOG?

From the inside of a patrol car, I watch through frosted windows, my forehead pressed against the frigid glass.

Adriana pleads with Gibson, with the officer who originally questioned her. Stu, eventually, betrays his right to keep his mouth shut, intervening at times with a fair amount of finger pointing. After a few minutes of this, the officer whose name I never got pulls Stu aside, begins collecting a separate statement, which, come the fuck on, they should have done from the start.

Gibson, meanwhile, ignores Adriana's desperation, nodding solemnly. I beg her—telepathically or whatever—to tell them I had permission. That computer in the back office, I only used it after she gave me the password. It wasn't unauthorized access. She told me I could use it, knew what I was doing, and who the hell cares if it was her dad's login info? She obviously had his username and password, had used both before, and she knew what I was up to, so why in the fuck aren't the cops returning to this car? Why on God's green earth are they not removing my handcuffs, issuing apologies, and thanking me for being a goddamn hero?

Vargas returns to the group, as does the second cop who joined her in pursuit.

My dad does not accompany them.

"Fuck." I slam my head—okay, it's more like a tap—against the window, my jaw set. I concentrate on my phone, on where it's tucked away amid chintzy treasure chests and faux coral reefs, attempting to mind meld again with Adriana, to tell her my phone is there, it's *right there*, that if she can grab it, if she can stop and save the recording before the phone dies, we can verify everything I said on the tip line, not to mention whatever she's included in her statement to the police.

Gibson closes his notepad, seems to thank Adriana before stepping away. Vargas remains a moment longer, her body language more open until one of the officers questioning Stu abandons their conversation, strides past Adriana.

Then, his flashlight trained on the space where the shelving stops just short of meeting the floor, he crouches, reaches for—and finds—the pepper spray I'd kicked away.

What comes next is worse than the bite of the cold steel against my wrists, is worse maybe, even, than my father's escape. The officer who found the pepper spray opens the fist he closed around it, showing it to Adriana. She nods.

Vargas hangs her head, but reaches for her handcuffs.

I don't have to watch to know what comes next. Even the glass—and the distance separating us—isn't enough to mute Adriana's shrieks.

CHAPTER 62
10-4

"You have to let her go."

In the front seats on the far side of the partition, Gibson and Vargas ignore me while their car glides down Willy Street, morning rush hour traffic having mostly cleared.

"I don't know what it is, exactly," I say, "but Adriana's got this thing about touching and routines and, damn it, I'm not a doctor or therapist or counselor, but you've got to know there's a mental health issue to consider here." Their radio buzzes. Dispatch calls in a fender bender on the west side. "You've got procedure to follow, sure, but the more distressed she gets, the worse—can you even hear me?"

Gibson's hands remain steady on the wheel. Vargas calls in our impending arrival, the name of the perpetrator they'll soon be processing. And, because the universe is a cold, indifferent expanse, that perpetrator isn't my dad. It's not him or Stu or, hell, even the Als of the world with their diligent, ceaseless attempts to take advantage of anyone and everyone in their path.

Nope, it's me. And, in another car not far behind ours, it's Adriana.

We're the ones who'll pose for mug shots and sit in cells and plead our cases before a judge. Ooh, and public defenders, won't *that* be exciting? Fuck.

I fold my arms except, right, no I don't. My handcuffs nip at my wrists, so I settle instead for staring out the window.

"At least go back," I say now, exhausted, my voice low, "and grab my phone. It's, like, literally all the evidence you'll need to lock up Stu and my dad, assuming you can find him." I shake my head, my gaze trained on the distant, frozen surface of Lake Monona. "Or try my apartment," I add. "Maybe you can still catch him there. My dad, I mean. You can catch him and find the note Stu originally left me, the one about my dog."

My stomach clenches. "Or please"—I lean forward now—"go to Stu's, at least, for the love of God. Are either of you dog people? You're not people-people, clearly, but if you're dog people, you wouldn't want to see anything terrible happen to the dog who's caught in the middle of all this, right? Right?"

Vargas turns, slowly, looking back at me over her shoulder. "The address on your I.D. current?"

"What does that have to do with my dog?"

Gibson pipes up. "Address is current. Said as much before I got him in the car."

I'd kick their seats—or, you know, the divider between me and their seats—if I weren't interested in getting the hell out of police custody as soon as I possibly can. "This has nothing to do with—"

Vargas activates her radio. "Can we get an officer to investigate a possible 10-31? Trespassing. Possible evasion of arrest."

The radio cracks, fizzles. "10-4. You got an address for that 10-31?"

Vargas relays my address, cites a possible suspect on the run. "We're looking for a suspect, male. Goes by Glenn

Amundsen. Physical description—" She glances at me in the back seat.

"Six-two," I say. "Probably, like, 260 pounds?"

She passes this info along, looks back to me for more.

"Uh, blond hair," I say. "Broad shoulders. Built like me, but if I worked out and also had an extra cheeseburger now and then."

Vargas rolls her eyes, shares with dispatch the *useful* information I gave her.

"Copy that," dispatch says. "We'll have someone take a look."

"10-4," Vargas says.

"10-4," I repeat, for reasons beyond my reckoning. I shake off my embarrassment, urge myself to the front of my seat. "What about the phone? If you find my dad, you're going to want that. He's on tape—or well, my phone—literally confessing to fraud. Or close enough to it. He confirms he faked his death, anyway, which has to be illegal. In some form or fashion."

"Have you forgotten," Gibson says, "you have the right to remain silent?"

"It's a right," I say, "not a command. And I'm the one helping *you* here. Please, you have to grab that phone. You have to free Adriana and check in on my dog. Neither of them did anything wrong, and—"

"We get it," Gibson says. "We've heard it all before, kid."

Kid. *Rapaz, rapaz.* It's like Caio all over again, but now it's Caio in an officer's uniform and a gun in a holster and my fate in his hands. Oh, how far I've fallen.

This is what I get, I guess, for trying to keep a promise.

CHAPTER 63
LEVERAGE

Once I've been fingerprinted, my photo taken, they ask me to take it from the top. No, the top-top, they say. The bit about your grandma, Eric, and how, exactly, she ended up giving her money to strangers on the internet, to strangers over the phone. You mentioned there was an inheritance. About how much was that worth? How much was lost? And a Saint Bernard? That feels like an inappropriately sized dog to foist upon your grandmother, which, yes it is, I tell them, but Grandma was so lonely and Boulder was, too, and he was about as old as she was—in doggy years, obviously—and he just so happened to be the only dog left for adoption that day.

"Huh. Nice gesture, kid."

"Can you please stop calling me *kid*?"

"Yeah, we heard you don't like that."

"Does anyone? "

"Kids, maybe."

I gesture to myself, a grown-ass man.

Point taken, they say, but now, again, the part about your dad, this first email contact of his—you hadn't heard from him for how long? Phew. Twenty years is some number of years, and we know you're happy to show us the actual emails if we get your phone; don't you worry about that right now. The phone will get here when the phone gets here. We don't know if they found it yet. You're better off answering our questions again, even if it does feel like we've asked you these, as you so eloquently put it, a million damn times.

The cop who's taken the lead in questioning me pauses for a moment, reviews his notes.

Without prompting, I walk him again through the ransomware setup at Kitten Caboodle, how I accessed the actual computer with Adriana's permission, and yes, he says, she gave you the username and password. We understand. But do you, I ask, because what I'm trying to tell you is that I essentially logged in, realized what I wanted to do wasn't going to work, and then all the changes I made—the thing that actually looks like a ransomware attack—was done on my own device. All I did was—yup, we know, he interrupts. All you did was plug it in, and you keep telling us Adriana will confirm everything you're saying, so there's really no need to keep repeating yourself.

"Okay, so are you going to ask her?" I venture. "Can you check on her? On my dog? On my phone and whatever happened with my dad at my apartment? I mean, these are important leads, right, and it feels like every minute we spend revisiting details I've already shared with you is a minute we lose trying to—"

"Eric, you know why we do this. We have to make sure your story checks out, even as you tell it a hundred times. We appreciate your cooperation, but for the love of God, please understand we've got people working on it. On all of it. Well, no, I don't know about the dog for sure, but everything else you've brought up *a million damn times* is certainly being investigated."

At this, I lean back in my chair.

"Don't sulk," the cop says. "You're not a kid, remember?"

"I have nothing further to say until we've got updates on Boulder, my phone, Adriana—my dad, too. And Stu. It's been hours, for Christ's sake, and if I have to tell this story one more time—can I get more water, by the way, or is dehydrating witnesses also part of procedure around here?"

A knock on the door. It's Vargas for the first time since she escorted me from her and Gibson's vehicle. She enters with—thank God—my phone.

"Was the battery still alive when you got to the store?" I ask. "Did you listen to the recording? Was everything my dad said—was everything Stu and Adriana said—audible?"

Instead of answering, Vargas begins by informing the others she and Gibson first went to my apartment and found, fuck *off*, no sign of my dad, though the place was a wreck and a moving crew was taking everything to the curb.

"Eviction day," I tell her, before asking about the note.

"No note to speak of," she says, "at least not amid the, uh, eviction, did you say?"

I defer to the cops who've been questioning me for what feels like hours, and they tell her, yes, I've brought them up to speed. It checks out.

"Anyway," Vargas says, "the eviction's on hold." The place is an active crime scene now, and units have been advised to keep their eyes peeled for anyone matching my dad's description.

At this, I stand, could give Vargas a hug, but holy shit, sit your ass down, man; these people aren't your friends and you are still in police custody. I apologize, say I needed to stretch my legs for a second, and ask Vargas what changed.

The pet store, she says. Officers were sent back to the store, but found it locked, the lights off, no one inside. They had to get a warrant to enter and grab the phone, which, thanks to my highly repetitive description—her words—was easy enough to spot through the front windows.

"What about the recording?" I ask.

"By the time my colleagues could retrieve the device, it was down to three percent battery. They confirmed it was recording, and they believe they saved the voice memo before the phone died, but we've been waiting for the damn thing to charge sufficiently before bringing it to you."

I lean away from the phone now, suspicious.

"Someone has to unlock this phone," Vargas says, "and we don't have your password."

I take the phone, begin entering my password. With two digits remaining, I stop myself.

"Something the matter?" asks the cop who'd been questioning me most while Vargas was away.

"I want to hear this recording as much as you do," I say, "but before any of that happens—my dog. Adriana. I want updates, damn it, and sorry for the language, but you have to understand the whole reason this escalated is because Stu—which, where is *he*, by the way?—broke into my apartment and stole him."

"We still have no verifiable proof—"

I wave my phone around. "I can show you the videos that upset Stu in the first place. The unedited footage will establish motive." Then, to Vargas—who's clearly more interested in hearing me out than anyone else—"But, again, the dog first. And Adriana. Look for the first. Check in on the second. Then the phone's all yours. Well, ours. I'll need it back. Eventually. It's really the only thing to my name at this point, aside from a car and the clothes on my back."

And Boulder, hopefully.

CHAPTER 64
I TOLD YOU SO

After another hour, I'm moved from holding to Gibson's office. A good sign, I think, though I caught no glimpse of Adriana when they first escorted me across the floor. And Gibson, since I wound up in a horribly uncomfortable plastic chair opposite his desk, has kept a not-so-watchful eye on me. This has freed me up to, well, continue my mental health freefall.

Desperate for distraction, I break the silence. "What are you playing?"

He continues mashing his phone screen with his thumbs.

"Can I use the bathroom?"

His phone chimes with some sort of unlocked power-up.

"What's your favorite color?"

The light illuminating his face shifts, flashes.

"How many pancakes does it take to shingle a doghouse?"

Another chime from his phone. "I can hear you."

"Here I was, worried I'd died and gone to—"

A knock on the door. Both Gibson and I snap our attention to Vargas, who stands in the doorframe.

I rise. "Boulder?"

She shakes her head.

"What does that mean?" I step closer. "He wasn't there, or—?"

"Easy." Her hand finds her hip.

I reset, try to swallow the knot in my throat as I take a step back.

"There was no one home. No Stu. No dog."

I curse under my breath. "Then we have to check the shelters. Unless Stu took Boulder with him, in which case—"

"We'll figure it out," Vargas says. "Won't we, Gibson?"

Gibson nods without looking up from his device, his thumbs still racing across its screen.

"Very reassuring," I say.

"I do have some good news," Vargas interjects.

A weight—a small one, anyway—is taken from me. "It's my dad. You caught him, didn't you? He couldn't have gotten far."

She gestures for me to sit and, after I do, takes the seat next to me.

"Can't you do this in your office?" Gibson says.

"Settle down, officer," Vargas snaps back.

Gibson does not protest further.

"We were able to confirm," Vargas continues, her hands on her knees, "most of your story."

"Of course," I say. "I had no reason to—"

"Including the bit about the Blueberry Pi."

"*Raspberry* Pi, but okay."

"Sure. Yes. I wasn't there when they examined the setup, so—"

I wave off her apology—or whatever it's meant to be. "Happens all the time."

"Anyway, the officers on site were able to unplug your motherboard-looking apparatus, return the office computer to its original configuration, and, with the login information

Adriana gave them, determine the computer was working just fine."

The gust of relief I breathe forces Vargas to lean away. "Sorry," I say. "But what about Adriana?"

"What about her?"

"She obviously started talking at some point."

"She did."

"So, she's doing okay? Relatively speaking."

"She won't leave the station until she knows how *you're* doing."

"Wait. Leave the station? As in, she's been released?"

Vargas chuckles. "Not that she's really taken advantage of it."

"Good," I say. "Good for her." I suck in a breath between my teeth. "But tell her it's complicated, I guess. Or, I don't know, what have you been telling her? About how I'm doing, I mean."

Vargas stands. "Why don't you tell her yourself?"

"What?"

"You're free to go," she says, and the tension in my neck dissipates. "On one condition."

Forget what I said about my shoulders and neck. "And that condition is?"

"We need you to unlock your phone."

I take it from her outstretched hand, enter my password, deactivate it entirely.

Then, my phone in her hand, a smile on her face, Vargas says, "Come on, kid."

I'm not even mad.

CHAPTER 65
ON THE PROWL

Her arms stiff at her sides, Adriana waits in the lobby, her eyes sunken. "I see you've managed to escape their clutches," she says.

"I am, uh, yeah. I'm clutch-free."

"And of Boulder?"

"Nothing," I say.

She bites her lower lip. "Well, we'll simply have to find him ourselves, then, won't we?"

I nod, my hands in my pockets. "Are you—are you okay?"

Adriana ignores me, fishing her phone from her peacoat pocket instead. "Let's call a cab."

We wait outside, in the cold, for our cab to arrive. The sky is bright and blue, a remarkably cloudless day for February. Wind swirls around the capitol loop, cutting across what skin remains exposed, and though the days are longer now than they were even a month ago, judging by how low the sun lies now, it'll be gone again soon enough.

Neither of us speaks until the cab has retrieved us, has dumped us outside Adriana's home.

"It was pepper spray," she says.

"What?"

"Only pepper spray." She digs around in her pockets, finds her house keys. "My father told them it was mace."

I narrow my eyes, trailing her along the walkway to her house.

"He knew it wasn't mace," she adds, stepping onto the porch.

"I don't understand."

"Mace," she says, holding onto the word, "is illegal in the state of Wisconsin. Pepper spray is not. My father and I discussed the very topic when I first purchased the deterrent." Her key in the lock, she glances over her shoulder at me. Her eyes water, look as if they might well over.

"I'm sorry," I say.

She blinks away the tears, turns the key in the lock. "It was as elucidating a moment as any, my father wanting me arrested. Heavens knows what he chose to do with the time it bought him." She leans into, pushes open the door, stops as it swings open.

"Adriana?" I say. "What's—?"

I don't have to finish my question. I see it, too, saw it when Stu did the same to my apartment.

Her home has been turned over. Ransacked. Completely upended.

CHAPTER 66
HOME BASE

Adriana sighs. "It seems we have our answer, then." She shuffles into her home before dropping to the floor, resting her back against the wall, her shoulders heaving with sobs.

I follow her in, survey the damage.

Her plushie collection has been scattered throughout the living room, some of them stomped upon, slush and snow having seeped into their fabric. In the kitchen, every cabinet remains flung open—the closet doors, too, along with the plastic storage drawers near where I hid in the closet. Their contents have been strewn throughout the dining area, the wood floor beneath the table a mess of scattered trinkets and what appear to be Yu-Gi-Oh cards.

"What was he looking for?" I ask.

Adriana takes a gasping breath. "The safe, I suspect."

"The safe?"

She sniffles, hyperventilates, fans herself.

"It's okay," I say. "Just, uh. Your breathing. Focus on your breathing. Can I get you anything?"

"Water," she gasps, and I find a glass, fill it, return with it a minute later. Before she takes the glass from me, she asks if

I'll help her up. I offer her my free hand, helping her to her feet before she takes the water from me, sucks it down in a few gulps.

"My father kept a personal safe here, in my home." She wipes her mouth.

"That much, I gathered."

"He had one at his home, too, and one at Kitten Caboodle."

"Why so many?"

"I imagine to mitigate the possibility of loss should he be forced to leave town on a moment's notice and not have access to the others. In case an event such as this transpired, essentially. One that forced him to get the hell out of Dodge." Her smile is flat, sad.

"Now you're getting it."

She kicks off her boots, steps into the living room where she retrieves one of her Pokémon plushies from the floor. Oddish, maybe? "It was empty last night," she volunteers, turning the plushie over in her hand.

"The safe? In your house?"

"The one at the store," she says. "We use the same safe to secure cash from customer transactions. When we were closing, as I finished verifying the contents of the register, I accessed the safe in the office and noticed his personal shelf had been emptied."

Finally, I get it. "So once you got home, you hid the safe he normally kept here."

"I returned to the store and hid it there, yes, where he certainly wouldn't think to look for it."

"But why?"

"The money doesn't belong to him. It belongs to his victims. Myself included."

I stroke my chin, watch as Adriana lets her Oddish plushie slip through her fingers and onto the carpet.

"It also means," she adds, "he'll have fewer funds available to him while he remains on the run. I suspect they'll freeze his assets soon enough."

"You really thought this out."

"Not that it's done us any good."

"We don't know that yet."

"No." She sighs. "I suppose we don't."

I run my hand through my hair. "We should probably call this in."

Adriana nods.

"Can I—can I use your phone? The police have mine, still, as evidence."

She offers me her phone, but as I dial, Adriana interrupts.

"Eric?" she asks.

"Yeah?"

"I might like to try a hug."

CHAPTER 67
DELOCATED

Once the police have come and gone, once they've advised us, needlessly, to stay elsewhere until they can confirm neither of our fathers poses an immediate threat, we pack into my car and drive to a motel across town.

"It should go without saying," Adriana says as we traverse the lobby for the check-in counter, "that we'll require separate beds."

"Is this another one of those *you think I'm going to ask you on a date* things?"

"I believe they call this establishing boundaries."

"I feel those have been established quite well."

"Mmm."

We manage—or, well, *Adriana* manages because I sure as hell have no money—to book a room with two twin beds, and our luggage has hardly hit the floor of our room before I'm asking her, again, for her phone.

"Why do you require my cellular?"

"To call animal shelters."

She nods to the room's phone on the nightstand.

"That'll cost a fortune," I say.

"For local calls, even?"

"Have you never stayed in a hotel?"

I take her silence as a no.

Ultimately, she relents, and while browsing the web on her phone, I compile a list of shelters and their phone numbers.

"There's no knowing for certain," she says, "Boulder will even be at a shelter. He could still be in my father's care."

"Care?" I ask, stretched out on my bed. "I don't think I'd call whatever your dad is doing with him *care*."

"Mmm."

"But you're right. He could still be with your dad, but that's not my favorite possibility to dwell on." I roll from my stomach onto my side, plop the list of phone numbers onto the bedside table. "So, we might as well give this a shot." I swallow. "Take turns on your phone?"

"Please—use the room phone while I use my cellular."

"Again, that's going to cost—"

"Let's do this efficiently," she says. "We can cover twice as many numbers the same amount of time if you use the room phone. I'll bear the cost."

"Thank you."

We attempt to contact as many shelters as we can, expanding our call radius as we go down the list. Most shelters, naturally, turn out to be closed, and those that do have someone taking calls haven't had any Saint Bernards brought in, no, but they'll let us know, they say, if anything turns up.

It's after eleven p.m. when I cross off the final shelter on our list.

Adriana emerges from the bathroom, her toothbrush in her mouth. "Per has tom row Darrell—"

"What?"

She removes her toothbrush, tries again. "Perhaps tomorrow there will be good news in store." After disappearing into the bathroom, she spits and the faucet runs. Still out of sight, she continues, "On several fronts, one hopes."

With only a frontage road separating us from the highway, the light in our room is never quite extinguished. We lie there, in separate beds, the sounds of cars whooshing past on the Beltline a constant refrain. I grip the sheets on either side of me, wondering, fearing what tomorrow will bring. Even the day's biggest wins feel small when pit against what it's cost to win them. No job. No home. No dog. Still no dad, no family to speak of.

And the shame—don't even get me started on the shame. Feels bad, man.

"Do you remain awake, Eric?" Adriana says.

After a long, tense breath, I finally respond. "Yes, *I remain awake.*"

"One hopes this isn't too distressing to recall, but why, exactly, did you choose to investigate my father and our store in the first place? I recall your video on YouTube mentioned something about your grandmother, but I fail to understand the connection."

My gaze remains trained on the popcorn ceiling. "It's kind of a long story."

"I shan't be sleeping any time soon."

I release my grip on the sheets, lean forward, give my pillow a couple of punches to fluff it.

"Well, if you're feeling violent about it—" Adriana lets her statement hang in the air between us.

"No. Fine. I'll—sure. I'll tell you. Just promise you won't take shots at me for my every blunder along the way."

"It's quite difficult to take shots when one isn't armed."

"Figurative language," I say.

"Yes, please keep it to a minimum."

I laugh, sigh, and take it from the top with Grandma Amundsen, with the scamming bastards who fleeced her for everything—almost everything—she had. Then there's the promise and scambaiting, the—

"Did you say scam*baiting*?" she interrupts.

"It's a whole thing."

"I didn't expect it to be half of something."

I elaborate, fill her in on how I spent my time at my day job.

"And this company, they paid you to do this?"

"Not technically. I mean, it wasn't part of my job, but it felt more meaningful. Besides, any profit-based enterprise is inherently denying those who work for it their share of the fruits of their labor."

"I was unaware you were a Marxist."

"I—what? You don't have to be a Marxist to—never mind." I grab the second pillow on my bed, hug it tight to my chest.

"Have I caused some offense? Did I inadvertently call attention to a blunder?"

"I—" My jaw clenches. "It's hard to explain. Like, they're all… everyone…"

"Mmm?"

"It's scammers forever and always, everywhere." At this, I sit up, yank the chain on the lamp to illuminate the room— well, to illuminate it more than it'd already been illuminated. "It's my dad. It's yours. It's the criminals who came for my grandma. It's Nortex and my Scambait Bros pretending to be my friends, even when they most certainly are not."

"I was unaware you had a brother."

I ignore her. "And then you sprinkle in an AI once in a while, a Gibson playing mobile games instead of, I don't know, upholding his oath—"

"Who's AI?"

"Hell, it's *me*," I say, "with all the on-the-clock scambaiting I did. I admit it. I'm not happy about it, but there's no denying it."

"That's quite the cynical view."

"It is, but you'll have a hard time convincing me it isn't the truth. Not with all the evidence piled up in support of it."

The sounds of the highway drone on. Down the hall, a door opens, closes. Adriana pulls her knees to her chest, rocking softly. I study her a moment, waiting for the other shoe to drop, not that I'd say that because, of course, figurative language. But with her eyes wide and the hug she gives herself as tight as it is, I wonder if I've broken her.

When at last she speaks, I'm certain I have. "Are you familiar with Sudoku, Eric?"

"Like the game with the numbers and the squares?"

"The same." Her soft rocking continues.

"Yeah, I know it. I hate it, but I know it."

"Mmm."

"What does *mmm* mean?"

Her attention snaps my direction. "Would you say I'm a scammer, Eric, for having done Sudoku while on shift at Kitten Caboodle?"

I laugh. "Is that what's bothering you?"

"No," she says smartly, "I think that's what's bothering you." Her rocking stops.

I swing my legs over the side of my bed. "How could I be bothered by you doing a thing I didn't even know you did?"

"That's the wrong question." She does the same as me, facing me now in full across the thin strip of carpet between us. "Would you say I'm a scammer?"

"You are not a scammer." I scratch my head. "You benefited from having one for a dad, for sure—with the job and the pet store and all—but you, personally, are not a scammer, I assure you."

"How is my doing Sudoku any different than you spending your time at work scambaiting?"

"It's—I don't know—a matter of degree. Of intent, maybe."

"So you intended to defraud North Ex—"

"Nortex."

"Nortex. You intended to defraud Nortex?"

"No, but my scambaiting was, like, all I did while on the clock."

"There's your matter of degree," she says.

"What?"

She sighs as if *I'm* the one who's not getting it. "Everything incurs a cost, Eric."

"I'm pretty familiar with what my actions have cost me, if that's what you mean."

"It isn't, really, but I suppose it's evidence in support of the hypothesis."

"Okay," I say, reaching for the light on the bedside table, "if we're going to turn this into an episode of Bill Nye, maybe it can wait until tomorrow." I turn off the light and, once my head hits the pillow, roll onto my side, my back to her.

"You're no scammer," she says. "You're someone who cares."

"Caring's not enough to keep out of trouble, apparently."

"It never is."

"For someone who doesn't do figurative language, you have a real knack for riddles."

"Let me be plain: everyone cares. They simply care about different things. Some people value themselves and their beliefs above all else. They value their success, their comfort, and their position in the world over everyone and everything."

"That doesn't give them an excuse to purposely harm others. To steal from them, I mean."

"No, but it justifies their actions to themselves, and many people feel they are only ever accountable to themselves. This is untrue. We live, as they say, in a society, and when what one cares about contradicts the established norms—or, in the strictly legal sense, the laws—of the community, friction becomes inevitable."

"Is any of this going to help me get my dog back?"

She yawns. "I suppose not." Sheets rustle. A mattress sighs. "But it might help you sleep better at night."

Sleep—despite Adriana's hypothesis—does not come easy. My eyes burn, and my wrists remain agitated from the handcuffs earlier today. Imagine, handcuffs! Now *that's* friction. The wrist pain is a problem caused by friction, anyway. And, if anything, it's just another example of friction hurting the undeserving.

Though I can't blame them, the police, for misunderstanding my call to the tip line. They hear a guy call in and talk about how he rigged up a computer with words like ransomware, and *voila*, easiest arrest of the day. Maybe. What do I know? Nothing, obviously.

Except friction. I know friction, and I sure would like a lot less of it around, which, hey, maybe that's a me problem. Water off a duck's back, right? If I were more flexible—if I weren't such a goddamn *either-or* of a man—I wouldn't have spent the last couple of weeks getting sandpapered at every possible opportunity.

Shit. That's it. My dad. Stu. Al. They're flexible. They shape-shift. They're who they need to be to the people they need to convince when those people need convincing, and look at them. No consequences for their actions. Well, okay, Al is losing his car dealership, and my dad did have to fake his own death before going on the run again, and Stu—Christ —his troubles are only just beginning.

And that's… that's me, too. I did it, did exactly what they were doing when I put off Dolores, when I ignored the Caios and Shawns of the world. I was flexible, all right, but to what end? Don't answer that. We know to what end, and that end is here, in this bed, dogless and homeless and, okay, let's not let ourselves spiral again.

Adriana's right, though. Kind of. Even the most flexible get ground down eventually, at least if they run against the grain. And not to overstate this because I am in no way anyone's hero, but this is what elevates rebels and revolutionaries, isn't it? It's friction. Friction defines them. It defines their legacy, and they *own* it.

Okay, settle down, Eric. Going after a couple of scammers is no hunger strike, and it's not like I was arrested willingly to prove a point. The real takeaway is there's no escaping the friction, in the end—no escaping the consequences of our actions, for better or for worse. At least not if we believe in something.

My eyelids grow heavy. The room still swells with the gliding hum of cars on the highway. Through the dark, I call out. "Adriana?"

She rolls over, her eyes still closed. "Mmm?"

"Thank you," I say.

"Whatever for?" she mumbles.

"For trying."

CHAPTER 68
KEEP HER MOVING

otel coffee. Those unlabeled drip machines, the thin layer of dust coating the columns of styrofoam cups. And the taste, the texture—brown water or, alternatively, tar. This place serves the latter. At least it's got caffeine in it, which will have the added benefit of staving off hunger because I'm not digging into this so-called continental breakfast.

Adriana, her glasses fogging when she sips from her styrofoam cup, eyes me while I inspect the underside of the miniature cereal boxes. "Is there something you fear you've lost beneath each package?" she asks.

"No," I say, setting down a box of, and I can't make this shit up, Fun-Bird Fruited Circle-O's. "These are all expired."

"I was unaware sugar could expire."

"We're learning a lot together, aren't we?"

She lowers her cup, her brows pinching together.

I set down an expired box of—yikes—Doctor O'Irish Marshmallow Bites. "Don't think too hard about it. I was being a smart-ass, is all."

"Your cynicism is this active in the mornings as well?"

"Is it still cynicism if it's my default world view?"

"Would it be presumptuous of me to assume you're thinking to yourself, *this breakfast, what a scam?*"

"I—no." My jaw hangs loose. I cover by taking a sip of my coffee. "I mean, maybe. So what if I was?"

"That's not really a question I'm meant to answer."

Before I can bite back, Adriana raises a finger, bites into one of the rock-hard croissants she nabbed from the platter next to the cereal stand.

"What?" I ask.

Between chews, she says, "I hoped only you'd pause a moment before replying as to give yourself ample time to truly consider whatever it is you intended to say."

And she wonders why she doesn't have friends. Okay, that's not even true insofar as I know, and that's the exact kind of comment better kept to myself, which, look, I did it. She probably doesn't have friends because she prefers to keep to herself anyway, and here's a thought—what if she and I are friends? Do I have a friend? Holy shit, did I not have friends before?

My stomach growls as if it has an opinion on the matter. I consider the box of Fruited Circle-O's, but no. I can't subject myself to that.

"Ah," Adriana says when her phone screen lights up on the counter next to her. "It's the constabulary." Instead of picking up the phone, she goes on chewing.

"Well," I say, "answer." This must be news about our dads, about one of them, maybe, and if it's Stu who's been apprehended, we've got an all-clear to return to her place. No more motel! No more tossing and turning at night! No more sludge coffee in dust cups! Or, and I didn't think of this first because, let's be honest, their priorities are going to be elsewhere, what if it's news about Boulder?

I reach for her phone.

She holds her hand up in a stop gesture. "I'm chewing."

"You're going to miss the call."

She swallows. "Everything in its right place." Then, the phone in her hand, she answers. "Hello? Yes, naturally. And of our fathers? I see. Well, then." Adriana offers a single-shoulder shrug, extends the phone to me.

"What?" I mouth. Her expression gives nothing away. I snatch the phone from her, my chest tightening. "This is Eric."

It's my apartment, they tell me. They've combed the place for any sign of my dad, and their work is complete.

"But you didn't find him?" I ask.

No, not in my place or anywhere else, they say, but there's the matter of all my belongings, some of which remain in the apartment while others sit on the curb, surrounded by police tape. Someone needs to come get them or, as management told the officers on the scene this morning, if someone wants to pay the rent that's owed, I can move back in.

"Good joke," I say.

They assure me this is no joke, that either my things need to be moved before noon today or they'll be disposed of or stored in accordance with the terms of my lease.

"What are those terms, if you don't mind me asking?"

They tell me they're not sure, that this is a question better asked of the landlord or of—and here they are again with the jokes—my lawyer. I'm ready to point out the unlikelihood of someone having a lawyer if they can't pay rent, but Adriana's phone beeps. I remove it from my ear, glance at the phone, notice a 262 area code. Milwaukee suburbs, maybe one of the shelters we called last night.

"Hey," I say, "can I call you back?"

There's no need, apparently, because what I do with my belongings is entirely up to me.

"I'll get them," I say. "I don't know where I'll put them, but I'll get them. And I've got another call coming in, sorry. Have to take this." I thumb END and try to grab the incoming call before it goes to voicemail.

"I beg your pardon." Adriana lunges across the table, swipes the phone from me.

"Hey!"

"My phone, my rules."

"I—"

"Hello?" she says into the receiver. "Just a moment." She returns the phone to me.

I shoot her a look that's something between a *god damn it* and *see?* before taking the call. "This is Eric."

"Eric," says the woman's voice on the other end, "this is Shelby with Paws and Claws of Kenosha. How are you this morning?"

Sweat seeps into the spaces between my fingers. "Did you find him? Is there a dog? A Saint Bernard at your shelter?"

"Well," Shelby says, her speech impossibly slow, "we did have a fella swing through last night with a big dog matching the description you left by voicemail, yes. Had a friend with him, too, but he stayed in the car. I told him his friend or husband or whatever could come on in as well, but—"

"Wait. What?"

"The guys who dropped off this dog last night."

"There were two of them?"

"Like I said, only the one came in, but—"

"What did they look like, these guys? And does the dog respond to Boulder?"

"Now, before I answer any questions," Shelby says, "I just have to be sure this isn't someone trying to adopt a dog back into a challenged home."

"What? A challenged home?"

"It's sad, really, but we see it often enough, a family member or friend removing a pet from someone else's custody for fear of abuse, you know."

"I? *Me?* I'm great to Boulder. That dog loves me. I mean, he smells horrible from time to time—"

"We noticed, yeah."

"—but he's my dog. Well, he was my grandma's and then he became my dog, but the guy who's been taking care of him, the one who dropped him off, he's far worse for Boulder than almost anyone else I could imagine."

Adriana leans in, attempt to listen to the conversation. I put the call on speakerphone.

Shelby is relentless. "Do you have anyone who can corroborate your story, Mr. Eric?"

"Greetings, Ms. Shelter-Owner," Adriana says. "My name is Adriana. I'm the woman who answered the phone, and I can corroborate."

"Oh, geez. I didn't know I was on speaker."

"You are now," I say. "As of, like, five seconds ago."

"Gotcha," Shelby replies, not that she needed to say that because, please, for the love of God, can we keep this conversation moving? "Now, are you two members of the same household?"

"We most certainly are not," Adriana says.

"You don't have to say it so incredulously," I say.

"It isn't personal," she says. "It's a statement of fact."

"Felt personal."

"Ah, I see what's going on here," Shelby says.

To the phone, I say, "What do you think is—?"

"A distressed couple makes for a challenging environment for a dog of any age and any size."

Adriana seizes the phone from me and paces while she speaks into the receiver. "It's important you understand several basic truths." While she carries the phone farther from me, my stomach clenches from hunger, yes, but from tension, too. Adriana's going to blow it, is going to upset this Shelby person, who'll keep Boulder from me forever.

Instead, as I should have expected by now, Adriana is nothing but facts. She's firm in their presentation, sure, but nothing she says about how she and I know each other, the situation with our fathers, or the police investigation is incorrect.

"This is why it is of critical importance," Adriana says, "that this dog be treated as much more than your typical shelter drop-off. He's evidence, you see."

"Oh my."

I hustle over, speak next. "We're happy to connect you with law enforcement," I say. "Maybe they can confirm everything we've told you while we drive to Kenosha to pick up the dog? Please? Yes?"

"This is quite the start to a Thursday morning," Shelby says.

Adriana interjects. "I found all of this quite precarious when it was dropped on me yesterday morning."

"Please just speak to the police," I say, trying to get this back on track. "I'll give you their number now."

"How soon do you think you can be here?" Shelby asks.

"Why? What's the problem?"

"Well, I run the shelter out of my home."

"And?"

"I'm leaving for Tampa this afternoon."

"You're leaving the dogs alone while you go to Tampa?"

"Heavens, no," she says. "I've got someone keeping an eye on the place while I'm gone. They'll live out of the second bedroom and take care of our four-legged friends. There certainly won't be any adoptions while I'm away, though."

My jaw clenches. "And how long will you be away?"

"Oh, about a month."

"A month?!"

"I'm what they like to call a snowbird, you know. The folks who—"

"You don't need to explain it." I glance at Adriana. "But we're coming. Now. We're on our way."

"My flight leaves at noon, like I said, so—"

"Yup, and we'll be at your place before you have to leave for the airport."

Adriana pipes up. "We'll have the constabulary ring you immediately to confirm the veracity of our tale."

"What?" Shelby says.

I roll my eyes. "The police will call you. They'll confirm everything we've said."

"Oh, sure."

We end the call, rushing for our room to grab our jackets before returning to the lobby and making for the exit. Before we reach the parking lot, my stomach complains again.

I double back.

"Whatever are you doing?" Adriana calls.

As I hustle to catch up with her, I hold up a box of Fun-Bird Fruited Circle-O's.

CHAPTER 69
FETCH

The final stretch of I-94 passes beneath us as we—or as I, the person driving—maintain speed, just enough to get to Kenosha before Shelby leaves home, but not so fast as to get pulled over.

"It must have been them," Adriana says. "My father. Yours. Traveling together. On their way out of state, perhaps."

"I don't think they were ever the brightest bulbs," I say, realizing I've gone the figurative language route again, "by which I mean they're not the smartest crooks around."

"They've gone much of our lifetimes without running afoul of the authorities."

"Good point."

"And," she adds, "if they felt they could only trust each other—or perhaps that they *couldn't* trust the other to not give them up were they to be captured—"

"It makes sense for them to keep the other close," I say. "Sure." I grind my teeth. "You're pretty good at this, you know."

"Whatever do you mean?"

"Just—people. You handle them well. You understand them."

"It rarely feels that way, though one supposes I've had a great deal of time to study."

"You're not that old."

"That isn't what I meant."

I almost give in, nearly ask her what she means, but she goes on before I have the chance.

"When you worked for North Ex—"

"Nortex."

"Right. Nortex. When you worked there, did you ever arrive at a meeting and realize, while in attendance, that you clearly missed some critical details about the goings-on in the room? That perhaps there was a gathering to which you weren't invited and at which the rules of engagement were established, so to speak?"

"The former? Yes. My God, yes."

"Mmm."

"But rules of engagement? I have no idea what you mean."

"People rarely do."

I drive for a time, an uneasy quiet between us while I keep an eye out for our exit. Eventually, Adriana glances up from her phone. "This is it," she says.

I signal, turn off, listen intently as she relays the lefts and rights, the tapping of my left foot increasing in frequency the nearer we get to the shelter.

When we turn into and snake through a residential neighborhood, I begin to worry. "You sure you put in the address correctly?"

She points ahead at an aging two-story with chipped white paint. "If the presence of the five-oh is any indication, we're in the correct location, yes."

Sure enough, a police vehicle is parked, running, at the curb. I pull in behind it, exit my Corolla, and give the patrol car a wide berth to signal to the officer inside. When he sees me, he rolls down the window a crack. "Eric Amundsen?"

"That's me."

He shuts off the car, exits, and approaches me in the street. "You have any I.D. on you? Just so we can verify—"

"Of course." I share my license with him.

He inspects it a moment.

"Is something the matter?" Adriana says. "We were under the impression this would be a matter of simply fetching the dog and returning—"

"We've got protocol to follow. And, in case you're unaware, Shelby is"—he returns my license to me—"a very particular individual."

"I can appreciate that," Adriana says.

The officer ignores her. "She asked me to wait in my car until you got here. Didn't want strangers upsetting the dogs."

"So," I say, letting the word hang.

"So," the officer says, "let's get the hell out of the cold and get you your dog back."

When he depresses the doorbell, the yips, yaps, and barks of at least a dozen dogs explode to life, and it takes a minute —and some shouting from inside the home—for the dogs to quiet, for Shelby to make it to the door.

Once she does, she stands before us in a bathrobe, not exactly looking like someone who'll be headed to the airport anytime soon.

"Shelby," the officer says, "this is Eric and, uh, Adriana, was it?"

"Yes," Adriana confirms.

"They're here about—"

"I know why they're here." She waves us in. "I'd have appreciated a knock, you know. The dogs don't mind the knocking as much as the bell."

"Slipped my mind, Shelby," the officer says. "I should've known better."

With Shelby in the lead, we follow the cop into the dim

entryway, this place more hoarder's paradise than dog shelter. Though, I suppose in Shelby's defense, much of what lines the walls—what's stacked from floor to ceiling—is dog cages and bags of food, some bags more full than others.

"Pardon the mess," Shelby says. "Dogs are through this way."

"Didn't you have a flight to catch?" I say.

"Honestly," she calls over her shoulder. "I didn't, no."

"Then why—?"

"I couldn't spend all day waiting around for you to show up, you know."

Is she—is she serious? Boulder was priority number one, yeah, but if we could have delayed our trip here by an hour, maybe there would have been enough time to move a few of my things before they disappeared into the void. But sure, yeah, okay. I guess we wouldn't have wanted to inconvenience anyone.

I almost say as much, but up ahead, Shelby enters what looks like it might be a kitchen, where she steps aside before the officer and Adriana do the same.

There, on the peeling linoleum, his tail wagging, is Boulder.

I drop to one knee, open my arms wide, and welcome him into my embrace. "Okay, easy. Yes, you're still huge and I am not as huge. And, sure, you're pretty excited and I am, too, but no barking, okay? No. This is my face, yes, and you don't need to lick every inch of it, but fine. I'll allow it. Good job." When he finally calms enough to simply sit before me, I hug him tight, tell him it's going to be okay, that he doesn't have to worry about Stu or my dad or any of the bad people ever again.

As I do this, Shelby gags, abandons the kitchen.

The officer, meanwhile, laughs to himself, and Adriana, her eyes wide, pinches her nose.

Still on the floor, my arms wrapped around Boulder, I glance at her, ignoring the smell.

"I don't care," I say. "I don't even care."

CHAPTER 70
A NEW ROUTINE

Despite the lack of K-Pop, Adriana guides us confidently on the two-hour drive back to Madison, while I, in the back seat with Boulder, do my best not to fret the status of my belongings at my apartment. Or, well, what *was* my apartment.

"We're fortunate to no longer require the motel," Adriana says.

"*You're* fortunate to no longer require the motel. I've got nowhere else to go," I say, scratching Boulder behind the ears. "We can stop at my apartment before we check out, right? Just to see if there's anything there to salvage?"

"Certainly."

Even if I—even if *Boulder and I*—have nowhere to go save for this car once we're back in Madison, Adriana's right. When we first left Kenosha, the call from Vargas came as some relief. That our dads were, by all indications, traveling together in the direction of the state line means there's no immediate threat, at least, so Adriana can get back to her routine, can return to living at her place and working at Kitten Caboodle as she would have were Stu still in town.

And, you know, not on the run with my dad.

Boulder recognizes our apartment building when we pull into the lot, and I tell him not to get too excited, that we don't know what—if anything—will be inside waiting for us. There's no longer anything on the curb, anyway, unless you count the single wooden stake with a bit of police tape still clinging to it, flapping in the wind.

My key fob to access the building still works—a good sign—and once inside, Boulder bounds up the stairs while Adriana and I follow. He tempers a bark once outside our apartment door, and I hang my head, drawing in an uneasy breath before I try the door.

It glides open, unlocked, and Boulder thunders forward into an empty apartment.

Adriana speaks up. "Perhaps your belongings have been relocated to a storage facility."

"If they were putting them on the curb originally, I seriously doubt it."

Boulder chases his tail in the middle of what was once the living room, his paws disturbing the pattern vacuumed into the carpet.

"I can give you a moment, if you'd like," Adriana says.

A moment. Ha! A moment for what? To piss and moan about a situation I put myself in? To throw another one of my pity parties?

"No," I say.

"No?"

"Come on, Boulder," I say. He ignores me until I say his name a second time, more excited this time around. Then, with him back in the hall, I close the door on my apartment—or, again, what was my apartment—and lead us down the stairs.

"Shall we make inquiries at the management office?" Adriana asks when we return to the parking lot.

"Forget the office," I say. "I don't need it. I don't want it. They can keep it for all I care."

"Mmm."

We return to the motel, where, after some unsuccessful haggling about whether Adriana will have to pay for a second night, Adriana examines the bill. "Oh my."

"What?"

She shows me the cost of the calls we made from the room last night.

"I told you so," I say.

She sighs. "Perhaps there really are scammers everywhere."

I want to tell her, again, that I told her so, but something about hearing her say there are scammers everywhere doesn't feel right. It's forced. A stretch, even. Have I sounded just as foolish when clinging so doggedly to the idea? I never bother to ask.

Eventually, we pile back into my Corolla to drop Adriana off at her place. While I drive this time, I realize I'm still without a plan, without any semblance of where Boulder and I will head next, without any notion of how we'll begin again. Adriana, in her silence, must also consider how she'll handle the coming days and weeks, the uncertainty she'll face, too, until our fathers are caught. Assuming they ever are.

A quarter of an hour later, I bring my car to a stop in her driveway, its engine still running.

"You know," Adriana says, "we're short-handed at Kitten Caboodle."

I chuckle. "Are you now?"

"Well, the store must remain open if I'm to have any income, and there are many hours to cover as a result of my father's absence."

"I *did* apply for a job a while back, if you'll recall."

"I recall quite well. You're more than qualified for a position, assuming you'd still like one."

I nod, my chest warm with gratitude. "When can I start?"

"Tomorrow, if you'd like. I'd open today, but I'm quite exhausted."

"Same."

"Well, then," Adriana says, throwing open the passenger side door before slamming it shut.

So much for goodbyes, I guess.

Unsure where we're going, I still throw the car into reverse, look over my shoulder, and begin backing out of the driveway.

A thud on the hood snaps my attention back around. Adriana has slapped a mittened hand against it, is waving at me through the windshield.

I roll down my window. "Did you forget something?"

"Aren't you coming?" she asks.

"What? Inside?"

"You need a place to stay, do you not?"

"I do, but what about your space? Your routines?"

"I'll make do."

"You sure?"

"Not at all."

"Wait. What?"

She grips the lapels of her pea coat. "To be quite honest, I loathe the idea of a roommate, but I squirm more at the thought of you and Boulder facing the elements on your own. Plus, with what few belongings you have to your name—"

"Are you saying if we *had* been able to get my things back you wouldn't have offered me a place to stay?"

"Let's not dwell on the matter any longer than we have to."

We don't, and a minute later, I'm inside helping her clean up after her father's rampage, or at least helping as much as she'll permit. After a half hour of protests and *no, please, don't touch that*, she assures me she has it all under control, and won't I please, as she believes the phrase goes, simply make myself at home?

I do, which entails moving the one suitcase I have to my name to a corner of the living room before excusing myself to take Boulder on a walk. A long walk. The kind of walk you never want to end because, well, you have no idea what you're going to do when it's over.

That feeling hangs over me—and Adriana, too, I suspect—for much of the subsequent weeks. As it turns out, we can't start working at Kitten Caboodle, at least not immediately. There's this whole thing called an *active investigation into the store's finances*, and with the pet store's assets being frozen, well, that investigation comes with a fair amount of thumb twiddling and staring absent-mindedly out windows until the operation's books are cleared. When they are, finally, it's because since Stu last reopened the store under a new name, his scamming operation has been so laughably ineffective that laundering was no longer necessary.

Score one for the good guys. Yeah, Team Scambait. Woot, I guess.

Once we've got the green light to open the store, Adriana and I arrive together every day, taking our shifts so neither of us is home alone, just in case. Boulder remains at my side on shift, too, with Adriana going so far as to order him an XL employee vest that, after a day of attempting to shimmy it from his doggy shoulders, he ultimately accepts. The customers love this newest employee of ours, many of them coming back more frequently than they otherwise would have, at least according to Adriana.

At night—or during the day, when we work closing shifts —I do not scambait. I never once check my inboxes and, after some deliberation, finally delete the document where I stored my passwords for those accounts. Discord never makes it to the old phone Adriana lends me, and at no point do I feel compelled to hop on Twitch, to tune in to my favorite scam-baiters' channels and watch them do the good work. It's still good work—and I'm happy they do it—but the fire is gone.

The fun of it, too, and what was once a rush I pined for nearly every hour of the day feels like little more than a high I chased in another life, as another person.

Despite these changes, and with all apologies to Grandma Amundsen, it never feels as though I'm letting someone down.

During the first week of my crashing on Adriana's couch, we phone the police daily, asking for updates on our fathers' whereabouts, on the investigation into them. Vargas remains polite—at least in the initial days—but it's apparent that, ten days after their disappearance, she'd really prefer this be a *don't call us, we'll call you* arrangement.

March thaws much of the snow February leaves behind, though on Saint Patrick's Day, we close early in anticipation of a major storm. There's at least a foot of snow coming, forecasters agree, and while mopping, I make a joke about the *bad* luck of the Irish.

"I don't understand," Adriana says, counting cash.

"Never mind," I say, and she doesn't press me further.

Gargantuan, gorgeous flakes are already falling by the time we arrive home, and once the blast of K-Pop has been silenced, Adriana examines her phone in the driver's seat. "I'll need a moment," she says.

I exit the car and open the rear door for Boulder, who attempts to catch the falling snow between his jaw. On the porch, I kick the snow off my boots and let Boulder inside. Before I can join him, however, Adriana calls out to me from her car.

"Eric," she says.

"You coming or what?"

"They've been apprehended," she says. "Your father. Mine."

CHAPTER 71
BE PREPARED

ndianapolis, Adriana says, or somewhere thereabouts. According to Vargas, a dine and dash gave them away— some restauranteur caught their license plate number before they could snake their way into traffic. The local authorities caught up with them and, after running Stu's license and discovering my dad lacked identification, they were connected to the warrants for their arrest in Wisconsin.

"Thank goodness I had the wherewithal to relocate one of my father's safes," Adriana says.

I furrow my brow.

"The one that caused my father to ransack my home in search of it."

"Right," I say, finally remembering.

"Dining without paying," Adriana adds. "Abhorrent."

"Did you expect any better from them?"

"Mmm."

With the two of them in custody, it should be over.

Instead, the following month is an absolute shitstorm of complication.

Though Stu's case, granted, is more straightforward given his in-state crimes were more recent, it turns out that when your dad has been dead—legally dead—for twenty years, it's kind of hard to put him on trial. What's more, the crimes he committed in Wisconsin would have been decades ago, and, of course, statutes of limitation are a thing.

"So what, then?" I ask Vargas one afternoon when I finally get her on the phone.

"You should really be talking to the district attorney's office."

"Can I do that, even?"

"You're a witness. I'm surprised they haven't already called you in for additional testimony." She passes along a phone number, wishes me luck.

And I have some, finally, once I get through to the prosecutor on the case.

"First and foremost," he says, "we have to get a court to pronounce your dad *not* dead."

"Can't they look at him and say *he looks alive to me*?"

The prosecutor assures me it's more complex than that. "And once—or, really, *even* if your father is declared to no longer be deceased, we have to prove he lived outside Wisconsin, and for how long." He goes on to explain tolling provisions, some legal mumbo-jumbo that puts a pause on statutes of limitation while the suspect is out of state.

"Do you really think that will work?" I ask. "Will a judge buy that?"

"My understanding is your father will be asking for a jury trial."

"The jury, then."

"Whether a jury convicts will come down to the final presentation of the evidence, much of which the defense will likely attempt to have dismissed as hearsay."

"I thought you were getting more of my dad's victims to come forward."

"We are, but that doesn't mean their recollection of events

will be convincing to a jury. What your dad did to them was years and years ago by now."

"I'll testify, then. I need to. I want to."

"Want to? Oh, you'll have to."

In the week leading up to Stu's trial, Adriana is inconsolable. "To think my father would rather cling to his pride than plead guilty—it's shameless. Shameless!"

"I'd offer you a hug, but—"

"I appreciate the thought." Her shoulders fall. "What infuriates me is that despite his guilt, he insists the trial proceed. It's as if he's goading me, his own daughter, to put herself at risk by testifying against him in court. He knows how I am. He knows who I am."

"Did you ever think," I say, "that's precisely why he's going through with it?"

Adriana wrinkles her nose, sniffling.

"It'll be all right," I say. "We'll testify together, just as we've been asked, and then—"

She leaves the living room, cinches shut the door to her room before I can finish.

I swallow hard, return my attention to the notebook I've been scribbling in at the prosecution's recommendation. Any memory, anything useful, they said. Write it down. Put it on a timeline. I've been at it now for weeks—months, at this point—and I've shared with them everything I can recall along the way.

Aside from helping the prosecution build its case, the journal's been an exercise in self-discovery. I've remembered, for the first time in years, the flashes of anger my father would display when I was a child, the odd hours he'd come and go from the house, the bits and pieces of conversation I caught, over time, when I came across him whispering hurriedly into the phone. In the process, my entire relationship to my past— my childhood relationship to my father—shifts even further. It's as if I spent my childhood staring into funhouse mirrors, unaware of the world's true shape until the illusion was shattered, first when I met my father again, then again, here, in pen and paper.

And the internet, as is tradition, is no help in making the process any easier to endure. Someone—and if I had to guess, the Scambait Bros and their comrades—connects the dots between my since-deleted YouTube channel and public records about the forthcoming trials. The press catches on. The *Wisconsin State Journal*, for one, followed by the *Journal-Sentinel* out of Milwaukee and, because the word's out my dad laid low there for twenty years, the *Chicago Tribune*. There are the smaller papers, too, the *Appleton Post-Crescent*s and the *Green Bay Press Gazette*s of the world, but it's not until a reporter from the *New York Times* lands in my inbox that I tell myself it's time to step away.

Not that I agreed to any interviews—at the district attorney's request—but good God.

Most days, I ignore my inbox. I minimize the number of apps I open on my phone, attempt to avoid the news. When I do check in with the world—I've got to follow up on the new wave of job applications I've been sending out—it's letdown after letdown. It's wince after wince, too, at what I used to do in my mail app, but I was keeping a promise, I tell myself, and it feels like it's one I'm so close to, at long last, being able to walk away from, to call complete.

One afternoon, during a fleeting glance at my email, I finally receive a job offer.

It's from, of all people, SalchichaSimon.

He's been trying to track me down, he says, after I disappeared from Discord, when he caught the news in one of the bajillion blogs that's covered the circumstances surrounding the trials. His real name is Victor, he says, and he wants to help—really, actually help this time. If I ever need to get away, he's got a job. He's got a job and a place. A place far from Wisconsin.

He's got a place in Arizona.

The job is nothing fancy, he adds, but it's mine if I want it. There'll always be a place for me.

"Something the matter?" Adriana asks, interrupting me as I consider the email.

"Déjà vu," I say. "Déjà vu."

I write him back immediately, thumbing an email that says thanks, but you might understand why I'm wary, Victor, of unsolicited opportunities of a lifetime sent to me by email.

Afterward, I talk it out with Adriana, who reminds me my father is one person. She reminds me not everyone is out to get me. She reminds me it's really okay, sometimes, to let a friend do you a favor. Some people are, in fact, just nice, and I think of Daniel at Willalby's, the kindness he showed me the morning of my arrest.

I send Victor another email. I ask if we can talk. Video chat. Something. Maybe seeing him, maybe getting a better feel for what he's really thinking will help, not that I'm leaving—not that I *can* leave—anytime soon.

Then, three days before Stu's trial, Adriana and I close Kitten Caboodle until further notice, asking our customers— or, if we're honest, Boulder's customers—to respect our privacy until the trial has concluded.

Two days before Stu's trial is to begin, Adriana learns she won't have to testify against her father. Neither of us will.

Stu has taken a plea deal, has become another witness for the prosecution.

And, on the final day of May, more than three months after he was arrested, my father is declared legally alive.

CHAPTER 72
TESTIFY

t's amazing the deal you can find on a suit when pressed for cash. Did mine come from the Target clearance rack? You bet. Was the jacket a little big in the shoulders, the pants long in the leg? Yes. Did Adriana pay to have it tailored so I didn't look like a buffoon in court? Also, yes.

Thank goodness for friends.

The judge proves to be the sullen, no-nonsense type, and I dare not look at the jury when I'm called to testify—not that I could size them up if I wanted to. My neck is stiff, my shoulders, too, and the undersides of my feet prickle when I take my seat, am asked to raise my right hand and take the oath.

As I do, my gaze falls to my dad. Mugshots and news clippings aside, I haven't seen him since he hightailed it out of Kitten Caboodle in February. He's more pale now, the lines in his face deeper, and there's a hint—yes!—of scars left behind from Adriana's slashing of his face. He looks sorrowful, even! Was his time in jail—there was no way he could make bail—enough for him to learn his lesson? No. I can't let myself buy into that. He'll never learn.

But maybe he has. I mean, he really looks like shit.

The prosecution goes first, and it's nothing I hadn't

planned for. Or, perhaps better put, it's nothing that *we* hadn't planned for, considering they informed me in advance what they'd be asking. I steady myself throughout by keeping my attention on the expanse of carpet between the stand and the prosecution's table, only occasionally glancing at the defense.

There are times when, as I detail our every relevant interaction, the weight of the moment seems to strike my dad, his eyes welling over. While he suffers, I'm struck with an incredible catharsis, a justice high like none I could have ever hoped to achieve while dumpster-diving through my scambait inboxes. It's enough to make me pity the man in fits and starts. I can relate, after all; I came close, however fleetingly, to following in his scamming footsteps.

"Thank you, your honor," the prosecutor says. "The prosecution rests."

The defense attorney approaches for cross-examination, a frigid man in an icy gray suit. As he steps nearer, it's as if a cold wind whips through the chamber, and the dark days of February are on me once more. I chew the inside of my cheek, look for Adriana—or, hell, even Stu—among the spectators. The defense attorney's wide shoulders block my view, and his questions begin while I'm still on my heels.

"Please state your name for the court."

I do, but we've done this already. What's the point? Why defend this man, that man, my dad, when you know he's as guilty as anyone else? I don't ask these things, don't say a word beyond that which is asked of me because no clapbacks, the prosecution told me. The facts are on our side.

"Are you the Eric Glenn Amundsen who worked for Nortex Medical Incorporated?"

I clench my jaw. "I am."

"Then you're familiar with an Ann Hagel?"

My eyebrows raise. "I'm sorry, who?"

"Ann Hagel. The Human Resources Manager at Nortex—"

"Yes. Sorry. Just not a name that's been on the top of my mind for a while."

"Frankly," the defense says, "I'm not surprised you don't remember her." He leaves the statement hanging. He wants me to bite, wants me to push him to make his next point, but I fight down the urge, remain with my hands clasped on my lap. "What about a Dolores Bestatter?"

"If your question is whether I know who she is, the answer is yes."

"One for two," the defense says. "Not bad, considering."

The judge intervenes. "Is there a point to this line of questioning?"

"Yes, your honor," the defense says, "because this so-called witness—who never once saw my client commit any of the crimes with which he's been charged, mind you—never managed to gain the trust of those with whom he worked for years."

Oh, Christ. Here we go.

The defense goes on, reading aloud from a sworn affidavit provided by Ann regarding my dismissal. It's all in there, the time theft—with no mention of what I was doing with that time or why, naturally—and the complete and total dereliction of duty. The ransomware attack and my responsibility for it figures into the affidavit, too, as well as what the company estimates the attack cost them in downtime.

"And," the defense says, "in case you're concerned this is perhaps just one former colleague who this witness rubbed the wrong way, I have a second affidavit from another professional who worked even more closely with Eric."

The affidavit sworn by Dolores is, somehow, even worse. It's personal, this one, throwing around words like "disrespectful" and "dismissive." There's a section on my "lack of engagement" and "relentless prevarication," so we can officially say this wasn't written by Dolores, just signed by her, not that it's going to matter.

As the defense continues reading, I study the jury. One woman tut-tuts, another shakes her head softly, and aren't they supposed to be emotionless, damn it all? And my dad. My dad! His chin is up now, his gaze piercing. If he hadn't presumably been coached not to, he'd absolutely be wearing some shit-eating grin right now, lording the moment over me like the dogshit excuse for a father he is.

The prosecution stands, raises an objection on grounds of hearsay. The judge allows it, asks the defense if either Ann or Dolores intend to testify.

My dad's attorney addresses the judge, his shoulders square. "They will, your honor, if necessary."

The judge instructs the jury to disregard the contents of the affidavits until they've been testified to by the parties who signed them. The prosecution shoots me a nod. What I'd love to do is fist bump, but instead, I settle for eye contact.

Any relief is short-lived. The defense pivots to my eviction, to my inability to care for a dog, which, what the fuck, that only happened because of Stu, not that, again, the defense is going to frame its questions in a way that actually illuminates the facts of the matter. Oh, and the YouTube channel! They've got that on me, too, information that was no doubt shared between Stu and my dad when they were on the same team.

"What you're saying, then, Eric," the defense says, "is that you uploaded a video with a slew of information you believed to be true before retracting it within a matter of days?"

"Under threat to my life and that of my dog."

"And how were those threats transmitted?"

"A note was left in my home."

"And who left that note in your home?"

I sigh. "Stuart Erwahrend."

"Stuart Erwahrend." He pushes away from the witness stand. "A man who has since turned state's witness against my client. A man who himself has pleaded guilty to the charges my client is accused of. Can Stuart Erwahrend, known criminal, be trusted? Can Eric, a man with so few scruples, be trusted?"

I clutch tight to the sides of my chair. Everything he's brought up, I've done. Objectively, anyway, but context is important, and as Adriana has said, it's a matter of degree, but maybe that's the point. We're all scammers, are all the bad guys when the light of justice is shone selectively.

And we—people like me—get to make those selections for ourselves.

None of this excuses what I've done. None of it excuses my father, either, and none of it materially changes the facts at hand, that some acts are good and others are bad, but it does mean, maybe, that we're all living in glass houses and it's only a matter of time before someone peers inside and sees what they want to see.

I just so happen to have the world peering in at a really bad time. Like, on one of those pants off, eating cereal by hand and straight from the box, not having showered days. Weeks, maybe.

"And then there's the matter," the defense says, "of the unhinged mob of internet vigilantes Eric unleashed on Kitten Caboodle as a result of his careless internet postings in the form the videos he would later retract."

Few questions follow, and I sit in silence, my head bowed, as the defense tears me limb from limb. My cheeks run hot. Sweat dots my brow. I turn the unbearable heat on its head by embracing it, channeling the desert, the Superstition Mountains and the hikes Grandma Amundsen longed to take. I force myself to consider SalchichaSimon—er, Victor—and his evergreen offer, as he put it, when we finally connected by phone. That job, the place to stay, they're both there, waiting for me, mere days away if I want them, and there's nothing I want more right now than to be far away from this place, far from whatever verdict this jury reaches, far from my eternally smirking should-still-be-dead father if he is, in fact, found not guilty.

"That's enough," the judge finally says. "Do you have any further questions for the witness?"

"I do not, your honor."

Once dismissed from the stand, I march past Adriana, past where I'd sat next to her, and exit the courtroom. She'll need all the strength she can muster; I'm not letting her see me break.

I'm not letting *my dad* see me break.

CHAPTER 73
STARTING OVER

The day after my testimony, Boulder and I leave Madison for good.

Before we hit the road, I thank Adriana, again, for everything.

"No," she says. "I should be thanking you."

"What for?"

"For leaving."

"Ouch."

"As roommates go, you weren't intolerable."

"I think this is you trying to give a compliment."

Adriana ignores me, squats, hugs Boulder. "Take care of Eric," she says. "Remember to feed him three times daily, and remind him to text now and then."

"He won't need to remind me."

"See to it he doesn't."

The interstate opens before me and Boulder, our westward trek stretching on well into the humidity of the midsummer night. We call it quits after twelve-plus hours, stopping at a budget motel in some no-name town between Wichita and Albuquerque, the kind of place it'll be easy enough to sneak a dog into and out of without drawing the attention of the front desk.

Then, at sunrise, our journey continues, the landscape shifting from prairie to desert by day's end, the sprawl of the greater Phoenix area taunting me until, at long last, I heave a sigh of relief at the city limits.

Victor greets me and Boulder when we pull up outside his place. He shows us to the mother-in-law suite out back, says he'll check in tomorrow morning and that, if we need anything before then, we'll know where to find him.

The mother-in-law suite is the size of a studio apartment, the queen bed a bit too large for a space that's to be shared, however temporarily, by a man and a dog Boulder's size. Not that I'm complaining. There's a refrigerator, after all, and running water, a bathroom. It's a place of our own, one far from the ongoing trial, the continuing deliberations of the jury, the danger posed if my dad is found not guilty.

But no more of that. I'm here to keep myself from dwelling on it. I'm here to try again.

And this room is cozy, really. It's simple. It's a start.

It's the kind of place Grandma Amundsen would have loved.

CHAPTER 74
VERDICT

Salchicha—or Victor, ugh—hollers from the kitchen. Another order ready. I carry a plate of chimichangas and a taco salad to table four, where I ask if there's anything else I can get them. More water, says the man at the table, and with a curt nod, I'm off to fetch the pitcher.

At the drink station, my phone buzzes. A call—a call?—from Adriana.

My heart thrashes, my mouth drying as I carry the pitcher back to table four, as I fill their water glasses, careful not to spill a drop despite the shaking of my hand. They thank me. I leave them be.

Then, after stepping outside and clinging to what little shade there is around high noon in the desert, I return her call.

"Eric Amundsen," she answers.

"Obviously, yeah. What is it?"

"Straight to the point, it seems." Her tone betrays nothing.

"I'm on shift right now, sorry, but I wanted to call back as soon as—"

"Guilty," she says.

"What?"

"Your father. The jury of his peers has reached a verdict. Several, really. They found him guilty of defrauding the state and two counts of mail fraud. These aren't all the charges levied against him, of course, but—"

"No." I lean against the alley wall, rest my head against the brick. "It isn't everything, but it's enough."

CHAPTER 75
SPAM

sit before my laptop on the wobbly aluminum desk in Victor's mother-in-law suite. At my laptop's side, a photo of me and Grandma stares back at me. I keep the framed image here, always, a reminder of the promise I made, the mistakes I committed in keeping it, the opportunities still before me where she has none. There's still time. There's always time.

Boulder, meanwhile, yawns on the tile at my feet, much of him stretched across the charging cord that connects my laptop to the wall. He sleeps more and more with each passing day, though whether from the desert heat, his old age, or both, I don't know. Our time together has always been limited, yes, but I can't help but feel as though every day we have together, every sunrise and sunset walk we take, is a gift.

This is why I was hoping he'd join me on my drive out to —on my hike of—the Superstition Mountains this afternoon, but for now, Boulder, snooze. Enjoy that nap, buddy, you old man. Old dog. Old dog-man. He knows what I mean.

I lean back in my chair—plastic, the cheap outdoor variety —and into a cool blast of arctic air from the conditioner.

We've adjusted to this space, no matter how cramped, by denying ourselves the little luxuries. There are debts to pay, of course, and a modest rent to make each month, but we'll be back on our own soon. Eventually. We'll have a place that's truly ours at some point, even if that point is years, not months, away.

My laptop dings. I inspect the screen, this challenge from my past, this surprise in my inbox. It reminds me of grief unmerited, of mistakes made and obstacles overcome. It reminds me of a friendship forged—Adriana—and a still-empty grave on Madison's west side.

Eric, this is your father.

It's rare to get a call from my father in prison—an email, rarer still.

It should be the easiest thing to delete this email, and it is.

ACKNOWLEDGMENTS

Unlike Eric, I'm fortunate to count on a number of friends, many of whom were integral in seeing this book to publication.

First, I need to thank early readers like Kathryn Keener and Scott Birrenkott. Your willingness to read *Scambait* in all of its iterations hasn't been forgotten (nor have I forgotten Adriana's long-lost brother and his iguana, both of which will have to make an appearance in future work). The next time I'm in town, the drinks are on me. See you at the usual joint.

I'd also like to thank early reader Madolyn Rogers for her kind insistence that I consider rewriting *Scambait* in the first person present, as it made all the difference in bringing Eric to life. Fellow writers and readers who echoed her sentiments include Dan Schiro, Jason Guy, Rick Richards, and Chuck Ogg —thanks to all of you for your feedback.

Thanks is also owed to the Writerverse Discord server. Unlike the server where SalchichaSimon and PrakashMoney hang out, the Writerverse is a supportive community with no equal. So, to Avery, Naomi, Audely, Alicia, and Jaedyn, thank you.

I'm also grateful for the feedback of Robb Grindstaff and Alex Aulisi. Thank you for your kindness.

Many thanks to Ekta Garg, who recommended I contact Kevin Stone about designing the cover for *Scambait*. Thanks to you, Ekta, and to you, Kevin, for being part of what makes this book really pop on—and hopefully *off*—the shelves.

I'd like to offer additional thanks to the likes of the

r/scambait subreddit, Pierogi, Jim Browning, and Kitboga, not only for the work you do, but for the countless free hours of entertainment and education you provide.

And where would I be without Lacey? That's not a question I want to know the answer to, so thank you, Lacey, for your unwavering love and support.

Lastly, thanks to the car dealership whose predatory practices during the purchase of my own 2014 Toyota Corolla planted the first seeds of motivation to write this book. It's the very least I could do.

ABOUT THE AUTHOR

Ryan R. Campbell is an author, speaker, and software engineer whose work as R.R. Campbell has earned him accolades including finalist placement in the International Book Awards and acclaim from *New York Times* bestselling authors.

He is the founder of the Writescast Network and the co-founder of Kill Your Darlings Candle Company. Previously, he taught for the University of Wisconsin's Division of Continuing Studies in Writing, and he is a regular speaker at conferences throughout Wisconsin and beyond.

His debut as Ryan R. Campbell, *And Ampersand: Short Stories on Endings and Beginnings (of a Sort)*, has been met with significant praise.

Ryan lives in Milwaukee, Wisconsin with his wife, Lacey, and their cats, Hashtag and Rhaegar.

for more
ryanrcampbell.com
@iamrrcampbell

ALSO BY RYAN R. CAMPBELL

ryan r. campbell

"Reminiscent of Hemingway and De Lillo."

- AWARD-WINNING AUTHOR IVY NGEOW

"To say so much with so few words is a gift."

- GREGORY LEE RENZ, AWARD-WINNING AUTHOR OF BENEATH THE FLAMES

Now available wherever books are sold.

www.ingramcontent.com/pod-product-compliance
Lightning Source LLC
Chambersburg PA
CBHW051218190726
48288CB00006B/2015